THE VORTEX BLASTER

—"Storm" Cloud, the only man who could destroy the ravening nuclear vortices that struck and killed at random

THE VORTEX BLASTER

was also the name of Cloud's spaceship, an incredibly advanced arsenal of modern science, in which Cloud and his crew of colorful space castaways hunted the source of the lethal vortices, battled a criminal mastermind, developed unheard-of sciences, and made an ultimate discovery of shattering importance to the destiny of the Universe!

THE VORTEX BLASTERS

team up in a saga of crisis and adventure in the worlds of the Lensmen—"Doc" Smith's most enduring creation.

A LENSMAN ADVENTURE
Seventh in the Great Series

E. E. "DOC" SMITH

A NOVEL OF THE LENSMAN UNIVERSE

MASTERS OF THE VORTEX

ORIGINAL TITLE: THE VORTEX BLASTER

BERKLEY BOOKS, NEW YORK

To
Bob Heinlein
With Admiration and Esteem

MASTERS OF THE VORTEX

A Berkley Book / published by arrangement with
Verna Smith Trestrail

PRINTING HISTORY
Jove/HBJ edition / November 1977
Berkley edition / August 1983

ISBN: 0-425-06046-2

CONTENTS

Chapter 1

————————————————CATASTROPHE

SAFETY DEVICES that do not protect.

"Unsinkable" ships that, before the days of Bergenholm and of atomic and cosmic energy, sank into the waters of Earth.

More particularly, safety devices which, while protecting against one agent of destruction, attract magnet-like another and worse. Such as the armored cable within the walls of a wooden house. It protects the electrical conductors within it against accidental external shorts; but, inadequately grounded, it may attract and upon occasion has attracted the stupendous force of lightning. Then, steel armor exploding into incandescence inside walls and ceilings, that house's existence thereafter is to be measured in minutes.

Specifically, four lightning rods. The lightning rods protecting the chromium, glass, and plastic home of Neal Cloud. Those rods were adequately grounded, with copper-silver cables the size of a big man's forefinger; for Neal Cloud, Doctor of Nucleonics, knew his lightning and was taking no chances whatever with the safety of his wife and children.

He did not know, did not even suspect, that under certain conditions of atmospheric potential and of ground-magnetic stress his perfectly-designed and perfectly-installed system would become a super-powerful attractor for flying vortices of atomic disintegration.

So now Neal Cloud, nucleonicist, sat at his desk in a strained, dull apathy. His face was a yellowish-gray white, his tendoned hands gripped rigidly the arms of his chair. His eyes, hard and lifeless, stared unseeingly past the small, three-dimensional block portrait of all that had made life worth living.

For his guardian against lightning had been a vortex-magnet at the moment when some luckless wight had tried to abate the nuisance of a "loose" atomic vortex. That wight dies, of course—they almost always did—and the vortex, instead of being destroyed, was simply broken up into a number of widely-scattered new vortices. And one of those bits of furious, uncontrolled energy, resembling a handful of substance torn from the depths of a sun, darted toward and shot downward to' earth through Neal Cloud's new house.

That house did not burn; it exploded. Nothing of it, in it, or near it stood a chance, for in a few seconds the place where it had been was a crater of seething, boiling lava—a crater which filled the atmosphere with poisonous vapors; which flooded all nearby space with lethal radiations.

Cosmically, the whole thing was infinitesimal. Ever since man learned how to use atomic power the vortices of disintegration had been breaking out of control. Such accidents had been happening, and would continue to happen. More than one world, perhaps, had been or would be consumed to the last gram by such loose atomic vortices. What of that? Of what real importance are a few grains of sand to a pile five thousand miles long, a hundred miles wide, and ten miles deep?

Even to that individual grain of sand called "Earth"—or, in modern parlance, "Sol Three," or "Tellus of Sol," or simply "Tellus"—the affair was negligible. One man had died; but, in dying, he had added one more page to the thick bulk of negative results already on file. That Mrs. Cloud and her children had perished was merely unfortunate. The vortex itself was not yet a real threat to Tellus. It was a "new" one, and thus it would be a long time before it would become other than a local menace.

Nor, to any except a tiny fraction of Earth's inhabitants, was the question of loose atomic vortices a matter of concern. It was unthinkable that Tellus, the point of origin and the very center of Galactic Civilization, could cease to exist. Long before such vortices could eat away much of her mass, or poison much of her atmosphere, Earth's scientists would have solved the problem.

But to Neal Cloud the accident was ultimate catastrophe. His personal universe had crashed in ruins; what was left was not worth picking up. He and Jo had been married for more than fifteen years and the bonds between them had grown stronger, deeper, truer with every passing day. And the kids ... it *couldn't* have happened ... fate COULDN'T do this to him ... but it had ... it could. Gone ... *gone* ... GONE!

And to Neal Cloud, sitting there at his desk in black abstraction, with maggots of thought gnawing holes in his mind, the catastrophe was doubly galling because of its cruel irony. For he was second from the top in the Vortex Control Laboratory; his life's work had been a search for a means or method of extinguishing loose atomic vortices.

His eyes focused vaguely upon the portrait. Wavy brown hair ... clear, honest gray eyes ... lines of character, of strength and of humor ... sweetly curved lips, ready to smile or to kiss ...

He wrenched his attention away and scribbled briefly upon a sheet of paper. Then, getting up stiffly, he took the portrait and moved woodenly across the room to a furnace. After the flaming arc had done its work he turned and handed the paper to a tall man, with a Lens glowing upon his wrist, who had been watching him with quiet, understanding eyes. Significant enough, to the initiate, of the importance of the laboratory is the fact that it was headed by a Lensman.

"As of now, Phil, if it's QX with you."

The Lensman took the document, glanced at it, and slowly, meticulously, tore it into sixteen equal pieces.

"Uh-uh, Storm," he denied, gently. "Not a resignation. Leave of absence, perhaps, but not severance."

"Why not?" It was scarcely a question; Cloud's voice was level, uninflected. "I wouldn't be worth the paper I'd waste."

"Now, no; but the future's another matter. I haven't said anything so far, because I knew you and Jo. Nothing could be said." Two hands gripped and held. "For the future, though, four words that were spoken long ago have never been improved upon. 'This, too, shall pass'."

"You think so?"

"I know so, Storm. I've been round a long time. You're too good a man to go down out of control. You've got a place in the world and a job to do. You'll be back—" a thought struck the Lensman and he went on, in a strangely altered tone: "But you wouldn't—of course you wouldn't—you couldn't."

"I don't think so. No." Suicide, tempting although it might be, was not the answer. "Good-bye, Phil."

"Not good-bye, Storm. Au revoir."

"Maybe." Cloud left the laboratory and took an elevator down to the garage. Into his big blue DeKhotinsky Special and away.

Through traffic so heavy that front-, rear-, and side-bumpers almost touched he drove with his wonted cool skill; even though he did not know, consciously, that the other cars were there. He slowed, turned, stopped, "shoveled on the coal," all correctly—and all purely automatically.

He did not know where he was going, nor care. His numbed brain was simply trying to run away from its own bitter imaginings—which, if he had thought at all, he would have known hopeless of accomplishment. But he did not think. He simply acted; dumbly, miserably.

Into a one-way skyway he rocketed; along it over the suburbs and into the trans-continental super-highway. Edging inward, lane after lane, he reached the "unlimited" way—unlimited, that is, except for being limited to cars of not less than seven hundred horsepower, in perfect mechanical condition, driven by registered, tested drivers at not less than one hundred twenty five miles per hour—flashed his number at the control station, and shoved his right foot down to the floor.

Everyone knows that an ordinary DeKhotinsky Sporter will do a hundred and forty honestly-measured miles in one honestly-timed hour; but very few drivers have ever found out how fast one of those brutal big souped-up Specials can wheel. Most people simply haven't got what it takes to open one up.

"Storm" Cloud found out that day. He held that six-thousand-pound Juggernaut onto the road, wide open, for mile after mile after mile. But it didn't help. Drive as he would, he could not out-run that which rode with him. Beside him and within him and behind him; for Jo was there.

Jo and the kids, but mostly Jo. It was Jo's car as much as it was his. "Babe, the big blue ox," was her pet name for it; because, like Paul Bunyan's fabulous beast, it was pretty nearly six feet between the eyes.

Jo was in the seat beside him. Every dear, every sweet,

every luscious, lovely memory of her was there . . . and behind him, just beyond eye-corner visibility, were the three kids. And a whole lifetime of this loomed ahead—a vista of emptiness more vacuous by far than the emptiest reaches of inter-galactic space. Damnation! he couldn't stand much more of . . .

High over the roadway, far ahead, a brilliant octagon flared red. That meant "STOP!" in any language. Cloud eased up on the accelerator; eased down on the brake-pedal; took his place in the line of almost-stalled traffic. There was a barrier and a trimly-uniformed policeman.

"Sorry, sir," the officer said, with a sweeping, turning gesture, "but you'll have to detour over to Twenty. There's a loose atomic vortex beside the road up ahead . . . Oh, it's you, Doctor Cloud! You can go ahead, of course. Couple of miles yet before you'll need your armor. They didn't tell us they were sending for *you*. It's just a little new one, and the dope we got was that they were going to shove it over into the badlands with pressors."

"They didn't send for me." Cloud tried to smile. "I'm just driving around. No armor, even, so I might as well go back."

He turned the Special around. A loose vortex—new. There might be three or four of them, scattered over that many counties. Sisters of the one that had murdered his family—spawn of that damned Number Eleven that that bungling nitwit had tried to blow out . . . Into his mind there leaped a picture, wire-sharp, of Number Eleven as he had last seen it, and simultaneously an idea hit him like the blow of a fist.

He thought. *Really* thought, now; intensely and clearly. If he could do it—could actually blow out the atomic flame of an atomic vortex . . . not exactly revenge, but . . . it *would* work . . . it would *have* to work—he'd *make* it work! And grimly, quietly, but alive now in every fiber, he drove back to the city almost as fast as he had come away.

If Philip Strong was surprised at Cloud's sudden reappearance in the laboratory he did not show it. Nor did he offer any comment as his erstwhile assistant went to various lockers and cupboards, assembling coils, tubes, armor, and other paraphernalia.

"Guess that's all I'll need, chief," Cloud remarked, finally. "Here's a blank check. If some of this stuff shouldn't happen to be in usable condition when I get done with it, fill it out to suit, will you?"

"No." The Lensman tore up the check just as he had torn up the resignation. "If you want the stuff for legitimate purposes, you're on Patrol business and it's the Patrol's risk. But if you're thinking of trying to snuff a vortex, the stuff stays here. That's out, Storm.

"But I'm going to *really* snuff 'em, starting with Number One and taking 'em in order. No suicide."

"Huh?" Skepticism incarnate. "It can't be done, except by an almost impossibly fortuitous accident, which is why you yourself have always been as opposed to such attempts as the rest of us. The charge of explosive must match, within very narrow limits, the activity of the vortex itself at the instant of detonation; and that activity varies so greatly and so unpredictably that all attempts at accurate extrapolation have failed. Even the Conference of Scientists couldn't develop a usable formula, any more than they could work out a tractor that could be used as a tow-line on one."

"Wait a minute!" Cloud protested. "They found that it could be forecast, for a length of time proportional to the length of the cycle in question, by an extension of the calculus of warped surfaces."

"Humph! I said a *usable* formula!" the Lensman snorted. "What good is a ten-second forecast when it takes a GOMEAC twice that long to solve . . . Oh!" he broke off, staring.

"Oh," he repeated, slowly. "I forgot for a minute that you were born with a super-GOMEAC in your head. But there are other things."

"There were. Now there are none."

"No?"

"NO. I couldn't take such chances before, and I'd've tied myself up into knots if I did. Now nothing can throw me. I can compute all the elements of a sigma curve in nothing flat. A ten-second prediction gives me ten seconds of action. That's plenty."

"I see." Strong pondered, his fingers drumming softly upon his desk. Lensmen did not ordinarily use their Lenses on their Lensless friends, but this was no ordinary occasion. "You aren't afraid of death any more. But you won't invite it? And do you mind if I Lens you on that?"

"Come in. I'll not invite it, but that's as far as I'll go in promising. I won't make any superhuman effort to avoid it. I'll take all due precautions, for the sake of the job, but if one gets me, what the hell?"

"QX." The Lensman withdrew from Cloud's mind. "Not too good, but good enough. What's your plan? You won't have time for the usual method of attack."

"Like this." Cloud found a sheet of drafting paper and sketched rapidly. "There's the crater, with the vortex at the bottom—there. From the sigma curve I estimate the most probable value of the activity I'll have to shoot at. Then I select three duodec bombs from the hundred or so I'll have made up in advance—one on the mark, one each five percent over and under the mark. The bombs, of course, will be cased in neocarballoy thick enough for penetration. Then I take off in a shielded armored flying suit, say about here. . . ."

"If you take off at all, you and your suit will be inside a flitter," the Lensman interrupted. "Too many instruments for a suit, to say nothing of bombs, and you'll need heavier screen than a suit can put out. We can adapt a flitter for bomb-throwing easily enough."

"That'd be better, of course. QX, I set my flitter into a projectile trajectory toward the center of disturbance. Twelve seconds away, at about this point here, I take my instantaneous readings, solve the equations of that particular warped surface for some definite zero time. . . ."

"But s'pose the cycle won't give you a ten-second solution?"

"Then I'll swing around and try again until a long-enough cycle *does* show up."

"QX. It will, sometime."

"Sure. Then, having everything set for zero time, and assuming that the activity is somewhere near my assumed value. . . ."

"Assume it isn't—it probably won't be."

"I accelerate or decelerate. . . ."

"Solving new equations—differential equations at that—all the while?"

"Certainly. Don't interrupt so. I stick around until the sigma curve, extrapolated to zero time, matches one of my bombs. I build up the right velocity, cut that bomb loose, shoot myself off in a sharp curve, and Z-W-E-E-T—POWIE! She's out." With an expressive, sweeping gesture.

"You hope." Strong was frankly dubious. "And there you are, right in the middle of the damndest explosion you ever saw."

"Oh, no. I've gone free in the meantime, so nothing can touch me."

"*I* hope! But do you realize just how busy you are going to be during those ten or twelve seconds?"

"Yes." Cloud's face grew somber. "But I'll be in full control. I won't be afraid of anything that can happen—of *anything* that can happen. From my standpoint, that's the hell of it."

"QX," the Lensman decided, "You can go. We'll iron out the kinks as we go."

"We?"

"I'll be in the lookout shack with the boys, at least on the first ones. When do you want to start?"

"How long will it take to fix up the flitter?"

"Two days. Say we meet you there Saturday morning?"

"I'll be there," and again Neal Cloud and Babe, the big blue ox, hit the road; and as he rolled along the physicist mulled over in his mind the assignment to which he had set himself.

Like fire, only worse, atomic energy was a good servant, but a very bad master. Man had liberated it before he could really control it. In fact, control was not yet, and probably never would be, perfect. True, all except a minute fraction of one percent of the multitudes of small, tame, self-limiting vortices were perfect servants. But at long intervals, for some unknown reason—science knew *so* little, fundamentally, of nuclear reactions—one of them flared, nova-like, into a huge, wild, self-sustaining monster. It ceased being a servant, then, and became a master.

Such flare-ups occurred very infrequently; the trouble was that the loose vortices were so utterly, so damnably *permanent*. They never went out; and no data were ever obtained. Every living thing in the vicinity of a flare-up died; every instrument and every other solid thing within a radius of hundreds of feet melted down into the reeking, boiling slag of its crater.

Fortunately, the rate of growth was slow—as slow, almost, as it was persistent. But even so, unless something could be done about loose vortices before too many years, the situation would become extremely serious. That was why the Laboratory had been established in the first place.

Nothing much had been accomplished so far. Tractor beams would not hold. Nothing material was of any use. Pressors worked after a fashion—vortices *could* be moved from one place to another. One or two, through sheer luck, had been blown out by heavy charges of duodecaplylatomate. But duodec had taken many lives; and since it scattered a vortex as often as it fed it, duodec had caused vastly more damage than it had cured.

No end of fantastic schemes had been proposed, of course; of varying degrees of fantasy. Some of them sounded almost practical. Some of them had been tried; some were still being tried. Some, such as the perennially-appearing one of installing a free drive and flinging the whole neighborhood off into space, were perhaps feasible from an engineering standpoint. They were potentially so capable of making things worse, however, that they could not be used except as last-ditch measures. In short, the control of loose atomic vortices was very much an unsolved problem.

Chapter 2

—————— CLOUD BLASTS A VORTEX

NUMBER ONE, the oldest and worst vortex on Tellus, had been pushed out into the badlands, and there, at eight o'clock of the indicated morning, Cloud started to work on it.

The "lookout shack" was in fact a fully-equipped nucleonics laboratory. Its staff was not large—eight men worked in three staggered eight-hour shifts—but the development of its instrumentation had required hundreds of man-years of intensive research. Every factor of the vortex's activity was measured and recorded continuously, throughout every minute of every day of every year; and all of these measurements were summed up, integrated, into the "sigma" curve. This curve, which to the layman's eye was only a senselessly zig-zagging line, told the expert everything he wanted to know.

Cloud glanced at the chart and scowled, for one jagged peak, less than half an hour old, almost touched the top line of the paper.

"Bad, huh, Frank?"

"Bad, Storm, and getting worse. I wouldn't wonder if 'Calamity' were right—it certainly looks like she's getting ready to blow her top."

"No equation, I suppose," Strong said. The Lensman ignored as completely as did the observer, if not as flippantly, the distinct possibility that at any moment the observatory and all that it contained might be resolved into their sub-atomic components.

"None," Cloud stated. He did not need to spend hours at a calculating machine; at one glance he knew, without knowing how he knew, that no equation could fit that wildly-shifting sigma curve. "But most of these recent cycles cut ordinate seven fifty, so I'll take that for my value. That means nine point nine six zero kilograms of duodec for my basic, and nine four six two and ten point three five eight as alternates. On the wire?"

"It went out as you said it," the observer replied. "They'll be here in five minutes."

"QX. I'll get dressed, then."

The Lensman and one of the observers helped him into his cumbersome, heavily-padded armor; then all three men went out to the flitter. A tiny speedster, really; a slim torpedo with the stubby wings and the ludicrous tail-surfaces, the multifarious driving-, braking-, side-, top-, and under-jets so characteristic of the tricky, cranky, but ultra-maneuverable breed. Cloud checked the newly installed triplex launcher, made sure that he knew which bomb was in each tube, and climbed into the tiny operating compartment. The massive door—flitters are too small to have airlocks—rammed shut upon its teflon gaskets, the heavy toggles drove home. A heavily-padded form closed in upon the pilot, leaving only his left arm and his right leg free to move.

"Everybody in the clear?"

"All clear."

Cloud shot the flitter into the air and toward the seething inferno which was Loose Atomic Vortex Number One. The crater was a ragged, jagged hole perhaps two miles from lip to lip and a quarter of a mile in depth. The floor, being largely molten, was almost level except for a depression at the center, where the actual vortex lay. The walls of the pit were steeply, unstably irregular, varying in pitch and shape with the refractoriness of the strata composing them. Now a section would glare into an unbearably blinding white, puffing away in sparkling vapor. Again, cooled by an inrushing blast of air, it would subside into an angry scarlet, its surface crawling in a sluggish flow of lava. Occasionally a part of the wall might even go black, into pockmarked scoriae or brilliant planes of obsidian.

For always, at some point or other, there was a torrent of air rushing into that crater. It rushed in as ordinary air. It came out, however, in a ragingly uprushing pillar, as—as something else. No one knows exactly what a vortex does to air. Or, rather, the composition of the effluent gases varies as frequently and as unpredictably as does the activity of the vortex. Thus, the atmosphere emitted from a vortex-crater may be corrosive, it may be poisonous, it may be merely different; but it is no longer the air which we human beings are used to breathing. This conversion and corruption of Earth's atmosphere, if it could not be stopped, would end the possibility of life upon the planet's surface long before the world itself could be consumed.

As to the vortex itself ... it is difficult indeed to describe such a phenomenon. Practically all of its frightful radiation lies in those octaves of the spectrum which are invisible to the human eye. Suffice it to say, then, that it was a continuously active atomic reactor, with an effective surface temperature of approximately twenty five thousand degrees Kelvin, and let it go at that.

Neal Cloud, driving his flitter through that murky, radiation-riddled atmosphere, extrapolating his sigma curve by the sheer power of his mathematical-prodigy's mind, sat appalled. For the activity level was, and even in its lowest dips remained, well above the figure he had chosen. Distant though he was from the rim of that hellish pit, his skin began to prickle and to burn. His eyes began to smart and to ache. He knew what those symptoms meant: even the flitter's powerful screens were leaking; even his suit-screens and his special goggles were not stopping the stuff. But he wouldn't quit yet: the activity might—probably would—take a nose-dive any second now. If it did, he'd have to be ready. On the other hand, it might blow up any second, too.

There were two schools of mathematical thought upon that point. One held that a vortex, without any essential change in its nature or behavior, would keep on growing bigger until, uniting with the other vortices of the planet, it had converted all the mass of the world into energy.

The second school, of which the forementioned "Calamity" Carlowitz was the loudest voice, taught that at a certain stage of development the internal energy of the vortex would become so great that generation-radiation equilibrium could not be maintained. This would of course result in an explosion, the nature and consequences of which this Carlowitz was wont to dwell upon in ghoulishly mathematical glee. Neither school could prove its point, however—or, rather, each school proved its point with eminently plausible mathematics—and each hated and de-rided the other, with heat and at length.

Neal Cloud, as he studied through his almost opaque defenses that indescribably ravening fireball, that ra-pacious monstrosity which might very well have come from the very center of the hottest hell of mythology, felt strangely inclined to agree with Carlowitz. It didn't seem possible that it *could* get any worse without exploding.

The activity stayed high; 'way too high. The tiny con-trol room grew hotter and hotter. His skin burned more and his eyes ached worse. He touched a stud and spoke.

"Phil? Better get me three more bombs. Like these, except up around. . . ."

"I don't check you. If you do that, it's apt to drop to a minimum and stay there. I'd suggest a wider interval."

"QX—that'd be better. Two, then, instead of three. Four point nine eight zero and thirteen point nine four zero. You might break out a jar of burn-dressing, too; some fairly warm stuff is leaking through."

"Will do. Come down, fast!"

Cloud landed. He stripped to the skin and his friends smeared him with the thick, gooey stuff that was not only added protection against radiation, but also a sovereign remedy for new burns. He exchanged his goggles for a heavier, darker pair. The two bombs arrived and were substituted for two of the original load.

"I thought of something while I was up there," Cloud said then. "Fourteen kilograms of duodec is nobody's firecracker, but it may be the least of what's going to go off. Have you got any idea of what's going to become of the intrinsic energy of the vortex when I snuff it?"

"Can't say I have." The Lensman frowned in thought. "No data."

"Neither have I. But I'd say you'd better go back to the new station—the one you were going to move to if it kept on getting worse. The clocks are ticking there, aren't they?"

"Yes. It might be the smart thing to do—just in case."

Again in air, Cloud found that the activity, while still very high, was not too high for his heaviest bomb, but that it was fluctuating too rapidly. He could not get even five seconds of trustworthy prediction, to say nothing of ten. So he waited, as close to the horrible center of disintegration as he dared.

The flitter hung poised in air, motionless, upon softly hissing under-jets. Cloud knew to a fraction his height above the ground. He knew to a fraction his distance from the vortex. He knew the density of the atmosphere and the velocity and direction of the wind. Hence, since he could also read, closely enough, the momentary variations in the cyclonic storms within the crater, he could compute very easily the course and velocity necessary to land the bomb in the exact center of the vortex at any given instant of time. The hard part—the thing that no one had as yet succeeded in doing—was to predict, for a time far enough ahead to be of any use, a usably close approximation to the vortex's quantitative activity.

Therefore Cloud concentrated upon the dials and gauges in front of him; concentrated with every fiber of his being and with every cell of his brain.

Suddenly, almost imperceptibly, the sigma curve gave signs of flattening out. Cloud's mind pounced. Simultaneous differential equations; nine of them. A quadruple integration in four dimensions. No matter—Cloud did not solve problems laboriously, one operation at a time. Without knowing how he had arrived at it, he knew the answer; just as the Posenian or the Rigellian can perceive every separate component particle of an opaque, three-dimensional solid, but without being able to explain to any Tellurian how his sense of perception works. It just *is*, that's all.

By virtue of whatever sense or ability it is which makes a mathematical prodigy what he is; Cloud knew that in exactly seven and three-tenths seconds from that observed instant the activity of the vortex would match precisely the rating of his heaviest bomb. Another flick of his mental switch and he knew exactly the velocity he would require. His hand swept over the studs, his right foot tramped down hard upon the firing pedal; and, even as the quivering flitter rammed forward under five Tellurian gravities of acceleration, he knew to the thousandth of a second how long he would have to hold that acceleration to attain that velocity. While not really long—in seconds— it was much too long for comfort. It would take him much closer to the vortex than he wanted to be; in fact, it would take him almost to the crater's rim.

But he stuck to the calculated course, and at the precisely correct instant he released his largest bomb and cut his dive. Then, in a continuation of the same motion, his hand slashed down through the beam of light whose cutting would activate the Bergenholm and make the vessel inertialess—safe from any form whatever of physical violence. For an instant nothing happened, and for that instant Cloud sat appalled. *Neutralization of inertia took time!* Not that he had ever been told that it was instantaneous—he had just assumed so. He had never noticed any time-lapse before, but now it seemed to be taking forever!

After that one instant of shocked inaction he went into ultra-speed action; kicking in the little vessel's all-out eight-G drive and whirling her around as only a flitter or a speedster can whirl; only to see in his plate the vortex opening up like a bell-flower, or like a sun going nova.

Cloud's forebodings were more than materialized then, for it was not only the bomb that was going off. The staggeringly immense energy of the vortex was merging with that of the detonating duodec to form an utterly indescribable explosion.

In part the flood of incandescent lava in the pit was beaten downward by the sheer, stupendous force of the blow; in part it was hurled abroad in masses, gouts, and streamers. And the raging blast of the explosion's front seized the fragments and tore and worried them to bits, hurling them still faster along their paths of violence. And air, so densely compressed as to act like a solid, smote the walls of the crater. Those walls crumbled, crushed outward through the hard-packed ground, broke up into jaggedly irregular blocks which hurtled screamingly in all directions.

The blast-wave or explosion front buffeted the flyer while she was still partially inert and while Cloud was almost blacked out and physically helpless from the frightful linear and angular accelerations. The impact broke his left arm and his right leg; the only parts of his body not pressure-packed. Then, milliseconds later, the debris began to arrive.

Chunks of solid or semi-molten rock slammed against the hull, knocking off wings and control-surfaces. Gobs of viscous slag slapped it liquidly, freezing into and clogging up jets and orifices. The little ship was knocked hither and thither by forces she could no more resist than can a floating leaf resist a cataract; Cloud's brain was addled as an egg by the vicious concussions which were hitting him so nearly simultaneously from so many different directions.

The concussions and the sluggings lightened . . . stopped . . . a vast peace descended, blanket-wise. The flitter was free—was riding effortlessly away on the outermost, most tenuous fringes of the storm!

Cloud wanted to faint, then, but he didn't—quite. With one arm and leg and what few cells of his brain were still in working order, he was still in the fight. It did not even occur to him, until long afterward, that he was not going to make any effort whatever to avoid death.

Foggily, he tried to look at the crater. Nine-tenths of his visiplates were dead, but he finally got a view. Good—it was out. He wasn't surprised—he knew it would be.

His next effort was to locate the secondary observatory, where he would have to land; and in that, too, he was successful. He had enough intelligence left to realize that, with practically all of his jets clogged and his wings and tail shot off, he couldn't land his flitter inert. He'd *have* to land her free.

Neal Cloud was not the world's best pilot. Nevertheless, by dint of light and somewhat unorthodox use of what few jets he had left, he did land her free. A very good landing, considering—he almost hit the observatory's field, which was only one mile square—and having landed her, he inerted her.

But, as has been intimated, his brain wasn't working quite so good; he had held his ship inertialess for quite a few seconds longer than he thought, and he did not even think of the terrific buffetings she had taken. As a result of these things, however, her intrinsic velocity did not match, anywhere nearly, that of the ground upon which she lay. Thus, when Cloud cut his Bergenholm, restoring thereby to the flitter the absolute velocity and the inertia she had before going free, there resulted a distinctly anticlimactic crash.

There was a last terrific bump as the motionless vessel collided with the equally motionless ground; and "Storm" Cloud, Vortex Blaster, went out like the proverbial light.

Help came, of course; on the double. Cloud was unconscious and the flitter's port could not be opened from the outside, but those were not insuperable obstacles. A plate, already loose, was torn away; the pilot was unclamped and rushed to Base Hospital in the "meat-crate" standing by.

Later, in a private office of that hospital, the head of the Vortex Control Laboratory sat and waited—not patiently.

"How is he, Lacy?" he demanded, as the surgeon-marshal entered the room. "He's going to live?"

"Oh, yes, Phil—definitely yes," Lacy replied, briskly. "A very good skeleton; very good indeed. His screens stopped all the really bad radiation, so the damage will yield quite readily to treatment. He doesn't really need the Phillips we gave him—for the replacement of damaged parts, you know—except for a few torn muscles and so on."

"But he was pretty badly smashed up—I helped take him out, you know—how about that arm and leg? He was a mess."

"Merely simple fractures—entirely negligible." Lacy

waved aside with an airy gesture such minor ills as broken bones. "He'll be out in a couple of weeks."

"How soon can I see him? Business can wait, but there's a personal matter that can't."

"I know what you mean." Lacy pursed his lips. "Ordinarily I wouldn't allow it, but you see him now. Not too long, though, Phil; he's weak. Ten minutes at most."

"QX. Thanks." A nurse led the visiting Lensman to Cloud's bedside.

"Hi, stupe!" he boomed, cheerfully. " 'Stupe' being short for 'stupendous', this time."

"Ho, chief. Glad to see somebody. Sit down."

"You're the most-wanted man in the galaxy, not excepting Kimball Kinnison. Here's a spool of tape, which you can look at as soon as Lacy will let you have a scanner. It's only the first one. As soon as any planet finds out that we've got a sure-enough-vortex-blower-outer who can really call his shots—and *that* news gets around mighty fast—it sends in a double-urgent, Class A Prime demand for you.

"Sirius IV got in first by a whisker, but it was a photo finish with Aldebaran II and all channels have been jammed ever since. Canopus, Vega, Rigel, Spica. Everybody, from Alsakan to Zabriska. We announced right off that we wouldn't receive personal delegations—we had to almost throw a couple of pink-haired Chickladorians out bodily to make them believe we meant it—that our own evaluation of necessity, not priority of requisition, would govern. QX?"

"Absolutely," Cloud agreed. "That's the only way to handle it, I should think."

"So forget this psychic trauma ... No, I don't mean that," the Lensman corrected himself hastily. "You know what I mean. The will to live is the most important factor in any man's recovery, and too many worlds need you too badly to have you quit now. Check?"

"I suppose so," Cloud acquiesced, but somberly, "and I've got more will to live than I thought I had. I'll keep on pecking away as long as I last."

"Then you'll die of old age, Buster," the Lensman assured him. "We got full data. We know exactly how long it takes to go from fully inert to fully free. We know exactly what to do to your screens. Next time nothing will come through except light, and only as much of that as you like. You can wait as close to a vortex as you please, for as long as is necessary to get exactly the conditions you want. You'll be as safe as if you were in Klono's hip pocket."

"Sure of that?"

"Absolutely—or at least, as sure as we can be of anything that hasn't happened yet. But your guardian angel here is eyeing her clock a bit pointedly, so I'd better do a flit before she tosses me out on my ear. Clear ether, Storm!"

"Clear ether, chief!"

Thus "Storm" Cloud, nucleonicist, became the most narrowly-specialized specialist in the long annals of science; became "Storm" Cloud, the Vortex Blaster.

And that night Lensman Philip Strong, instead of sleeping, thought and thought and thought. What could he do—what could *anybody* do—if Cloud should get himself killed? *Somebody* would have to do *something* ... but who? And what? Could—or could not—another Vortex Blaster be found? Or trained?

And next morning, early, he Lensed a thought.

"Kinnison? Phil Strong. I've got a high-priority problem that will take a lot of work and a lot more weight than I carry. Are you free to listen for a few minutes?"

"I'm free. Go ahead."

Chapter 3

CLOUD LOSES AN ARM

TELLURIAN PHARMACEUTICALS, INC., was Civilization's oldest and most conservative drug house. "Hidebound" was the term most frequently used, not only by its younger employees, but also by its more progressive competitors. But, corporatively, Tellurian Pharmaceuticals, Inc., did not care. Its board of directors was limited by an iron-clad, if unwritten, law to men of seventy years more; and against the inertia of that ruling body the impetuosity of the younger generation was exactly as efficacious as the dashing of ocean waves against an adamantine cliff—and in very much the same fashion.

Ocean waves do in time cut into even the hardest rock; and, every century or two, TPI did take forward step—after a hundred years of testing by others had proved conclusively that the "new" idea conformed in every particular with the exalted standards of the Galactic Medical Association.

TPI's plant upon the planet Deka (Dekanore III, on the charts) filled the valley of Clear Creek and the steep, high hills on its sides, from the mountain spring which was the creek's source to its confluence with the Spokane River.

The valley floor was a riot of color, devoted as it was to the intensive cultivation of medicinal plants. Along both edges of the valley extended row after row of hydroponics sheds. Upon the mountains' sides there were snake dens, lizard pens, and enclosures for many other species of fauna.

Nor was the surface all that was in use. The hills were hollow: honeycombed into hundreds of rooms in which, under precisely controlled environments of temperature, atmosphere, and radiation, were grown hundreds of widely-variant forms of life.

At the confluence of creek and river, just inside the city limits of Newspoke—originally New Spokane—there reared and sprawled the Company's headquarters buildings; offices, processing and synthesizing plants, laboratories, and so on. In one of the laboratories, three levels below ground, two men faced each other. Works Manager Graves was tall and fat; Fenton V. Fairchild, M.D., Nu.D., F.C.R., Consultant in Radiation, was tall and thin.

"Everything set, Graves?"

"Yes. Twelve hours, you said."

"For the full cycle. Seven to the point of maximum yield."

"Go ahead."

"Here are the seeds. Treconian broadleaf. For the present you will have to take my word for it that they did not come from Trenco. These are standard hydroponics tanks, size one. The formula of the nutrient solution, while complex and highly critical, contains nothing either rare or unduly expensive. I plant the seed, thus, in each of the two tanks. I cover each tank with a plastic hood, transparent to the frequencies to be used. I cover both with a larger hood—so. I align the projectors—thus. We will now put on armor, as the radiation is severe and the atmosphere, of which there may be leakage when the pollenating blast is turned on, is more than slightly toxic. I then admit Trenconian atmosphere from this cylinder . . ."

"Synthetic or imported?" Graves interrupted.

"Imported. Synthesis is possible, but prohibitively expensive and difficult. Importation in tankers is simple and comparatively cheap. I now energize the projectors. Growth has begun."

In the glare of blue-green radiance the atmosphere inside the hoods, the very ether, warped and writhed. In spite of the distortion of vision, however, it could be seen that growth was taking place, and at an astounding rate. In a few minutes the seeds had sprouted; in an hour the thick, broad, purplish-green leaves were inches long. In seven hours each tank was full of a lushly luxuriant tangle of foliage.

"This is the point of maximum yield," Fairchild remarked, as he shut off the projectors. "We will now process one tank, if you like."

"Certainly I like. How else could I know it's the clear quill?"

"By the looks," came the scientist's dry rejoinder. "Pick your tank."

One tank was removed. The leaves were processed. The full cycle of growth of the remaining tank was completed. Graves himself harvested the seeds, and himself carried them away.

Six days, six samples, six generations of seed, and the eminently skeptical Graves was convinced.

"You've got something there, Doc," he admitted then. "We can really go to town on that. Now, how about notes, or stuff from your old place, or people who may have smelled a rat?"

"I'm perfectly clean. None of my boys know anything important, and none ever will. I assemble all apparatus myself, from standard parts, and disassemble it myself. I've been around, Graves."

"Well, we can't be too sure." The fat man's eyes were piercing and cold. "Leakers don't live very long. We don't want you to die, at least not until we get in production here."

"Nor then, if you know when you're well off," the scientist countered, cynically. "I'm a fellow of the College of Radiation, and it took me five years to learn this technique. None of your hatchetmen could *ever* learn it. Remember that, my friend."

"So?"

"So don't get off on the wrong foot and don't get any funny ideas. I know how to run things like this and I've got the manpower and equipment to do it. If I come in I'm running it, not you. Take it or leave it."

The fat man pondered for minutes, then decided. "I'll take it. You're in, Doc. You can have a cave—two hundred seventeen is empty—and we'll go up and get things started right now."

* * * * *

Less than a year later, the same two men sat in Graves' office. They waited while a red light upon a peculiarly complicated deskboard faded through pink into pure white.

"All clear. This way, Doc." Graves pushed a yellow button on his desk and a section of blank wall slid aside.

In the elevator thus revealed the two men went down to a sub-basement. Along a dimly-lit corridor, through an elaborately locked steel door, and into a steel-lined room. Four inert bodies lay upon the floor.

Graves thrust a key into an orifice and a plate swung open, revealing a chute into which the bodies were dumped. The two retraced their steps to the manager's office.

"Well, that's all we can feed to the disintegrator." Fairchild lit an Alsakanite cigarette and exhaled appreciatively.

"Why? Going soft on us?"

"No. The ice is getting too thin."

"Whaddya mean, 'thin'?" Graves demanded. "The Patrol inspectors are ours—all that count. Our records are fixed. Everything's on the green."

"That's what *you* think," the scientist sneered. "You're supposed to be smart. Are you? Our accident rate is up three hundredths; industrial hazard rate and employee turnover about three and a half; and the Narcotics Division alone knows how much we have upped total bootleg sales. Those figures are all in the Patrol's books. How can you give such facts the brush-off?"

"We don't have to." Graves laughed comfortably. "Even a half of one percent wouldn't excite suspicion. Our distribution is so uniform throughout the galaxy that they can't center it. They can't possibly trace anything back to us. Besides, with our lily-white reputation, other firms would get knocked off in time to give us plenty of warning. Lutzenschiffer's, for instance, is putting out Heroin by the ton."

"So what?" Fairchild remained entirely unconvinced. "Nobody else is putting out what comes out of cave two seventeen—demand and price prove that. What you don't seem to get, Graves, is that some of those damnèd Lensmen have *brains*. Suppose they decide to put a couple of Lensmen onto this job—then what? The minute anybody runs a rigid statistical analysis on us, we're done for."

"Um . . . . m." This was a distinctly disquieting thought, in view of the impossibility of concealing anything from a Lensman who was really on the prowl. "That wouldn't be so good. What would you do?"

"I'd shut down two seventeen—and the whole hush-hush end—until we can get our records straight and our death-rate down to the old ten-year average. That's the only way we can be really safe."

"Shut down! The way they're pushing us for production? Don't be an idiot—the chief would toss us both down the chute."

"Oh, I don't mean without permission. Talk him into it. It'd be best for everybody, over the long pull, believe me."

"Not a chance. He'd blow his stack. If we can't dope out something better than that, we go on as is."

"The next-best thing would be to use some new form of death to clean up our books."

"Wonderful!" Graves snorted contemptuously. "What would we add to what we've got now—bubonic plague?"

"A loose atomic vortex."

"Wh-o-o-o-sh!" The fat man deflated, then came back up, gasping for air. "Man, you're completely *nuts!* There's only one on the planet, and it's ... or do you mean ... but *nobody* ever touched one of those things off deliberately ... can it be done?"

"Yes. It isn't simple, but we of the College of Radiation know how—theoretically—the transformation can be made to occur. It has never been done because it has been impossible to extinguish the things; but now Neal Cloud is putting them out. The fact that the idea is new makes it all the better."

"I'll say so. Neat ... *very* neat." Graves' agile and cunning brain figuratively licked its chops. "Certain of our employees will presumably have been upon an outing in the upper end of the valley when this terrible accident takes place?"

"Exactly—enough of them to straighten out our books. Then, later, we can dispose of undesirables as they appear. Vortices are absolutely unpredictable, you know. People can die of radiation or of any one of a mixture of various toxic gases and the vortex will take the blame."

"And later on, when it gets dangerous, Storm Cloud can blow it out for us," Graves gloated. "But we won't want him for a long, long time!"

"No, but we'll report it and ask for him the hour it happens ... use your head, Graves!" He silenced the manager's anguished howl of protest. "Anybody who gets one wants it killed as soon as possible, but here's the joker. Cloud has enough Class-A-double-prime-urgent demands on file already to keep him busy from now on, so we won't be able to get him for a long, long time. See?"

"I see. Nice, Doc. ... very, *very* nice. But I'll have the boys keep an eye on Cloud just the same."

* * * * *

At about this same time two minor cogs of TPI's vast machine sat blissfully, arms around each other, on a rustic seat improvised from rocks, branches, and leaves. Below them, almost under their feet, was a den of highly venemous snakes, but neither man or girl saw them. Before them, also unperceived, was a magnificent view of valley and steam and mountain.

All they saw, however, was each other—until their attention was wrenched to a man who was climbing toward them with the aid of a thick club which he used as a staff.

"Oh . . . Bob!" The girl stared briefly; then, with a half-articulate moan, shrank even closer against her lover's side.

Ryder, left arm tightening around the girl's waist, felt with his right hand for a club of his own and tensed his muscles, for the climbing man was completely mad.

His breathing was . . . horrible. Mouth tight-clamped, despite his terrific exertion, he was *sniffing*—sniffing loathsomely, lustfully, each whistling inhalation filling his lungs to bursting. He exhaled explosively, as though begrudging the second of time required to empty himself of air. Wide-open eyes glaring fixedly ahead he blundered upward, paying no attention whatever to his path. He tore through clumps of thorny growth; he stumbled and fell over logs and stones; he caromed away from boulders; as careless of the needles which tore clothing and skin as of the rocks which bruised his flesh to the bone. He struck a great tree and bounced; felt his frenzied way around the obstacle and back into his original line.

He struck the gate of the pen immediately beneath the two appalled watchers and stopped. He moved to the right and paused, whimpering in anxious agony. Back to the gate and over to the left, where he stopped and howled. Whatever the frightful compulsion was, whatever he sought, he could not deviate enough from his line to go around the pen. He looked, then, and for the first time saw the gate and the fence and the ophidian inhabitants of the den. They did not matter. Nothing mattered. He fumbled at the lock, then furiously attacked it and the gate and the fence with his club—fruitlessly. He tried to climb the fence, but failed. He tore off his shoes and socks and, by dint of jamming toes and fingers ruthlessly into the meshes, he began to climb.

No more than he had minded the thorns and the rocks did he mind the eight strands of viciously-barbed wire surmounting that fence; he did not wince as the inch-long steel fangs bit into arms and legs and body. He did, however, watch the snakes. He took pains to drop into an area temporarily clear of them, and he pounded to death the half-dozen serpents bold enough to bar his path.

Then, dropping to the ground, he writhed and scuttled

about; sniffing ever harder; nose plowing the ground. He halted; dug his bleeding fingers into the hard soil; thrust his nose into the hole; inhaled tremendously. His body writhed, trembled, shuddered uncontrollably, then stiffened convulsively into a supremely ecstatic rigidity utterly horrible to see.

The terribly labored breathing ceased. The body collapsed bonelessly, even before the snakes crawled up and struck and struck and struck.

Jacqueline Comstock saw very little of the outrageous performance. She screamed once, shut both eyes, and, twisting about within the man's encircling arm, burrowed her face into his left shoulder.

Ryder, however—white-faced, set-jawed, sweating— watched the thing to its ghastly end. When it was over he licked his lips and swallowed twice before he could speak.

"It's all over, dear—no danger now," he managed finally to say. "We'd better go. We ought to turn in an alarm . . . make a report or something."

"Oh, I can't, Bob—I can't!" she sobbed. "If I open my eyes I just know I'll look, and if I look I'll . . . I'll simply turn inside out!"

"Hold everything, Jackie! Keep your eyes shut. I'll pilot you and tell you when we're out of sight."

More than half carrying his companion, Ryder set off down the rocky trail. Out of sight of what had happened, the girl opened her eyes and they continued their descent in a more usual, more decorous fashion until they met a man hurrying upward.

"Oh, Dr. Fairchild! There was a . . ." But the report which Ryder was about to make was unnecessary; the alarm had already been given.

"I know," the scientist puffed. "Stop! Stay exactly where you are!" He jabbed a finger emphatically downward to anchor the young couple in the spot they occupied. "Don't talk—don't say a word until I get back!"

Fairchild returned after a time, unhurried and completely at ease. He did not ask the shaken couple if they had seen what had happened. He knew.

"Bu . . . buh . . . but, doctor," Ryder began.

"Keep still—don't talk at all." Fairchild ordered, bruskly. Then, in an ordinary conversational tone, he went on: "Until we have investigated this extraordinary occurrence thoroughly—sifted it to the bottom—the possibility of sabotage and spying cannot be disregarded. As the only eye-witnesses, your reports will be exceedingly valuable; but you must not say a word until we are in a place which I *know* is proof against any and all spy-rays. Do you understand?"

"Oh! Yes, we understand."

"Pull yourselves together, then. Act unconcerned, casual; particularly when we get to the Administration Building. Talk about the weather—or, better yet, about the honeymoon you are going to take on Chickladoria."

Thus there was nothing visibly unusual about the group of three which strolled into the building and into Graves' private office. The fat man raised an eyebrow.

"I'm taking them to the private laboratory," Fairchild said, as he touched the yellow button and led the two toward the private elevator. "Frankly, young folks, I am a scared—yes, a badly scared man."

This statement, so true and yet so misleading, resolved the young couple's inchoate doubts. Entirely unsuspectingly, they followed the Senior Radiationist into the elevator and, after it had stopped, along, a corridor. They paused as he unlocked and opened a door; they stepped unquestioningly into the room at his gesture. He did not, however, follow them in. Instead, the heavy metal slab slammed shut, cutting off Jackie's piercing shriek of fear.

"You might as well cut out the racket," came from a speaker in the steel ceiling of the room. "Nobody can hear you but me."

"But Mr. Graves, I thought ... Dr. Fairchild told us ... we were going to tell him about ..."

"You're going to tell nobody nothing. You saw too much and know too much, that's all."

"Oh, *that's* it!" Ryder's mind reeled as some part of the actual significance of what he had seen struck home. "But listen! Jackie didn't see anything—she had her eyes shut all the time—and doesn't know anything. You don't want to have the murder of such a girl as *she* is on your mind, I know. Let her go and she'll never say a word—we'll both swear to it—or you could ..."

"Why? Just because she's got a face and a shape?" The fat man sneered. "No soap, Junior. She's not that much of a ..." He broke off as Fairchild entered his office.

"Well, how about it? How bad is it?" Graves demanded.

"Not bad at all. Everything's under control."

"Listen, doctor!" Ryder pleaded. "Surely you don't want to murder Jackie here in cold blood? I was just suggesting to Graves that he could get a therapist . . ."

"Save your breath," Fairchild ordered. "We have important things to think about. You two die."

"But why?" Ryder cried. He could as yet perceive only a fraction of the tremendous truth. "I tell you, it's . . ."

"We'll let you guess," said Fairchild.

Shock upon shock had been too much for the girl's overstrained nerves. She fainted quietly and Ryder eased her down to the cold steel floor.

"Can't you give her a better cell than this?" he protested then. "There's no . . . it isn't *decent!*"

"You'll find food and water, and that's enough." Graves laughed coarsely. "You won't live long, so don't worry about conveniences. But keep still. If you want to know what's going on, you can listen, but one more word out of you and I cut the circuit. Go ahead, Doc, with what you were going to say."

"There was a fault in the rock. Very small, but a little of the finest smoke seeped through. Barney must have been a sniffer before to be able to smell the trace of the stuff that was drifting down the hill. I'm having the whole cave tested with a leak-detector and sealed bottle-tight. The record can stand it that Barney—he was a snake-tender, you know—died of snake-bite. That's almost the truth, too, by the way."

"Fair enough. Now, how about these two?"

"Um . . . m. We've got to hold the risk at absolute minimum." Fairchild pondered briefly. "We can't disintegrate them this month, that's sure. They've got to be found dead, and our books are full. We'll have to keep them alive—where they are now is as good a place as any—for a week."

"Why alive? We've kept stiffs in cold storage before now."

"Too chancey. Dead tissues change too much. You weren't courting investigation then; now we are. We've got to keep our noses clean. How about this? They couldn't wait any longer and got married today. You, big-hearted philanthropist that you are, told them they could take their two weeks vacation now for a honeymoon—you'd square it with their department heads. They come back in about ten days, to get settled; go up the valley to see the vortex; and out. Anything in that set-up we can't fake a cover for?"

"It looks perfect to me. We'll let 'em enjoy life for ten days, right where they are now. Hear that, Ryder?"

"Yes, you pot-bellied . . ."

The fat man snapped a switch.

It is not necessary to go into the details of the imprisonment. Doggedly and skillfully though he tried, Ryder could open up no avenue of escape or of communication; and Jacqueline, facing the inevitability of death, steadied down to meet it. She was a woman. In minor crises she had shrieked and had hidden her face and had fainted: but in this ultimate one she drew from the depths of her woman's soul not only the power to overcome her own weakness, but also an extra something with which to sustain and fortify her man.

Chapter 4

————"STORM" CLOUD ON DEKA

IN THE VORTEX CONTROL LABORATORY on Tellus, Cloud had just gone into Philip Strong's office.

"No trouble?" the Lensman asked, after greetings had been exchanged.

"Uh-huh. Simple as blowing out a match. You quit worrying about me long ago, didn't you?"

"Pretty much, except for the impossibility of training anybody else to do it. We're still working on that angle, though. You're looking fit."

He was. He carried no scars—the Phillips treatment had taken care of that. His face looked young and keen; his hard-schooled, resilient body was in surprisingly fine condition for that of a man crowding forty so nearly. He no longer wore his psychic trauma visibly; it no longer obtruded itself between him and those with whom he worked; but in his own mind he was *sure* that it still was, and always would be, there. But the Lensman, studying him narrowly—and, if the truth must be known, using his Lens as well—was *not* sure, and was well content.

"Not bad for an old man, Phil. I could whip a wildcat, and spot him one bite and two scratches. But what I came in here for, as you may have suspected, is—where do I go from here? Spica or Rigel or Canopus? They're the worst, aren't they?"

"Rigel's is probably the worst in property damage and urgency. Before we decide, though, I wish you'd take a good look at this data from Dekanore III. See if you see what I do."

"Huh? Dekanore III?" Cloud was surprised. "No trouble there, is there? They've only got one, and it's 'way down in Class Z somewhere."

"Two now. It's the new one I'm talking about. It's acting funny—*damned* funny."

Cloud went through the data, brow furrowed in concentration; then sketched three charts and frowned.

"I see what you mean. '*Damned* funny' is right. The toxicity is too steady, but at the same time the composition of the effluvium is too varied. Inconsistent. However, there's no real attempt at a gamma analysis—nowhere near enough data for one—this *could* be right; they're so utterly unpredictable. The observers were inexperienced, I take it, with medical and chemical bias?"

"Check. That's the way I read it."

"Well, I'll say this much—I never saw a gamma chart that would accept half of this stuff, and I can't even imagine what the sigma curve would look like. Boss, what say I skip over there and get us a full reading on that baby before she goes orthodox—or, should I say, orthodoxly unorthodox?"

"However you say. it, that's my thought exactly; and we have a good excuse for giving it priority. It's killing more people than all three of the bad ones together."

"If I can't fix the toxicity with exciters I'll throw a solid cordon around it to keep people away. I won't blow it out, though, until I find out why it's acting so—if it is. Clear ether, chief, I'm practically there!"

It did not take long to load Cloud's flitter aboard a Dekanore-bound liner. Half-way there however, an alarm rang out and the dread word "Pirates!" resounded through the ship.

Consternation reigned, for organized piracy had disappeared with the fall of the Council of Boskone. Furthermore, this was not in any sense a treasure ship; she was an ordinary passenger liner.

She had had little enough warning—her communications officer had sent out only a part of his first distress call when the blanketing interference jammed his channels. The pirate—a first-class superdreadnought—flashed up and a visual beam drove in.

"Go inert," came the terse command. "We're coming aboard."

"Are you completely crazy?" The liner's captain was surprised and disgusted, rather than alarmed. "If not, you've got the wrong ship. Everything aboard—including any ransom you could get for our passenger list—wouldn't pay your expenses."

"You wouldn't know, of course, that you're carrying a package of Lonabarian jewelry, or would you?" The question was elaborately skeptical.

"I know damned well I'm *not*."

"We'll take the package you *haven't* got, then!" the pirate snapped. "Go inert and open up, or I'll do it for you—like this." A needle-beam lashed out and expired. "That was through one of your holds. The next one will be through your control room."

Resistance being out of the question, the liner went inert. While the intrinsic velocities of the two vessels were being matched, the pirate issued further instructions.

"All officers now in the control room, stay there. All other officers, round up all passengers and herd them into the main saloon. Anybody that acts up or doesn't do exactly what he's told will be blasted."

The pirates boarded. One squad went to the control room. Its leader, seeing that the communications officer was still trying to drive a call through the blanket of interference, beamed him down without a word. At this murder the captain and four or five other officers went for their guns and there was a brief but bloody battle. There were too many pirates.

A larger group invaded the main saloon. Most of them went through, only half a dozen or so posting themselves to guard the passengers. One of the guards, a hook-nosed individual wearing consciously an aura of authority, spoke.

"Take it easy, folks, and nobody'll get hurt. If any of you've got guns, don't go for 'em. That's a specialty that . . ."

One of his DeLameters flamed briefly. Cloud's right arm, almost to the shoulder, vanished. The man behind him dropped—in two different places.

"Take it easy, I said," the pirate chief went calmly on. "You can tie that arm up, fella, if you want to. It was in line with that guy who was trying to pull a gun. You nurse over there—take him to sick-bay and fix up his wing. If anybody stops you tell 'em Number One said to. Now, the rest of you, watch your step. I'll cut down every damn one of you that so much as looks like he wanted to start something."

They obeyed.

In a few minutes the looting parties returned to the saloon.

"Did you get it, Six?"

"Yeah. In the mail, like you said."

"The safe?"

"Sure. Wasn't much in it, but not too bad, at that."

"QX. Control room! QX?"

"Ten dead," the intercom blatted in reply. "Otherwise QX."

"Fuse the panels?"

"Natch."

"Let's go!"

They went. Their vessel flashed away. The passengers rushed to their staterooms. Then:

"Doctor Cloud!" came from the speaker. "Doctor Neal Cloud! Control room calling Doctor Cloud!"'

"Cloud speaking."

"Report to the control room, please."

"Oh—excuse me—I didn't know you were wounded," the officer apologized as he saw the bandaged stump and the white, sweating face. "You'd better go to bed."

"Doing nothing wouldn't help. What did you want me for?"

"Do you know anything about communicators?"

"A little—what a nucleonics man has to know."

"Good. They killed all our communications officers and

blasted the panels, even in the lifeboats. You can't do much with your left hand, of course, but you may be able to boss the job of rigging up a spare."

"I can do more than you think—I'm left-handed. Give me a couple of technicians and I'll see what we can do."

They set to work, but before they could accomplish anything a cruiser drove up, flashing its identification as a warship of the Galactic Patrol.

"We picked up the partial call you got off," its young commander said, briskly. "With that and the plotted center of interference we didn't lose any time. Let's make this snappy." He was itching to be off after the marauder, but he could not leave until he had ascertained the facts and had been given clearance. "You aren't hurt much—don't need to call a tug, do you?"

"No," replied the liner's senior surviving officer.

"QX," and a quick investigation followed.

"Anybody who ships stuff like that open mail ought to lose it, but it's tough on innocent bystanders. Anything else I can do for you?"

"Not unless you can lend us some officers, particularly navigators and communications officers."

"Sorry, but we're short there ourselves—four of my best are in sick-bay. Sign this clearance, please, and I'll be on that fellow's tail. I'll send your copy of my report to your head office. Clear ether!"

The cruiser shot away. Temporary repairs were made and the liner, with Cloud and a couple of electronics technicians as communications officers, finished the voyage to Dekanore III without more interruption.

The Vortex Blaster was met at the dock by Works Manager Graves himself. The fat man was effusively sorry that Cloud had lost an arm, but assured him that the accident wouldn't lay him up very long. He, Graves, would get a Posenian surgeon over here so fast that . . . .

If the manager was taken aback to learn that Cloud had already had a Phillips treatment, he did not show it. He escorted the specialist to Deka's best hotel, where he introduced him largely and volubly. Graves took him to supper. Graves took him to a theater and showed him the town. Graves told the hotel management to give the scientist the best rooms and the best valet they had, and that Cloud was not to be allowed to spend any of his own money. All of his activities, whatever their nature, purpose, or extent, were to be charged to Tellurian Pharmaceuticals, Inc. Graves was a grand guy.

Cloud broke loose, finally, and went to the dock to see about getting his flitter.

It had not been unloaded. There would be a slight delay, he was informed, because of the insurance inspections necessitated by the damage—and Cloud had not known that there had been any! When he had learned what had been done to his little ship he swore bitterly and sought out the liner's senior officer.

"Why didn't you tell me we got holed?" he demanded.

"Why, I don't know . . . just that you didn't ask, is all, I guess. I don't suppose it occurred to anybody—I know it didn't to me—that you might be interested."

And that was, Cloud knew, strictly true. Passengers were not informed of such occurrences. He had been enough of an officer so that he could have learned anything he wished; but not enough of one to have been informed of such matters as routine. Nor was it surprising that it had not come up in conversation. Damage to cargo meant nothing whatever to the liner's overworked officers, standing double watches; a couple of easily-patched holes in the hull were not worth mentioning. From their standpoint the *only* damage was done to the communicators, and Cloud himself had set them to rights. This delay was his own fault as much as anybody else's. Yes, more.

"You won't lose anything, though," the officer said, helpfully. "Everything's covered, you know."

"It isn't the money I'm yowling about—it's the time. That apparatus can't be duplicated anywhere except on Tellus, and even there it's all special-order stuff. OH, DAMN!" and Cloud strode away toward his hotel.

During the following days TPI entertained him royally. Not insistently—Graves was an expert in such matters— but simply by giving him the keys to the planet. He could do anything he pleased. He could have all the company he wanted, male or female, to help him to do it. Thus he did—within limits—just about what Graves wanted him to do; and, in spite of the fact that he did not want to enjoy life, he liked it.

One evening, however, he refused to play a slot machine, explaining to his laughing companion that the laws of chance were pretty thoroughly shackled in such mechanisms—and the idle remark backfired. What was the mathematical probability that all the things that had happened to him could have happened by pure chance?

That night he analyzed his data. Six incidents; the probability was extremely small. Seven, if he counted his arm. If it had been his *left* arm—jet back! Since he wrote with his right hand, very few people knew that he was left-handed. Seven it was; and that made it virtually certain. Accident was out.

But if he *was* being delayed and hampered deliberately, who was doing it, and why? It didn't make sense. Nevertheless, the idea would not down.

He was a trained observer and an analyst second to none. Therefore he soon found out that he was being shadowed wherever he went, but he could not get any really significant leads. Wherefore:

"Graves, have you got a spy-ray detector?" he asked boldly—and watchfully.

The fat man did not turn a hair. "No, nobody would want to spy on me. Why?"

"I feel jumpy. I don't know why anybody would be spying on me, either, but—I'm neither a Lensman nor an esper, but I'd swear that somebody's peeking over my shoulder half the time. I think I'll go over to the Patrol station and borrow one."

"Nerves, my boy; nerves and shock," Graves diagnosed. "Losing an arm would shock hell out of anybody's nervous system, I'd say. Maybe the Phillips treatment—the new one growing on—sort of pulls you out of shape."

"Could be," Cloud assented, moodily. His act had been a flop. If Graves knew anything—and he'd be damned if he could see any grounds for such a suspicion—he hadn't given away a thing.

Nevertheless, Cloud went to the Patrol office, which was of course completely and permanently shielded. There he borrowed the detector and asked the lieutenant in charge to get a special report from the Patrol upon the alleged gems and what it knew about either the cruiser or the pirates. To justify his request he had to explain his suspicions.

After the messages had been sent the young officer drummed thoughtfully upon his desk. "I wish I could do something, Dr. Cloud, but I don't see how I can," he decided finally. "Without a shred of evidence, I *can't* act."

"I know. I'm not accusing anybody, yet. It may be anybody between here and Andromeda. Just call me, please, as soon as you get that report."

The report came, and the Patrolman was round-eyed as he imparted the information, that, as far as Prime Base could discover, there had been no Lonabarian gems and the rescuing vessel had not been a Patrol ship at all. Cloud was not surprised.

"I thought so," he said, flatly. "This is a hell of a thing to say, but it now becomes a virtual certainty—six sigmas out on the probability curve—that this whole fantastic procedure was designed solely to keep me from analyzing and blowing out that new vortex. As to where the vortex fits in, I haven't got even the dimmest possible idea, but one thing is clear. Graves represents TPI—on this planet he *is* TPI. Now what kind of monkey business would TPI—or, more likely, somebody working under cover *in* TPI, because undoubtedly the head office doesn't know anything about it—be doing? I ask you."

"Dope, you mean? Cocaine—heroin—that kind of stuff?"

"Exactly; and here's what I'm going to do about it." Bending over the desk, even in that ultra-shielded office, Cloud whispered busily for minutes. "Pass this along to Prime Base immediately, have them alert Narcotics, and have your men ready in case I strike something hot."

"But listen, man!" the Patrolman protested. "Wait—let a Lensman do it. They'll almost certainly catch you at it, and if they're clean *nothing* can keep you from doing ninety days in the clink."

"But if we wait, the chances are it'll be too late; they'll have had time to cover up. What I'm asking you is, will you back my play if I catch them with the goods?"

"Yes. We'll be here, armored and ready. But I still think you're nuts."

"Maybe so, but even if my mathematics is wrong, it's still a fact that my arm will grow back on just as fast in the clink as anywhere else. Clear ether, lieutenant—until tonight!"

Cloud made an engagement with Graves for luncheon. Arriving a few minutes early, he was of course shown into the private office. Since the manager was busily signing papers, Cloud strolled to the side window and seemed to gaze appreciatively at the masses of gorgeous blooms just outside. What he really saw, however, was the detector upon his wrist.

Nobody knew that he had in his sleeve a couple of small, but highly efficient, tools. Nobody knew that he was left-handed. Nobody saw what he did, nor was any signal given that he did anything at all.

That night, however, that window opened alarmlessly to his deft touch. He climbed in, noiselessly. He might be walking straight into trouble, but he had to take that chance. One thing was in his favor; no matter how crooked they were, they couldn't keep armored troops on duty as night-watchmen, and the Patrolmen could get there as fast as their thugs could.

He had brought no weapons. If he was wrong, he would not need any and being armed would only aggravate his offense. If right, there would be plenty of weapons available. There were. A whole drawer full of DeLameters—fully charged—belts and everything. He leaped across the room to Graves' desk; turned on a spy-ray. The subbasement—"private laboratories," Graves had said—was blocked. He threw switch after switch—no soap. Communicators—ah, he was getting somewhere now—a steel-lined room, a girl and a boy.

"Eureka! Good evening, folks."

"Eureka? I hope you rot in hell, Graves . . ."

"This isn't Graves. Cloud. Storm Cloud, the Vortex Blaster, investigating . . ."

"Oh, Bob, the Patrol!" the girl screamed.

"Quiet! This is a zwilnik outfit, isn't it?"

"I'll say it is!" Ryder gasped in relief. "Thionite . . ."

"Thionite! How could it be? How could they bring it in here?"

"They don't. They're growing broadleaf and *making* the stuff. That's why they're going to kill us."

"Just a minute." Cloud threw in another switch. "Lieutenant? Worse than I thought. *Thionite!* Get over here fast with everything you got. Armor and semi-portables. Blast down the Mayner Street door. Stairway to right, two floors down, corridor to left, half-way along left side. Room B-Twelve. Snap it up, but keep your eyes peeled!"

"But wait, Cloud!" the lieutenant protested. "Wait 'til we get there—you can't do anything alone!"

"Can't wait—got to get these kids out—evidence!" Cloud broke the circuit and, as rapidly as he could, one-handed, buckled on gun-belts. Graves would *have* to kill these two youngsters, if he possibly could.

"For God's sake save Jackie, anyway!" Ryder prayed. He knew just how high the stakes were. "And watch out for gas, radiation, and traps—you must have sprung a dozen alarms already."

"What kind of traps?" Cloud demanded.

"Beams, deadfalls, sliding doors—I don't know what they haven't got. Graves said he could kill us in here with rays or gas or . . ."

"Take Graves' private elevator, Dr. Cloud," the girl broke in.

"Where is it—which one?"

"It's in the blank wall—the yellow button on his desk opens it. Down as far as it will go."

Cloud jumped up listening with half an ear to the babblings from below as he searched for air-helmets. Radiations, in that metal-lined room, were out—except possibly for a few beam-projectors, which he could deal with easily enough. Gas, though, would be bad; but every drug-house had air-helmets. Ah! Here they were!

He put one on, made shift to hang two more around his neck—he had to keep his one hand free. He punched the yellow button; rode the elevator down until it stopped of itself. He ran along the corridor and drove the narrowest, hottest possible beam of a DeLameter into the lock of B-12. It took time to cut even that small semi-circle in that refractory and conductive alloy—altogether too much time —but the kids would know who it was. Zwilniks would open the cell with a key, not a torch.

They knew. When Cloud kicked the door open they fell upon him eagerly.

"A helmet and a DeLameter apiece. Get them on quick! Now help me buckle this. Thanks. Jackie, you stay back there, out of the way of our feet. Bob, you lie down here in the doorway. Keep your gun outside and stick your head out just far enough so you can see. No farther. I'll join you after I see what they've got in the line of radiation."

A spot of light appeared in a semi-concealed port, then another. Cloud's weapon flamed briefly.

"Projectors like those aren't much good when the prisoners have DeLameters," he commented, "but I imagine our air right now is pretty foul. It won't be long now. Do you hear anything?"

"Somebody's coming, but suppose it's the Patrol?"

"If so, a few blasts won't hurt 'em—they'll be in G P armor." Cloud did not add that Graves would probably rush his nearest thugs in just as they were; to kill the two witnesses before help could arrive.

The first detachment to round the corner was in fact unarmored. Cloud's weapon flamed white, followed quickly by Ryder's, and those zwilniks died. Against the next to arrive, however, the DeLameters raved in vain. But only for a second.

"Back!" Cloud ordered, and swung the heavy door shut as the attackers' beams swept past. It could not be locked, but it could be, and was, welded to the jamb with dispatch, if not with neatness. "We'll cut that trap-door off, and stick it onto the door, too—and any more loose metal we can find."

"I hope they come in time," the girl's low voice carried a prayer. Was this brief flare of hope false? Would not only she and her Bob, but also their would-be rescuer, die? "Oh! That noise—s'pose it's the Patrol?"

It was not really a noise—the cell was sound-proof—it was an occasional jarring of the whole immense structure.

"I wouldn't wonder. Heavy stuff—probably semi-portables. You might grab that bucket, Bob, and throw some of that water that's trickling in. Every little bit helps."

The heavy metal of the door was glowing bright-to-dull red over half its area and that area was spreading rapidly. The air of the room grew hot and hotter. Bursts of live steam billowed out and, condensing, fogged the helmets.

The glowing metal dulled, brightened, dulled. The prisoners could only guess at the intensity of the battle being waged. They could follow its progress only by the ever-shifting temperature of the barrier which the zwilniks were so suicidally determined to burn down. For hours, it seemed, the conflict raged. The thuddings and jarrings grew worse. The water, which had been a trickle, was now a stream and scalding hot.

Then a blast of bitterly cold air roared from the ventilator, clearing away the gas and steam, and the speaker came to life.

"Good work, Cloud and you other two," it said, chattily. "Glad to see you're all on deck. Get into this corner over here, so the Zwilniks won't hit you when they hole through. They won't have time to locate you—we've got a semi right at the corner now."

The door grew hotter, flamed fiercely white. A narrow pencil sizzled through, burning steel sparkling away in all directions—but only for a second. It expired. Through the hole there flared the reflection of a beam brilliant enough to pale the noon-day sun. The portal cooled; heavy streams of water hissed and steamed. Hot water began to spurt into the cell. An atomic-hydrogen cutting torch sliced away the upper two-thirds of the fused and battered door. The grotesquely-armored lieutenant peered in.

"They tell me all three of you are QX. Check?"

"Check."

"Good. We'll have to carry you out. Step up here where we can get hold of you."

"I'll walk and I'll carry Jackie myself," Ryder protested, while two of the armored warriors were draping Cloud tastefully around the helment of a third.

"You'd get boiled to the hips—this water is deep and hot. Come on!"

The slowly rising water was steaming; the walls and ceiling of the corridor gave mute but eloquent testimony of the appalling forces that had been unleashed. Tile, concrete, plastic, metal—nothing was as it had been. Cavities yawned. Plates and pilasters were warped, crumbled, fused into hellish stalactites; bare girders hung awry. In places complete collapse had necessitated the blasting out of detours.

Through the wreckage of what had been a magnificent building the cavalcade made its way, but when the open air was reached the three rescued ones were not released. Instead, they were escorted by a full platoon of soldiery to an armored car, which was in turn escorted to the Patrol station.

"I'm afraid to take chances with you until we find out

who's who and what's what around here," the young
commander explained. "The Lensmen will be here in the
morning, with half an army, so I think you'd better spend
the rest of the night here, don't you?"

"Protective custody, eh?" Cloud grinned. "I've never
been arrested in such a polite way before, but it's QX with
me. You, too, I take it?"

"Us, too, decidedly," Ryder assented. "This is a very
nice jail-house, especially in comparison with where
we've . . ."

"I'll say so!" Jackie broke in, giggling almost hysterical-
ly. "I never thought I'd be tickled to death at getting
arrested, but I am!"

Lensmen came, and companies of Patrolmen equipped
in various fashions, but it was several weeks before the
situation was completely clarified. Then Ellington—
Councillor Ellington, the Unattached Lensman in charge
of all Narcotics—called the three into the office.

"How about Graves and Fairchild?" Cloud demanded
before the councillor could speak.

"Both dead," Ellington said. "Graves was shot down
just as he took off, but he blasted Fairchild first, just as he
intimated he would. There wasn't enough of Fairchild left
for positive identification, but it couldn't very well have
been anyone else. Nobody left alive seems to know much
of anything of the real scope of the thing, so we can
release you three now. Thanks, from me as well as the
Patrol. There is some talk that you two youngsters have
been contemplating a honeymoon out Chickladoria way?"

"Oh, no, sir—that is . . . ." Both spoke at once. "That
was just talk, sir."

"I realize that the report may have been exaggerated,
or premature, or both. However, not as a reward, but
simply in appreciation, the Patrol would be very glad to
have you as its guests throughout such a trip—all expense
—if you like."

They liked.

"Thank you. Lieutenant, please take Miss Cochran and
Mr. Ryder to the disbursing office. Dr. Cloud, the Patrol
will take cognizance of what you have done. In the meantime, however, I would like to say that in uncovering this
thing you have been of immense assistance to us."

"Nothing much sir, I'm afraid. I shudder to think of

what's coming. If zwilniks can grow Trenconian broadleaf anywhere . . ."

"Not at all, not at all," Ellington interrupted. "If such an entirely unsuspected firm as Tellurian Pharmaceuticals, with all their elaborate preparations and precautions, could not do much more than start, it is highly improbable that any other attempt will be a success. You have given us a very potent weapon against zwilnik operations—not only thionite, but heroin, ladolian, nitrolabe, and the rest."

"What weapon?" Cloud was puzzled.

"Statistical analysis and correlation of apparently unrelated indices."

"But they've been used for years!"

"Not the way you used them, my friend. Thus, while we cannot count upon any more such extraordinary help as you gave us, we should not need any. Can I give you a lift back to Tellus?"

"I don't think so, thanks. My stuff is en route now. I'll have to blow out this vortex anyway. Not that I think there's anything unusual about it—those were undoubtedly murders, not vortex casualties at all—but for the record. Also, since I can't do any more extinguishing until my arm finishes itself up, I may as well stay here and keep on practising."

"Practising? Practising what?"

"Gun-slinging—the lightning draw. I intend to get at least a lunch while the next pirate who pulls a DeLameter on me is getting a square meal."

* * * * *

And Councillor Ellington conferred with another Gray Lensman; one who was not even vaguely humanoid.

"Did you take him apart?"

"Practically cell by cell."

"What do you think the chances are of finding and developing another like him?"

"With a quarter of a million Lensmen working on it now, and the number doubling every day, and with a hundred thousand million planets, with almost that many different cultures, it is my considered opinion that it is merely a matter of time."

Chapter 5

_____THE BONEHEADS

SINCE BECOMING the Vortex Blaster, Neal Cloud lived alone. Whenever he decently could, he traveled alone and worked alone. He was alone now, hurtling through a barren region of space toward Rift Seventy One and the vortex next upon his list. In the interests of solitude, convenience, and efficiency he was now driving a scout-class ship which had been converted to one-man and automatic operation. In one hold was his vortex-blasting flitter; in the others his duodec bombs and other supplies.

During such periods of inaction as this, he was wont to think flagellantly of Jo and the three kids; especially of Jo. Now, however, and much to his surprise and chagrin, the pictures which had been so vividly clear were beginning to fade. Unless he concentrated consciously, his thoughts strayed elsewhere: to the last meeting of the Society; to the new speculations as to the why and how of super-novae; to food; to bowling—maybe he'd better start that again, to see if he couldn't make his hook roll smoothly into the one-two pocket instead of getting so many seven-ten splits. Back to food—for the first time in the Vortex Blaster's career he was really hungry.

Which buttons would he push for supper? Steak and Venerian mushrooms would be mighty good. So would fried ham and eggs, or high-pressured gameliope . . . .

An alarm bell jangled, rupturing the silence; a warm-blooded oxygen-breather's distress call, pitifully weak, was coming in. It would have to be weak, Cloud reflected, as he tuned it in as sharply as he could; he was a good eighty five parsecs—at least an hour at maximum blast—away from the nearest charted traffic lane. It was getting stronger. It hadn't just started, then; he had just gotten into its range. He acknowledged, swung his little ship's needle nose into the line and slammed on full drive. He had not gone far on the new course, however, when a tiny but

48

brilliant flash of light showed on his plate and the distress-call stopped. Whatever had occurred was history.

Cloud had to investigate, of course. Both written and unwritten laws are adamant that every such call must be heeded by any warm-blooded oxygen-breather receiving it, of whatever race or class or tonnage or upon whatever mission bound. He broadcast call after call of his own. No reply. He was probably the only being in space who had been within range.

Still driving at max, he went to the rack and pulled down a chart. He had never been in on a space emergency before, but he knew the routine. No use to investigate the wreckage; the brilliance of the flare was evidence enough that the vessel and everything near it had ceased to exist. It was lifeboats he was after. They were supposed to stick around to be rescued, but out here they wouldn't. They'd have to head for the nearest planet, to be sure of air. Air was far more important than either food or water; and lifeboats, by the very nature of things, could not carry enough air.

Thus he steered more toward the nearest T-T (Tellus-Type) planet than toward the scene of disaster. He put his communicators, both sending and receiving, on automatic, then sat down at the detector panel. There might not be anything on the visuals or the audio. There had been many cases of boats, jammed with women and children, being launched into space with no one aboard able to operate even a communicator. If any lifeboats had gotten away from the catastrophe, his detectors would find them.

There was one; one only. It was close to the planet, almost into atmosphere. Cloud aimed a solid communicator beam. Still no answer. Either the boat's communicator was smashed or nobody aboard could run it. He'd have to follow them down to the ground.

But what was that? Another boat on the plate? Not a lifeboat—too big—but not big enough to be a ship. Coming out from the planet, apparently . . . to rescue? No—what the hell? The lug was *beaming* the lifeboat!

"Let's go, you sheet-iron lummox!" the Blaster yelled aloud, kicking in his every remaining dyne of drive. Then, very shortly, his plate came suddenly to life. To semi-life, rather, for the video was blurred and blotchy; the audio full of breaks and noise. The lifeboat's pilot was a Chickladorian; characteristically pink except for red-matted hair and red-streamed face. He was in bad shape.

"Whoever it is that's been trying to raise me, snap it up!" the pink man said in "Spaceal," the lingua franca of deep space. "I couldn't answer until I faked up this jury rig. The ape's aboard and he means business. I'm going to black out, I think, but I've undogged the locks. Take over, pal!"

The picture blurred, vanished. The voice stopped. Cloud swore, viciously.

* * * * *

The planet Dhil and its enormous satellite Lune are almost twin worlds, revolving around their common center of gravity and traversing as one the second orbit of their sun. In the third orbit revolves Nhal, a planet strikingly similar to Dhil in every respect of gravity, atmosphere, and climate. Thus Dhilians and Nhalians are, to intents and purposes, identical.*

The two races had been at war with each other, most of the time, for centuries; and practically all of that warfare had been waged upon luckless Lune. Each race was well advanced in science. Each had atomic power, offensive beams, and defensive screens. Neither had any degree of inertialessness. Neither had ever heard of Civilization or of Boskonia.

At this particular time peace existed, but only on the surface. Any discovery or development giving either side an advantage would rekindle the conflagration without hesitation or warning.

Such was the condition obtaining when Darjeeb of Nhal blasted his little space-ship upward from Lune. He was glowing with pride of accomplishment, suffused with self-esteem. Not only had he touched off an inextinguishable atomic flame exactly where it would do the most good, but also, as a crowning achievement, he had captured Luda of Dhil. Luda herself; the coldest, hardest, most efficient Minister of War that Dhil had ever had!

---

* For the explanation of these somewhat peculiar facts, which is too long to go into here, the student is referred to *Transactions of the Planetographical Society;* Vol. 283, *No.* 11, *P.* 2745. E.E.S.

As soon as they could extract certain data from Luda's mind, they could take Lune in short order. With Lune solidly theirs, they could bomb Dhil into submission in two years. The goal of many generations would have been reached. He, Darjeeb of Nhal, would have wealth, fame, and—best of all—power!

Gazing gloatingly at his captive with every eye he could bring to bear, Darjeeb strolled over to inspect again her chains and manacles. Let her radiate! No mentality in existence could break *his* blocks. Physically, however, she had to be watched. The irons were strong; but so was Luda. If she could break free he'd probably have to shoot her, which would be a very bad thing indeed. She hadn't caved in yet, but she would. When he got her to Nhal, where proper measures could be taken, she'd give up every scrap of knowledge she had ever had!

The chains were holding, all eight of them, and Darjeeb kept on gloating as he backed toward his control station. To him Luda's shape was normal enough, since his own was the same, but in the sight of any Tellurian she would have been more than a little queer.

The lower part of her body was somewhat like that of a small elephant; one weighing perhaps four hundred pounds. The skin, however, was clear and fine and delicately tanned; there were no ears or tusks; the neck was longer. The trunk was shorter, divided at the tip to form a highly capable hand; and between the somewhat protuberant eyes of this "feeding" head there thrust out a boldly Roman, startlingly human nose. The brain in this head was very small, being concerned only with matters of food.

Above this not-too-unbelievable body, however, there was nothing familiar to us of Tellus. Instead of a back there were two pairs of mighty shoulders, from which sprang four tremendous arms, each like the trunk except longer and much stronger. Surmounting those massive shoulders there was an armored, slightly retractile neck which bore the heavily-armored "thinking" head. In this head there were no mouths, no nostrils. The four equally-spaced *pairs* of eyes were protected by heavy ridges and plates; the entire head, except for its junction with the neck, was solidly sheathed with bare, hard, thick, tough bone.

Darjeeb's amazing head shone a clean-scrubbed white. But Luda's—the eternal feminine!—was really something to look at. It had been sanded, buffed, and polished. It had been inlaid with bars and strips and scrolls of variously-colored metals; then decorated tastefully in red and green and blue and black enamel; then, to cap the climax, *lacquered!*

But that was old stuff to Darjeeb; all he cared about was the tightness of the chains immobilizing Luda's hands and feet. Seeing that they were all tight, he returned his attention to his visiplates; for he was not yet in the clear. Enemies might be blasting off after him any minute.

A light flashed upon his detector panel. Behind him everything was clear. Nothing was coming from Dhil. Ah, there it was, coming in from open space. But nothing *could* move that fast! A space-ship of some kind ... Gods of the Ancients, *how* it was coming!

As a matter of fact the lifeboat was coming in at less than one light; the merest crawl, as space-speeds go. That velocity, however, was so utterly beyond anything known to his system that the usually phlematic Nhalian stood spellbound for a fraction of a second. Then he drove a hand toward a control. Too late—before the hand had covered half the distance the incomprehensibly fast ship struck his own without impact, jar, or shock.

Both vessels should have been blasted to atoms; but there the stranger was, poised motionless beside him. Then, under the urge of a ridiculously tiny jet of flame, she leaped away; covering miles in an instant. Then something equally fantastic happened. She drifted heavily *backward, against* the full force of her driving blasts!

Only one explanation was possible—inertialessness! What a weapon! With that and Luda—even without Luda—the solar system would be his. No longer was it a question of Nhal conquering Dhil. He himself would become the dictator, not only of Nhal and Dhil and Lune, but also of all other worlds within reach. That vessel and its secrets *must* be his!

He blasted, then, to match the inert velocity of the smaller craft, and as his ship approached the other he reached out both telepathically—he could neither speak nor hear—and with a spyray to determine the most feasible method of taking over this Godsend.

Bipeds! Peculiar little beasts—repulsive. Only two arms and eyes—only one head. Weak, no weapons—good! Couldn't *any* of them communicate? Ah yes, there was one—an unusually thin, reed-like creature, bundled up in layer upon layer of fabric. . . .

"I see that you are survivors of a catastrophe in outer space," Darjeeb began. He correlated instantly, if not sympathetically, the smashed panel and the pilot's bleeding head. If the creature had had a head worthy of the name, it could have wrecked a dozen such frailties with it, and without taking hurt. "Tell your pilot to let me in, so that I may guide you to safety. Hurry! Those will come at any moment who will destroy us all without warning or palaver."

"I am trying, sir, but I cannot get through to him direct. It will take a few moments." The strange telepathist began to make motions with her peculiar arms, hands, and fingers. Others of the outlanders brandished various repulsive members and gesticulated with ridiculous mouths. Finally:

"He says he would rather not," the interpreter reported. "He asks you to go ahead. He will follow you down."

"Impossible. We cannot land upon this world or its primary, Dhil," Darjeeb argued, reasonably. "These people are enemies—savages—I have just escaped from them. It is death to attempt to land anywhere in this system except on my own world Nhal—that bluish one over there."

"Very well, we'll see you there. We're just about out of air, but we can travel that far."

But that wouldn't do, either, of course. Argument took too much time. He'd have to use force, and he'd better call for help. He hurled mental orders to a henchman, threw out his magnetic grapples, and turned on a broad, low-powered beam.

"Open up or die," he ordered. "I do not want to blast you open, but time presses and I will if I must."

Pure heat is hard to take. The portal opened and Darjeeb, after donning armor and checking his ray-guns, picked Luda up and swung nonchalantly out into space. Luda was tough—a little vacuum wouldn't hurt her much. In side the lifeboat, he tossed his captive into a corner and strode toward the pilot.

"I want to know right now what it is that makes this

ship to be without inertia!" Darjeeb radiated, harshly. He had been probing vainly at the pink thing's mind-block. "Tell your pilot to tell me or I will squeeze it out of his brain."

As the order was being translated he slipped an arm out of his suit and clamped a huge hand around the pilot's head. But just as he made contact, before he put on any pressure at all, the weakling fainted.

Also, two of his senses registered disquieting tidings. He received, as plainly as though it was intended for him, a welcome which the swaddled-up biped was radiating in delight to an unexpected visitor rushing into the compartment. He saw that that visitor, while it was also a biped, was not at all like the frightened and harmless creatures already cluttering the room. It was armed and armored, in complete readiness for strife even with Darjeeb of Nhal.

The bonehead swung his ready weapon—with his build there was no need, ever to turn—and pressed a stud. A searing lance of flame stabbed out. Passengers screamed and fled into whatever places of security were available.

Chapter 6

_____DRIVING JETS ARE WEAPONS

CLOUD'S SWEARING wasted no time; he could swear and act simultaneously. He flashed his vessel up near the lifeboat, went inert, and began to match its intrinsic velocity.

He'd have to board, no other way. Even if he had anything to blast it with, and he didn't—his vessel wasn't armed—he couldn't, without killing innocent people. What did he have?

He had two suits of armor; a G-P regulation and his vortex special, which was even stronger. He had his DeLameters. He had four semi-portables and two needlebeams, for excavating. He had thousands of duodec bombs, not one of which could be detonated by anything less violent than the furious heart of a loose atomic vortex.

What else? Well, there was his sampler. He grinned as

he looked at it. About the size of a carpenter's hand-axe, with a savage beak on one side and a wickedly-curved, razor-sharp blade on the other. It had a double-grip handle, three feet long. A deceptive little thing, truly, for it was solid dureum. It weighed fifteen pounds, and its ultra-hard, ultra-tough blade could shear through neocarballoy as cleanly as a steel knife slices cheese. Considering what terrific damage a Valerian could do with a space-axe, he should be able to do quite a bit with this—it ought to qualify at least as a space-hatchet.

He put on his armor, set his DeLameters to maximum intensity at minimum aperture, and hung the sampler on a belt-hook. He eased off his blasts. There, the velocities matched. A minute's work with needle-beam, tractors, and pressor sufficed to cut the two smaller ships apart and to dispose of the Nhalian's magnets and cables. Another minute of careful manipulation and his scout was in place. He swung out, locked the port behind him, and entered the lifeboat.

He was met by a high-intensity beam. He had not expected instantaneous, undeclared war, but he was ready for it. Every screen he had was full out, his left hand held poised at hip a screened DeLameter. His return blast was, therefore, a reflection of Darjeeb's bolt, and it did vastly more damage. The hand in which Darjeeb held the projector was the one that had been manhandling the pilot, and it was not quite back inside the Nhalian's screens. In the fury of Cloud's riposte, then, gun and hand disappeared, as did also a square foot of panel behind them. But Darjeeb had other hands and other guns and for seconds blinding beams raved against unyielding screens.

Neither screen went down. The Tellurian holstered his weapons. It wouldn't take much of this stuff to kill the passengers remaining in the saloon. He'd go in with his sampler.

He lugged it up and leaped straight at the flaming projector, with all of his mass and strength going into the swing of his "space-hatchet." The monster did not dodge, but merely threw up a hand to flick the toy aside with his gun-barrel. Cloud grinned fleetingly as he realized what the other must be thinking—that the man must be puny indeed to be making such ado about wielding such a trifle—for to anyone not familiar with dureum it is sheerly unbelievable that so much mass and momentum can possibly reside in a bulk so small.

Thus when fiercely-driven cutting edge met opposing ray-gun it did not waver or deflect. It scarcely even slowed. Through the metal of the gun that vicious blade sliced resistlessly, shearing flesh as it sped. On down, urged by everything Cloud's straining muscles could deliver. Through armor it slashed, through the bony plating covering that tremendous double shoulder, deep into the flesh and bone of the shoulder itself; being stopped only by the impact of the hatchet's haft against the armor.

Then, planting one steel boot on the helmet's dome, he got a momentary stance with the other between barrel body and flailing arm, bent his back, and heaved. The deeply-embedded blade tore out through bone and flesh and metal, and as it did so the two rear cabled arms dropped useless. That mighty rear shoulder and its appurtenances were out of action. The monster still had one good hand, however, and he was still full of fight.

That hand flashed out, to seize the weapon and to wield it against its owner. It came fast, too, but the man, strongly braced, yanked backward. Needle point and keen edge tore through flesh and snicked off fingers. Cloud swung his axe aloft and poised, making it limpidly clear that the next blow would be straight down into the top of the head.

That was enough. Darjeeb backed away, every eye glaring, and Cloud stepped warily over to Luda. A couple of strokes of his blade gave him a length of chain. Then, working carefully to keep his foe threatened at every instant, he worked the chain into a tight loop around the monster's front neck, pulled it unmercifully taut around a stanchion, and welded it there with his DeLameter. He did not trust the other monster unreservedly, either, bound as she was. In fact, he did not trust her at all. In spite of family rows, like sticks to like in emergencies and they'd gang up on him if they could. Since she wasn't wearing armor, however, she didn't stand a chance with a DeLameter, so he could take time now to look around.

The pilot, lying flat upon the floor, was beginning to come to. Not quite flat, either, for a shapely Chickladorian girl, wearing the forty one square inches of covering which were *de rigueur* in her eyes, had his bandaged head in her lap—or, rather, cushioned on one bare leg—and was sobbing gibberish over him. That wouldn't help. Cloud started for the first-aid locker, but stopped; a white-wrapped figure was already bending over the injured man with a black bottle in her hand. He knew what it was. Kédeselin. That was what he was after, himself; but he wouldn't have dared give a hippopotamus the terrific jolt she was pouring into him. She must be a nurse, or maybe a doctor; but Cloud shivered in sympathy, nevertheless.

The pilot stiffened convulsively, then relaxed. His eyes rolled; he gasped and shuddered; but he came to life and sat up groggily.

"What the hell goes on here?" Cloud demanded urgently, in spaceal.

"I don't know," the pink man replied. "All the ape said, as near as I could get it, was that I had to give him our free drive." He then spoke rapidly to the girl—his wife, Cloud guessed; if she wasn't, she ought to be—who was still holding him fervently.

The pink girl nodded. Then, catching Cloud's eye, she pointed at the two monstrosities, then at the nurse standing calmly near by. Startlingly slim, swathed to the eyes in billows of glamorette, she looked as fragile as a wisp of straw; but Cloud knew Manarkans. She, too, nodded at the Tellurian, then "talked" rapidly with her hands to a short, thick-set, tremedously muscled woman of some race entirely strange to the Blaster. She was used to going naked; that was very evident. She had been wearing a light "robe of convention," but it had been pretty well demolished in the melee and she did not realize that what was left of it was hanging in tatters down her broad back. The "squatty" eyed the gesticulating Manarkan and spoke, in a beautifully modulated deep bass voice, to a supple, lithe, pantherish girl with vertically-slitted yellow eyes, pointed ears, and a long and sinuous, meticulously-groomed tail. The Vegian—by no means the first of her race Cloud had seen—spoke to the Chickladorian eyeful, who in turn passed the message along to her husband.

"The bonehead you had the argument with says to hell with you," the pilot translated to Cloud in spaceal. "He says his mob will be out here after him directly, and if you don't cut him loose and give him the dope he wants they'll burn us all to cinders."

Luda was, meanwhile, trying to attract attention. She was bouncing up and down, rattling her chains, rolling her eyes, and in general demanding notice. More communication ensued, culminating in:

"The one with fancy-worked skull—she's a frail, but not the other bonehead's frail, I guess—says pay no attention to the ape. He's a murderer, a pirate, a bum, a louse, and so forth, she says. Says to take your axe—it's *some* cleaver, she says, and I check her to ten decimals on that—cut his goddam head clean off, chuck his stinking carcass out the port, and get the hell out of here as fast as you can blast."

That sounded to Cloud like good advice, but he didn't want to take such drastic action without more comprehensive data.

"Why?" he asked.

But this was too much for the communications relays to handle. Cloud did not know spaceal any too well, since he had not been out in deep space very long. Also, spaceal is a very simple language, not well adapted to the accurate expression of subtle nuances of thought; and all those intermediate translations were garbling things up terrifically. Hence Cloud was not surprised that nothing much was coming through, even though the prettied-up monster was, by this time, just about throwing a fit.

"She's quit trying to spin her yarn," the pilot said finally. "She says she's been trying to talk to you direct, but she can't get through. Says to unseal your ports—cut your screens—let down your guard—something like that, anyway. Don't know what she does mean, exactly. None of us does except maybe the Manarkan, and if she does she can't get it across on her fingers."

"Perhaps my thought-screen?" Cloud cut it.

"More yet," the Chickladorian went on, shortly. "She says there's another one, just as bad or worse. On your head, she says . . . No, on your head-bone—what the hell! Skull? No, *inside* your skull, she says now . . . Hell's bells! I don't know what she *is* trying to say!"

"Maybe I do—keep still a minute, all of you." A telepath undoubtedly, like the Manarkans—that was why she had to talk to her first. He'd never been around telepaths much—never tried it. He walked a few steps and stared directly into one pair of Luda's eyes—large, expressive eyes, now soft and gentle.

"That's it, chief! Now blast away . . . baffle your jets . . . relax, I guess she means. Open your locks and let her in."

Cloud did relax, but gingerly. He didn't like this mind-to-mind stuff at all, particularly when the other mind belonged to such a monster. He lowered his mental barriers skittishly, ready to revolt at any instant; but as soon as he began to understand the meaning of her thoughts he forgot completely that he was not talking man to man. And at that moment—such was the power of Luda's mind and the precision of her telepathy—every nuance of thought became sharp and clear.

"I demand Darjeeb's life!" Luda stormed. "Not because he is the enemy of all my race—that would not weigh with you—but because he has done what no one else, however base, has ever been so lost to shame as to do. In our city upon Lune he kindled an atomic flame which is killing us in multitudes. In case you do not know, such flames can never be extinguished."

"I know. We call them loose atomic vortices; but they can be extinguished. In fact, putting them out is my business."

"Oh—incredible but glorious news . . ." Luda's thought seethed, became incomprehensible for a space. Then: "To win your help for my race I perceive that I must be completely frank. Observe my mind closely, please—see for yourself that I withhold nothing. Darjeeb wants at any cost the secret of your vessel's speed. With it, his race would destroy mine utterly. I want it too, of course—with it we would wipe out the Nhalians. However, since you are so much stronger than would be believed possible— since you defeated Darjeeb in single combat—I realize my helplessness. I tell you, therefore, that both Darjeeb and I have long since summoned help. Warships of both sides are approaching, to capture one or both of these vessels. The Nhalians are the nearer, and these secrets *must not,* under any conditions, go to Nhal. Dash out into space with both of these ships, so that we can plan at leisure. First, however, kill that unspeakable murderer—you have scarcely injured him the way it is—or give me that so-deceptive little axe and I'll be only too glad to do it myself."

A chain snapped ringingly; metal clanged against metal. Only two of Darjeeb's major arms had been incapacitated; his two others had lost only a few fingers apiece from their hands. His immense bodily strength was almost unimpaired. He could have broken free at any time, but he had waited; hoping to take Cloud by surprise or that some opportunity would arise for him to regain control of the lifeboat. But now, feeling sure that Luda's emminently sensible advice would be taken, he decided to let inertialessness go, for the moment, in the interest of saving his life.

"Kill him!" Luda shrieked the thought and Cloud swung his weapon aloft, but Darjeeb was not attacking. Instead, he was rushing into the airlock—escaping!

"Go free, pilot!" Cloud commanded, and leaped; but the inner valve swung shut before he could reach it.

As soon as he could operate the lock Cloud went through it. He knew that Darjeeb could not have boarded the scout, since her ports were locked. He hurried to his control room and scanned space. There the Nhalian was, falling like a plummet. There also were a dozen or so space-ships, too close for comfort, blasting upward.

Cloud cut in his Bergenhom, kicked on his driving blasts, cut off, and went back into the lifeboat.

"Safe enough now," he thought. "They'll never get out here inert. I'm surprised he jumped—didn't figure him as a suicidal type."

"He isn't. He didn't," Luda thought, dryly.

"Huh? He must have. That was a mighty long flit he took off on, and his suit wouldn't hold air."

"He would stuff something into the holes. If necessary he could have made it without air—or armor, either. He's tough. He still lives, curse him! But it is of no use for me to bewail that fact now. Let us make plans. You must put out the flame, and the leaders of our people will convince you . . ."

"Just a second—some other things come first." He fell silent.

First of all, he had to report to the Patrol, so they could get some Lensmen and a task force out here to straighten up this mess. With ordinary communicators, that would take some doing—but wait, he had a double-ended tight beam to the laboratory. He could get through on that, probably, even from here. He'd have to mark the lifeboat as a derelict and get these people aboard his cruiser. No space-tube. The women could wear suits, but this Luda . . .

"Don't worry about me!" that entity cut in. "You saw how I came aboard. I don't *enjoy* breathing vacuum, but I'm as tough as Darjeeb is. So *hurry!* During every moment you delay, more of my people are dying!"

"QX. While we're transferring, give me the dope."

Luda did so. Darjeeb's coup had been carefully planned and brilliantly executed. Drugged by one of her own staff, she had been taken without a struggle. She did not know how far-reaching the stroke had been, but she was pretty sure that most, if not all, of the Dhilian fortresses were now held by the enemy.

Nhal probably had the advantage in numbers and in firepower then upon Lune—Darjeeb would not have made his bid unless he had found a way to violate the treaty of strict equality. Dhil was, however, much the nearer of the two worlds. Hence, if this initial advantage could be overcome, Dhil's reenforcements could be brought up much sooner than the enemy's. If, in addition, the vortex could be extinguished before it had done irreparable damage, neither side would have any real advantage and the conflict would subside instead of flaring into another tri-world holocaust.

Cloud pondered. He would have to do something, but what? That vortex had to be snuffed; but, with the whole Nhalian army to cope with, how could he make the approach? His vortex-bombing flitter was screened against radiation, not war-beams. His cruiser was clothed to stop anything short of G-P primaries, but it would take a month at a Patrol base to adapt her for vortex work . . . and he'd have to analyze it, anyway, preferably from the ground. He had no beams, no ordinary bombs, no nega-bombs. How could he use what he had to clear a station?

"Draw me a map, will you, Luda?" he asked.

She did so. The cratered vortex, where an immense building had been. The ring of fortresses: two of which were unusually far apart, separated by a parkway and a shallow lagoon.

"Shallow? How deep?" Cloud interrupted. She indicated a depth of a couple of feet.

"That's enough map, then. Thanks." Cloud thought for minutes. "You seem to be quite an engineer. Can you give me exact details on your defensive screen? Power, radius, weave-form, generator type, phasing, interlocking, blow-off, and so on?"

She could. Complex mathematical equations and electrical formulae flashed through his mind, each leaving a residue of fact.

"Maybe we can do something," the Blaster said finally, turning to the Chickladorian. "Depends pretty much on our friend here. Are you a pilot, or just an emergency assignment?"

"Master pilot, Rating unlimited, tonnage or space."

"Good! Think you're in shape to take three thousand centimeters of acceleration?"

"Pretty sure of it. If I was right I could take three thousand standing on my head. I'm feeling better all the time. Let's hot 'er up and find out."

"Not until after we've unloaded these passengers somewhere," and Cloud went on to explain what he had in mind.

"Afraid it can't be done." The pilot shook his head glumly. "Your timing has got to be too ungodly fine. I can do the piloting, meter the blast, and so on. I can balance her down on her tail, steady to a hair, but piloting's only half what you got to have. Pilots never land on a constant blast, and your leeway here is damn near zero. To hit it as close as you want, your timing has got to be accurate to a tenth of a second. You don't know it, mister, but it'd take a master computer half a day to . . ."

"I know all about that. I'm a master computer and I'll have everything figured. I'll give you a zero exact to plus-or-minus a hundredth."

"QX, then. Let's dump the non-combatants and flit."

"Luda, where shall we land them? And maybe you'd better call out your army and navy—we can't blow out that vortex until we control both air and ground."

"Land them there." Luda swung the plate and pointed. "The call was sent long since. They come."

They landed; but four of the women would not leave the vessel. The Manarkan *had* to stay aboard, she declared, or be disgraced for life. What would happen if the pilot passed out again, with only laymen around? She was right, Cloud conceded, and she could take it. She was a Manarkan, built of whalebone and rubber. She'd bend under 3 + G's, but she wouldn't break.

The squatty insisted upon staying. Since when had a woman of Tominga hidden from danger or run away from a fight? She could hold the pilot's head up through an acceleration that would put any damn-fragile Tellurian into a pack—or give her that funny ·axe and she'd show him how it *ought* to be swung!

The Chickladorian girl, too, stayed on. Her eyes— not pink, but a deep, cool green, brimming with unshed tears— flashed at the idea of leaving her man to die alone. She just knew they were all going to die. Even if she couldn't be of any use, what of it? If her Thlaskin died she was going to die too, right then, and that was all there was to it. If they made her go ashore she'd cut her own throat that very minute, so there! So that was that.

So did the Vegian. Tail-tip twitching slightly, eyes sparkling, she swore by three deities to claw the eyes out of, and then to strangle with her tail, anyone who tried to put her off ship. She had come on this trip to *see* things, and did Cloud think she was going to miss seeing *this?* Hardly!

Cloud studied her briefly. The short, thick, incredibly soft fur—like the fur on the upper lip of a week-old kitten, except more so—did not conceal the determined set of her lovely jaw; the tight shorts and the even tighter, purely conventional breastband did not conceal the tigerish strength and agility of her lovely body. It'd be better, the Blaster decided, not to argue the point.

A dozen armed Dhilians came aboard, as pre-arranged, and the cruiser blasted off. Then, while Thlaskin was maneuvering inert, to familiarize himself with the controls and to calibrate the blast, Cloud brought out the four semi-portable projectors. They were frightful weapons, designed for tripod mounting; so heavy that it took a very strong man to lift one on Earth. They carried no batteries or accumulators, but were powered by tight beams from the mother ship.

Luda was right; such weapons were unknown in that solar system. They had no beam transmission of power. The Dhilians radiated glee as they studied the things. They had stronger stuff, but it was fixed-mount and far too heavy to move. This was wonderful—these were magnificent weapons indeed!

High above the stratosphere, inert, the pilot found his spot and flipped the cruiser around, cross-hairs centering the objective. Then, using his forward, braking jets as drivers, he blasted her straight downward.

She struck atmosphere almost with a thud. Only her fiercely-driven meteorite-screens and wall-shields held her together.

"I hope to Klono you know what you're doing, chum," the Chickladorian remarked conversationally as the fortress below leaped upward with appalling speed. "I've made hot landings before, but I always had a hair or two of leeway. If you don't hit this to a couple of hundredths we'll splash when we strike. We won't bounce, brother."

"I can compute it to a thousandth and I can set the clicker to within five, but it's *you* that'll have to do the real hitting." Cloud grinned back at the iron-nerved pilot. "Sure a four-second call is enough to get your rhythm, allow for reaction time and lag, and blast right on the click?"

"Absolutely. If I can't get it in four I can't get it at all. Got your stuff ready?"

"Uh-huh." Cloud, staring into the radarscope, began to sway his shoulders. He knew the exact point in space and the exact instant of time at which the calculated deceleration must begin; by the aid of his millisecond timer—two full revolutions of the dial every second—he was about to set the clicker to announce that instant. His hand swayed back and forth—a finger snapped down—the sharp-toned instrument began to give out its crisp, precisely-spaced clicks.

"Got it!" Cloud snapped. "Right on the middle of the click! Get ready, Thlaskin—seconds! Four! Three! Two! One! Click!"

Exactly with the click the vessel's brakes cut off and her terrific driving blasts smashed on. There was a cruelly wrenching shock as everything aboard acquired suddenly a more-than-three-times-Earthly weight.

Luda and her fellows merely twitched. The Tomingan, standing behind the pilot, supporting and steadying his wounded head in its rest, settled almost imperceptibly, but her firmly gentle hands did not yield a millimeter. The Manarkan sank deeply into the cushioned bench upon which she was lying; her quick, bright eyes remaining fixed upon her patient.

The Chickladorian girl, in her hammock, fainted quietly.

The Vegian, who had flashed one hand up to an overhead bar at the pilot's first move, stood up—although she seemed to shorten a good two inches and her tight upper garment parted with a snap as back- and shoulder-muscles swelled to take the strain. *That* wouldn't worry her. Cloud knew—what *was* she stewing about? Oh—her tail! It was too heavy for its own strength, great as it was, to lift! Her left hand came down, around, and back; with its help the tail came up. To the bar above her head, around it, tip pointing stiffly straight upward. Then, smiling gleefully at both Thlaskin and the Blaster, she shouted something that neither could understand, but which was the war-cry of her race:

"Tails high, brothers!"

Downward the big ship hurtled, toward the now glowing screens of the fortress. Driving jets are not orthodox weapons, but properly applied, they can be deadly ones indeed: and these were being applied with micromatric exactitude.

Down! DOWN!! The threatened fortress and its neighbors hurled their every beam; Nhalian ships dived frantically at the invader and did their useless best to blast her down.

Down she drove, the fortress' screens flaming ever brighter under the terrific blast.

Closer! Hotter! Still closer! Hotter still! Nor did the furious flame waver—the Chickladorian was indeed a master pilot.

"Set up a plus ten, Thlaskin," Cloud directed. "Air density and temperature are changing. Their beams, too, you know."

"Check. Plus ten, sir—set up."

"Give it to her on the fourth click from . . . this."

"On, sir." The vessel seemed to pause momentarily, to stumble; but the added weight was almost imperceptible.

A bare hundred yards now, and the ship of space was

still plunging downward at terrific speed. The screens were furiously incandescent, but were still holding.

A hundred feet, Velocity appallingly high, the enemy's screens still up. Something *had* to give now! If that screen stood up the ship would vanish as she struck it, but Thlaskin the Chickladorian made no move and spoke no word. If the skipper was willing to bet his own life on his computations, who was he to squawk? But . . . he must have miscalculated!

No! While the vessel's driving projectors were still a few yards away the defending screens exploded into blackness; the awful streams of energy raved directly into the structures beneath. Metal and stone glared white, then flowed—sluggishly at first, but ever faster and more mobile—then boiled coruscantly into vapor.

The cruiser slowed—stopped—seemed to hang for an instant poised. Then she darted upward, her dreadful exhausts continuing and completing the utter devastation.

"That's computin', mister," the pilot breathed as he cut the fierce acceleration to a heavenly one thousand. "To figure a dive like that to three decimals and have the guts to hold to it cold—skipper, that's com-pu-*tation!*"

"All yours, pilot," Cloud demurred. "All I did was give you the dope. You're the guy that made it good. Hurt, anybody?"

Nobody was. "QX. We'll repeat, then, on the other side of the lagoon."

As the ship began to descend on the new course the vengeful Dhilian fleet arrived. Looping, diving, beaming, oftentimes crashing in suicidal collision, the two factions went maniacally to war. There were no attacks, however, against the plunging Tellurian ship. The Nhalians had learned that they could do nothing about that vessel.

The second fortress fell exactly as the first had fallen. The pilot landed the cruiser in the middle of the shallow lakelet. Cloud saw that the Dhilians, overwhelmingly superior in numbers now, had cleared the air of Nhalian craft.

"Can you fellows and your ships keep them off of my flitter while I take my readings?"

"We can," the natives radiated happily.

Four of the armored boneheads were *wearing* the semiportable. They had them perched lightly atop their feeding heads, held immovably in place by two arms apiece.

One hand sufficed to operate the controls, leaving two hands free to do whatever else might prove in order.

"Let us out!"

The lock opened, the Dhilian warriors sprang out and splashed away to meet the enemy, who were already dashing into the lagoon.

Cloud watched pure carnage. He hoped—yes, there they were! The loyalists, seeing that their cause was not lost, after all, had armed themselves and were smashing into the fray.

The Blaster broke out his flitter then, set it down near the vortex, and made his observations. Everything was normal. He selected three bombs from his vast stock, loaded them into the tubes, and lofted. He set his screens, adjusted his goggles, and waited; while far above him and wide around him his guardian Dhilian war-vessels toured watchfully, their drumming blasts a reassuring thunder.

He waited, eyeing the sigma curve as it flowed backward from the recording pen, until he got a ten-second prediction. He shot the flitter forward, solving instantaneously the problems of velocity and trajectory. At exactly the correct instant he released a bomb. He cut his drive and went free.

The bomb sped truly, striking the vortex dead center. It penetrated deeply enough. The carefully-weighed charge of duodec exploded; its energy and that of the vortex combining in a detonation whose like no inhabitant of that solar system had ever even dimly imagined.

The noxious gases and the pall of smoke and pulverized debris blew aside; the frightful waves of lava quieted down. The vortex was out and would remain out. The Blaster drove back to the cruiser and put his flitter away.

"Oh—you did it! Thanks! I didn't believe that you— that anybody—really could!" Luda was almost hysterical in her joyous relief.

"Nothing to it," Cloud deprecated. "How are you doing on the mopping up?"

"Practically clean," Luda answered, grimly. "We now know who is who. Those who fought against us or who did not fight for us are, or very soon will be, dead. But the Nhalian fleet comes. Does yours? Ours takes off in moments."

"Wait a minute!" Cloud sat down at his plate, made

observations and measurements, calculated mentally. He turned on his communicator and conferred briefly.

"The Nhalian fleet will be here in seven hours and eighteen minutes. If your people go out to meet them it will mean a war that not even the Patrol can stop without destroying most of the ships and men both of you have in space. The Patrol task force will arrive in seven hours and thirty one minutes. Therefore, I suggest that you hold your fleet here, in formation but quiescent, under instructions not to move until you order them to, while you and I go out and see if we can't stop the Nhalians."

"*Stop* them!" Luda's thought was not at all ladylike. "What with, pray?"

"I don't know," Cloud confessed, "but it wouldn't do any harm to try, would it?"

"Probably not. We'll try."

All the way out Cloud pondered ways and means. As they neared the onrushing fleet he thought at Luda:

"Darjeeb is undoubtedly with that fleet. He knows that this is the only inertialess ship in this part of space. He wants it more than anything else in the universe. Now if we could only make him listen to reason ... if we could make him see ..."

He broke off. No soap. You couldn't explain "green" to a man born blind. These folks didn't know and wouldn't believe what real fire-power was. The weakest vessel in this oncoming task-force could blast both of these bone-heads' fleets into a radiant gas in fifteen seconds flat—and the superdreadnoughts' primaries would be starkly incredible to both Luda and Darjeeb. They simply *had* to be seen in action to be believed; and then it would be too late.

These people didn't stand the chance of a bug under a sledgehammer, but they'd have to be killed before they'd believe it. A damned shame, too. The joy, the satisfaction, the real advancement possible only through cooperation with each other and with the millions of races of Galactic Civilization—if there were only some means of *making* them believe ...

"We—and they—*do* believe." Luda broke into his somber musings.

"Huh? What? You do? You were listening?"

"Certainly. At your first thought I put myself en rapport with Darjeeb, and he and our peoples listened to your thoughts."

"But . . . you really believe me?"

"We all believe. Some will cooperate, however, only as far as it will serve their own ends to do so. Your Lensmen will undoubtedly have to kill that insect Darjeeb and others of his kind in the interest of lasting peace."

The insulted Nhalian drove in a protesting thought, but Luda ignored it and went on:

"You think, then, Tellurian, that your Lensmen can cope with even such as Darjeeb of Nhal?"

"I'll say they can!"

"It is well, then. Come aboard, Darjeeb—unarmed and unarmored, as I am—and we will together go to confer with these visiting Lensmen of Galactic Civilization. It is understood that there will be no warfare until our return."

"Holy Klono!" Cloud gasped. "He wouldn't do *that,* would he?"

"Certainly." Luda was surprised at the question. "Although he is an insect, and morally and ethically beneath contempt, he is, after all, a reasoning being."

"QX." Cloud was dumbfounded, but tried manfully not to show it.

Darjeeb came aboard. He was heavily bandaged and most of his hands were useless, but he seemed to bear no ill-will. Cloud gave orders; the ship flashed away to meet the Patrolmen.

The conference was held. The boneheads, after being taken through a superdreadnought and through a library by Lensmen as telepathic as themselves, capitulated to Civilization immediately and whole-heartedly.

"You won't need me any more, will you, admiral?" Cloud asked then.

"I don't think so—no. Nice job, Cloud."

"Thanks. I'll be on my way, then; the people I picked up must be off my ship by this time. Clear ether."

Chapter 7

__THE BLASTER ACQUIRES A CREW

CLOUD, RETURNING to his cruiser, found that most of his shipwrecked passengers had departed. Five of them, however—the two Chickladorians, the Manarkan, the squatty, and the Vegian—were still on board. Thlaskin, now back to normal, came to attention and saluted crisply; the women bowed or nodded and looked at him with varying degrees of interrogation.

"How come, Thlaskin? I thought all the passengers were going back with the task-force."

"They are, boss. They've gone. We followed your orders, boss—chivied 'em off. I checked with the flagship about more crew besides us, and he says QX. Just tell me how many you want of what, and I'll get 'em."

"I don't want anybody!" Cloud snapped. "Not even you. Not *any* of you."

"Jet back, boss!" Spaceal was a simple language, and inherently slangy and profane, but there was no doubt as to the intensity of the pilot's feelings. "I don't know why you were running this heap alone, or how long, but I got a couple questions to ask. Do you know just how many million ways these goddam automatics can go haywire in? Do you know what to do about half of 'em when they do? Or are you just simply completely nuts?"

"No. Not too much. I don't think so." As he answered the three questions in order Cloud's mind flashed back to what Phil Strong and several other men had tried so heatedly to impress upon him—the stupidity, the lunacy, the sheer, stark idiocy of a man of *his* training trying to go it solo in deep space. How did one say "You have a point there, but before I make such a momentous decision we should explore the various possibilities of what is a completely unexpected development" in spaceal? One didn't! Instead:

"Maybe QX, maybe not. We'll talk it over. Tell the

Manarkan to try to work me direct—maybe I can receive her now, after working the boneheads."

She could. Communication was not, perhaps, as clear as between two Manarkans or two Lensmen, but it was clear enough.

"You wish to know why I have included myself in your crew," the white-swathed girl began, as soon as communication was established. "It is the law. This vessel, the *Vortex Blaster I*, of Earth registry, belonging to the Galactic Patrol, is of a tonnage which obligates it to carry a medical doctor; or, in and for the duration of an emergency only, a registered graduate nurse. I am both R.N. and M.D. If you prefer to employ some other nursing doctor or doctor and nurse that is of course your right; but I can not and will not leave this ship until I am replaced by competent personnel. If I did such a thing I would be disgraced for life."

"But I haven't got a payroll—I never have had one!" Cloud protested.

"Don't quibble, please. It is also the law that any master or acting master of any ship of this tonnage is authorized to employ for his owner—in this case the Galactic Patrol—whatever personnel is necessary, whenever necessary, at his discretion. With or without pay, however, I stay on until replaced."

"But I don't *need* a doctor—or a nurse, either!"

"Personally, now, no," she conceded, equably enough. "I checked into that. As the chief of your great laboratory quoted to you, 'This too, shall pass.' It is passing. But you *must* have a crew; and any member of it, or you yourself, may require medical or surgical attention at any time. The only question, then, is whether or not you wish to replace me. Would you like to examine my credentials?"

"No. Having been en rapport with your mind, it is not necessary. But are you, after your position aboard the ship which was lost, interested in such a small job as this?"

"I would like it very much, I'm sure."

"Very well. If any of them stay, you can—at the same pay you were getting."

"Now, Thlaskin, the Vegian. No, hold it! We've got to have something better than spaceal, and a lot of Vegians go in for languages in a big way. She may know English or Spanish, since Vegia is one of Tellus' next-door neighbors. I'll try her myself."

Then, to the girl, "Do you speak English, miss?"

"No, eggzept in glimzzez only," came the startling reply. "Two Galactic Zdandard yearzz be pazz—come? Go?—'ere I mazzter zhe, zo perverze mood and tenze. Zhe izz zo difficult and abzdruze."

Switching to Galactic Spanish, which language was threatening to become the common tongue of Galactic Civilization, she went on:

"But I heard you say 'Zbanidge.' I know Galactic Spanish very well. I speak it well, too, except for the sounds of 'ezz' and 'zeta,' which all we Vegians must make much too hard—z-z-z-, zo. One hears that nearly all educated Tellurians have the Spanish, and you are educated, of a certainty. You speak it, no?"

"Practically as well as I do English." Cloud made relieved reply. "You have very little accent, and that little is charming. My name is Neal Cloud. May I ask yours?"

"Neelcloud? I greet you. Mine is Vezzptkn . . . but no, you couldn't pronounce it. 'Vezzta,' it would have to be in your tongue."

"QX. We have a name very close to that—Vesta."

"That's exactly what I said—Vezz-ta."

"Oh—excuse me, please. You were talking to this lady—Tomingan, she said? What language were you using?"

"Fourth-continent Tomingan, Middle Plateau dialect. Hers. She was an engineer in a big power plant on Manarka, is how she came to learn their sign language. Tomingans don't go in for linguistics much."

"And you very evidently do. How many languages do you know, young lady?"

"Only fifty so far—plus their dialects, of course. I'm only half-way to my Master of Languages degree. Fifty more to learn yet, including your cursed *Englidge*. P-f-zt-k!" Vesta wrinkled her nose, bared her teeth, and emitted a noise very similar to that made by an alley cat upon meeting a strange dog. "I don't know whether spaceal will count for credit or not, but I'm going to learn it anyway."

"Nice going, Vesta. Now, why did *you* appoint yourself a member of this party?"

"I wanted to go, and since I can't pay fare . . ."

"You wouldn't have had to!" Cloud interrupted. "If you

lost your money aboard that ship, the Patrol would take you anywhere . . ."

"Oh, I didn't mean *that*." She dipped into her belt-bag and held out for the man's inspection a book of Travelers' Cheques good for fifty thousand G-P credits! "I wanted to continue with you, and I knew this wasn't a passenger ship. I can be useful—who do you think lined up that translation relay?—and besides, I can work. I can cook—keep house—and I can learn any other job fast. You believe me?"

Cloud looked at her. She was as tall as he was, and heavier; stronger and faster. "Yes, you can work, if you want to, and I think you would. But you haven't said why you want to go along."

"Mostly because it's the best chance I'll ever have to learn English. I went to Tellus once before to learn it—but there are too many Vegians there. Young Vegians, like me, like to play too much. You know?"

"I've heard so. But teachers, courses . . .?"

"I need neither teachers nor courses. What I need is what you have in your library—solid English."

"QX. I'll reserve judgment on you, too. Now let's hear what the Tomingan has to say. What's *her* name?"

"You'd be surprised!" Vesta giggled in glee. "Literally translated, it's 'Little flower of spring, dwelling bashfully by the brook's damply sweet brink.' And that's an *exact* transliteration, so help me—believe it or not!"

"I'll take your word for it. What shall we call her?"

"Um . . . m . . . 'Tommie' would be as good as anything, I guess."

"QX. Tommie of Tominga. Ask her why she thinks she has to be a member of our crew."

"Who else do you have who can repair one of your big atomic engines if it lets go?" came the answering question, in Vesta's flawlessly idiomatic Galactic Spanish.

Cloud was amazed at Tommie's changed appearance. She was powdered, perfumed, and painted: made up to the gills. Her heavy blonde hair was elaborately waved. If it wasn't for her diesel-truck build, Cloud thought—and for the long black Venerian cigar she was smoking with such evident relish—she'd be a knockout on anybody's tri-di screen!

"I can." The profoundly deep, but pleasantly and musi-

cally resonant voice went on; the fluent translation continued. "What I don't know about atomic engines hasn't been
found out yet. I don't know much about Bergenholms and
a couple of other things pertaining solely to flight, and I
don't know *anything* about communicators or detectors,
which aren't engineers' business. I've laid in a complete
supply of atomic service manuals for class S-C ships, and I
tell you this—if anything with a motor or an engine in it
aboard this vessel ever has run, I can take it apart and put
it back together so it'll run again. And by the way, you
didn't have half enough spare parts aboard, but you have
now. Besides, you might need somebody to really swing
that axe of yours, some day."

Cloud studied the Tomingan narrowly. She *wasn't* bragging, he decided finally. She was simply voicing what to
her were simple truths.

"Your arguments have weight. Why do you want the
job?"

"Several reasons. I've never done anything like this
before, and it'll be fun. Main reason, though, is that I
think I'll be able to talk you into doing a job on Tominga
that has needed doing for a long time. I was a passenger,
not an officer, on my way to talk to a party about ways of
getting it done. You changed my mind. You and I, with
some others who'll be glad to help, will be able to do it
better."

Tommie volunteered no more information, and Cloud
asked no more questions. Explanation would probably
take more time than could be spared.

"Now you, Thlaskin," the Blaster said in spaceal. "What
have you got to say for yourself?"

"You've got me on a hell of a spot, boss," the pilot
admitted, ruefully. "You've *got* to have a pilot, no question about that. You already know I'm one. I know
automatics, and communicators, and detectors—the
works. Ordinarily I'd say you'd *have* to have *me*. But this
ain't a regular case. I wasn't a pilot on the heap that got
knocked out of the ether, but a passenger. Maluleme—
she's my . . . say, ain't there no word for . . ."

He broke off and spoke rapidly to his wife, who relayed
it to Vesta.

"They're newlyweds," the Vegian translated. "He was
off duty and they were on their honeymoon . . ."

Vesta's wonderfully expressive face softened, saddened. She appeared about to cry. "I wish *I* were old enough to be a newlywed." she said, plaintively.

"Huh? Aren't you?" the Blaster demanded. "You look old enough to me."

"Oh, I'm as big as I ever will be, and I won't change outside. It's inside. About half a year yet. But she's saying—

"We know that pilots on duty, in regular service, can't have their wives aboard. But this isn't a regular run, I know, so couldn't you—just this once—keep Thlaskin on as pilot and let me come too? *Please*, Mr. Neelcloud—she didn't know your name, but asked me to put it in—I can work my way. I'll do any of the jobs nobody else wants to do—I'll do *anything*, Mr. Neelcloud!"

The pink girl jumped up and took Cloud's left hand in both her own. Simultaneously Vesta took his right hand in her left, brought it up to her face, and laid the incredibly downy softness of her cheek against the five-hour bristles of his; sounding the while a soft, low-pitched but unmistakable *purr!*

"Just this once wouldn't do any harm, would it, Captain Neelcloud?" Vesta purred. "You zmell *zo* wonderful, and she zmells nice, too. *Pleeze* keep her on!"

"QX. You win!" The Blaster pulled himself loose from the two too-demonstrative females and addressed the group at large. "I think I ought to have my head examined, but I'm signing all of you on as crew. But *nobody else*. I'll get the book."

He got it. He signed them on. Chief Pilot Thlaskin. Chief Engineer Tommie. Linguist Vesta. Doctor . . . what? He tried to call her attention by thinking at her, but couldn't. Then, through Vesta: Manarkans didn't have names, but were known by their personality patterns. Didn't they sign something to documents? No, they used finger-prints only, without signatures.

"But we've got to have *something* we can put in the book!" Cloud protested. "Tell her to pick one."

"No preference," Vesta reported. "I'm to do it. I knew a lovely Tellurian named "Nadinevandereckelberg" once. Let's call her that."

"Nadine van der Eckelberg? Better not. Not common enough—there might be repercussions. We can use part of it, though. 'Nadine,' bracketed with her prints . . . there. Now how about Maluleme?" He turned to the "Classification" listing and frowned. "What to class *her* as I'll never know. She's got just about as much business aboard this bucket as I would have in a sultan's harem."

"You might find quite a lot—and *that* I'd like to see!" Vesta snickered. "But look under 'Mizzelaneouz,' there."

Her stiff, sharp fingernail ran down the column almost to the end. " 'Zupercargo'? We have no cargo. 'Zupernumerary'? That's it! See? I read: 'Zupernumerary—Perzonnel beyond the nezezzary or uzhual; ezpedjially thoze employed not for regular zervize, but only to fill the plazez of otherz in caze of need.' Perfect!"

"Whose place could *she* fill?"

"The cook's—if the automatics break down," Vesta explained, gleefully. "She says she can really cook—so even if they didn't break down she can tape lots of nice things to eat that aren't in your kitchen banks."

"Could be. I can get away with that. 'Supernumerary (cook 1/c) Maluleme' and her prints . . . there. Now we're organized—let's flit. Ready, Thlaskin?"

"Ready, sir," and the good ship *Vortex Blaster I* took off.

"Now, Vesta, I s'pose you've all picked out your cabins and got located?"

"Yes, sir."

"QX. Tell 'em all, except Tommie, to go and do whatever they think they ought to be doing. Tell Tommie to sit down at the chart-table. We'll join her. I want to find out what she's got on her mind."

Pulling a chart and rolling it out flat on the table, Cloud went on: "We're in this unexplored region, here, about thirty two dash twenty five.* We're headed for Nixson II, about sixty one dash forty six."

"Nixson? Why, that's only three thousand parsecs—a day and a half, say—from Tominga, where I want you to go!" Tommie exclaimed.

"Check. That's why I'm going to listen to what you

---

* Rough locations are expressed in degrees of galactic longitude and hundredths of the distance from Centralia to the Arbitrary Rim of the galaxy. This convention ignores the galaxy's thickness and is used only in first approximations. E.E.S.

have to say. We can pick Manarka up—sixty five dash
thirty five, here; they've got two really bad ones—on the
way back. It's a long flit to Chickladoria—'way over
there, one seventy seven dash thirty four—but I've got to
go there pretty quick, anyway. It's way up on the A list.
So, Tommie, start talking."

* * * * *

The run to Nixson II was uneventful, and Cloud rid
that planet of its loose atomic vortices in a few hours. The
cruiser then headed directly for Tominga, one man short,
for Tommie was not aboard.

"Now remember, no matter what happens, you don't
know any one of us," had been the Blaster's parting
instructions to her. "After we've checked in at the hotel
we'll meet in the lobby. Be sure you're sitting—or standing—some place where Vesta can pass a couple of words
with you without anybody catching on. Check?"

"Check."

Chapter 8

_____VESTA THE VEGIAN

IMMEDIATELY AFTER SUPPER Cloud called Vesta
and Nadine into his cabin.

"You first, Nadine." He caught her eyes and stopped
talking, but went on thinking. He was amazed at how easy
it had been to learn the knack of telepathy with both
Luda and the Manarkan. "How did you make out with
Tommie? Can't she read you at all?"

"Not at all. I can read her easily enough, but she can
neither send nor receive."

"How about Vesta, then? Any more progress?"

"No. Just like you. She learned very quickly to receive,
but that is all. She cannot tune her mind; I have to do it
all." It also amazed the Blaster that, after learning one
half of telepathy so easily, he had been unable even to get

a start on the other half. "We might try it again, though, all three of us together?"

They tried, but it was no use. Think as they would, of even the simplest things—squares, crosses, triangles, and circles—staring eye to eye and even holding hands, neither the Blaster nor the Vegian could touch the other's mind. Nor could the Manarkan tell them or show them what to do.

"Well, that's out, then." Cloud frowned in concentration, the fingers of his left hand drumming almost soundlessly on the table's plastic top. "Nadine, you can't send simultaneously to both Vesta and me, because we can't tune ourselves into resonance with you, as a real telepath could. However, could you read me and send my thoughts to Vesta, and do it fast enough to keep up? As fast as I talk, say?"

"Oh, easily. I don't have to tune sharply to receive— unless there's a lot of interference, of course—and even then, Vesta can read my shorthand. She learned it before we met you."

"Hm...m. Interesting. Let's try it out. I'll think at you, you put it down in shorthand. You, Vesta, tape it in Spanish. Get your notebook and recorder ... ready? Let's go!"

There ensued a strange spectacle. Cloud, leaning back in his seat with his eyes closed, mumbled to himself in English, to slow his thoughts down to approximately two hundred words per minute. Nadine, paying no visible attention to the man, wrote unhurried, smoothly-flowing— most of the time—symbols. Vesta, throat-mike in place and yellow-eyed gaze nailed to the pencil's point, kept pace effortlessly—most of the time.

"That's all. Play it back, Vesta. If you girls got half of that, you're *good*."

The speaker came to life, giving voice to a completely detailed and extremely technical report on the extinction of an imaginary atomic vortex, and as the transcription proceeded Cloud's amazement deepened. It was evident, of course, that neither of the two translators knew anything at all about many of the scientific technicalities involved. Nevertheless the Manarkan had put down—and Vesta had recorded in good, idiomatic Galactic Spanish— an intelligent layman's idea of what it was that had been left out. That impromptu, completely unrehearsed report would have been fully informative to any expert of the Vortex Control Laboratory!

"Girls, you *are* good—*very* good." Cloud paid deserved tribute to ability. "First chance we get, I'll split a bottle of fayalin with you. Now we'd better hit the sack. We land early in the morning, and since we're going to stay here a while we'll have to go through quarantine and customs. So pack your bags and have 'em ready for inspection.

They landed at the spaceport of Tommie's home town, which Cloud, after hearing Vesta's literal translation of its native name, had entered in his log as "Mingia." They passed their physicals and healths easily enough—the requirements for leaving a planet of warm-blooded oxygen-breathers are so severe and so comprehensive that the matter of landing on a similar one is almost always a matter of simple routine.

"Manarkan doctors we know of old; you are welcome indeed. We see very few Tellurians or Vegians, but the standards of those worlds are very high and we are glad to welcome you. But Chickladoria? I never heard of it— we've had no one from that planet since I took charge of this port of entry . . ."

The Tomingan official punched buttons, gabbled briefly, and listened.

"Oh, yes. Excellent! The health, sanitation, and exit requirements of Chickladoria are approved by the Galactic Medical Society. We welcome you. You all may pass."

They left the building and boarded a copter for their hotel.

". . . and part of its name is 'Forget-me-not'! Isn't that a dilly of a name for a hotel?" Vesta, who had been telepathing busily with Nadine, was giggling sunnily.

Suddenly, however, she stopped laughing and, eyes slitted, leaped for the door. Too late: the craft was already in the air.

"Do you know what that . . . that *clunker* back there *really* thought of us?" she flared. "That we're weak, skinny, insipid, underdeveloped little *runts!* By Zevz and Tlazz and Jadkptn, I'll show him—I'll take a tail-wrap around his neck and . . ."

"Pipe down, Vesta—listen!" Cloud broke in, sharply. "You're smart enough to know better than to explode that way. For instance, you're stronger than I am, and faster—admitted. So what? I'm still your boss. And Tommie isn't, even though, as you ought to know by this time, she could pull your tail out by the roots and beat you to death with the butt end of it in thirty seconds flat."

"Huh?" Vesta's towering rage subsided miraculously into surprised curiosity. "But you're *admitting* it!" she marvelled. "Even that *I* am stronger and faster than *you* are!"

"Certainly. Why not? Servos are faster still, and ordinary derricks are stronger. It's *brains* that count. I'd much rather have your linguistic ability than the speed and strength of a Valerian."

"So would I, really," Vesta purred. "You're the *nicest* man!"

"So watch yourself, young lady," Cloud went on evenly, "and behave yourself. If you don't, important as you are to this project, I'll send you back to the ship in irons. That's a promise."

"P-f-z-t-k!" Vesta fairly spat the expletive. Her first thought was sheer defiance, but under the Blaster's level stare she changed her mind visibly. "I'll behave myself, Captain Neelcloud."

"Thanks, Vesta. You'll be worth a whole platoon of Tomingans if you do."

The copter landed on the flat roof of the hotel. The guests were registered and shown to their rooms. The Forget-Me-Not's air was hot and humid, and the visitors wore the only clothing to be seen. Nevertheless, Cloud was too squeamish to go all the way, so he still wore shorts and sandals, as well as the side-arm of his rank, when he went back up to the lobby to meet his crew.

Vesta, tail-tip waving gracefully a foot and a half above her head, was wearing only her sandals. Thlaskin wore shorts and space-boots. Maluleme had reduced her conventional forty one square inches of covering to a daring twenty five—two narrow ribbons and a couple of jewels. Nadine, alone of them all, had made no concession to that stickily sweltering climate. She'd be disgraced for life, Cloud supposed, if she cut down by even one the hundreds of feet of white glamorette in which she was swathed. But Manarkans didn't sweat like Tellurians, he guessed—if they did, she'd either peel or smother before this job was over!

Cloud scanned the lobby carefully. Were they attracting too much attention? They were not. They had had to pose for Telenews shots, of course—the Chickladorians in particular had been held in the spots for all of five minutes—but that was all. Like any other space-port city, Mingia was used to outlandish forms of warm-blooded, oxygen-breathing life. Not counting his own group, he could see members of four different non-Tomingan races, two of which were completely strange to him. And Tommie, standing alone in front of one of the row of shop-windows comprising one wall of the lobby—and very close to a mirrored pillar—was intently studying a tobacconist's display of domestic and imported cigars.

"QX," the Blaster said then. "We aren't kicking up any fuss. Do your stuff, Vesta."

The girl sauntered over to the mirror, licked her forefinger, and began to smooth an imaginary roughness out of one perfect eyebrow. Thus, palm covering mouth—

"He still hangs out here, Tommie?"

"He still eats supper here every night, in the same private room." Tommie did not move or turn her head; her voice could not be heard three feet away.

"When he comes in, take one good look at him and think 'This is the one'—Nadine'll take over from there. Then sneak down to the chief's suite and join us."

Vesta, with a final approving pat at her sleek head, sauntered on; past a display of belt-pouches in which she was not interested, pausing before one of ultra-fancy candies in which she very definitely was, and back to her own group.

"On the green," she reported.

"Then I'll go on about my business of getting things lined up to blow out vortices. You, Thlaskin and Maluleme, just run around and play. Act innocent—you're just atmosphere for now. Nadine and Vesta, go down to my suite—here's a key—and get your recorder and stuff ready. I'll see you later."

Cloud came back, however, rather sooner than he had intended.

"I didn't get far—I'll have to take you along if I want to get any business done," he explained to Vesta. "Up to now, I've got along very nicely with English, Spanish, and spaceal, but not here. We're a long ways from either Tellus or Vegia."

"We are indeed. I don't know what they do use for an interstellar language here—I'll have to find out and see if I know it yet." Vesta then switched to English. "While we wait, do you mind if I zpeak at you in Englizh? And will you ztop me and correct, please, the errors I will make? My pronunziazïon is getting better, but I ztill have much trouble with your irregular verbs and pronouns. I come, but I am not yet arrive."

"I'll say you're better!" Cloud knew that she had been studying hard; studying with an intensity of concentration comparable only to that of a cat on duty at a mouse-hole; but he had expected no such progress as this. "It's amazing—you have scarcely any more accent now in English than in Spanish. I'll be glad to coach you. What you just said was QX except for the last sentence. Idiomatically, you should have said 'I'm coming along, but I'm not there yet,'" and Cloud explained in detail. "Now, for practice, brief me on this job we've got here."

"Thankz a lot. Tommie's brother, whom we'll call Jim, runs a tobacco zhop here in town." Cloud had had to explain what "briefing" meant, and he corrected many slight errors which are not given here. "A man who called himself 'Number One' organized a Protective Azzoziazion. Anyone not joining, he zaid, would zuffer the conzequenzez of a looze atomic vortex in his power plant. When he zhowed he meant buzzinez by exploding one right where and when he zaid he would, many merchants joined and began to pay. Jim did not. Inztead, he ... I forget the idiom?"

"'Stalled.' That means delayed, played for time."

"Oh, yez. Jim ztalled, and Tommie went looking for help, knowing the government here thoroughly corrupt. Impozzible to alleviate intolérable zituazion."

"*What* a vocabulary!"

"Iz wrong?" Vesta demanded.

"No, is *right*," Cloud assured her. "I was complimenting you, young lady—you'll be teaching *me* English before this trip is over."

The class in English Conversation went on until the Manarkan warned its two participants to get ready; that

Tommie, having identified the gangster, had left the lobby, had joined her brother, and was bringing him with her.

"Is that safe, do you think?" Vesta asked.

"For now, before anything starts, yes." Cloud replied. "After tonight, no."

The Tomingans arrived; Vesta let them in and introduced Jim to Nadine and Cloud. The brother was taller, heavier, craggier than the sister; his cigar was longer, thicker, and blacker than hers. Otherwise, they were very much alike. Cloud waved them both into comfortable chairs, for there was no time for conversation. Nadine began to write; Vesta to record.

The Big Shot—Nadine took an instant to flash into Cloud's mind a very good picture of the fellow—was in his private room, but if a dinner were to be on the program it would be later. There were two men in the room; Number One and another man, whom he thought of and spoke to as "Number Nine." At present the affair was strictly business. Number Nine was handing money to Number One, who was making notes in a book. Twenty credits from Number Seventeen; 50 from No. 20; 25 from No. 26; 175 from No. 29; 19 credits—all he could raise—from No. 30; 125 from No. 31, and so on . . . .

The gangsters thought that they were being very smart and cagey in using numbers instead of names, but neither had any idea of the power of a really good telepathic mind, or of that of a really good linguist. Each of those numbers meant something to either or to both of those men, and whatever it was—a name, a picture, a store-front or address, or a fleeting glimpse of personality pattern—Nadine seized and transmitted, either in shorthand or by force of mind, or both; and Vesta taped, in machine-gun-fast Spanish, every written word and every nuance of thought.

The list was long. At its end:

"Three more didn't pay up, huh? The same ones holding out as last time, and three more besides, huh?" This was Number One, thinking deeply. "I don't like it . . . Ninety Two, huh? I don't like it a bit—or him, either. I'll have to do something about him."

"Yeah. Ninety Two. The others all give the same old tear-jerker that they didn't have it, that our assessments were too stiff for their take, and so on, but Ninety Two didn't, this time. He simply blew his top. He was hotter than the business end of a blow-torch." Not much to Cloud's surprise, Nadine at this point poured into his mind the picture of excessively angry Jim. "Not only he didn't fork over, he told me to tell you something."

There was a long pause.

"Well, spill it!" Number One barked. "What did he say?"

"Shall I give it to you straight boss, or maybe I better tone it down some?"

"Straight!"

"He said for you to go roast, for fourteen thousand years, in the hottest corner you can find of the hottest hell of Telemachia, and take your Srizonified association with you. Take your membership papers and stick 'em. Blow his place up and be damned to you, he says. If you kill him in the blast he's left stuff in a deposit box that'll blow all the Srizonified crooked politicians and lawmen in the Fourth Continent off of their perches and down onto their Srizonified butts. An' if you *don't* get him, he says, he'll come after you with blasters in both hands. Make it plain, he says, that it's *you* he'll be after—not me. That's exactly what he told me to tell you, boss."

"Me? ME?" Number One demanded. The towering rage, which he had been scarcely able to control, subsided into a warily intense speculation. "How did he find out about *me?* Somebody'll burn for this!"

"I dunno, boss, but it looks like you said a mouthful about having to do something about him. We got to make an example of *somebody*, boss—or else—in my book it'd better be 92. He's organizing, sure as hell, and if we don't knock him off it'll spread fast."

"Hm ... m ... m. Yes, but just him personally, not his place. I'm not afraid of any evidence he can leave, of itself, but in connection with the other thing it might be bad. His place is too big; too centrally located. No matter what time of night it goes off it'll kill too many people and do too much damage. Yellow Castle might dump us instead of trying to ride out such a storm."

"Yeah, they might, at that. Prob'ly would. And the dogooders might get some of them Srizonified Lensmen in here besides. But an ordinary bomb would do the job."

"No. Got to be a vortex. We promised 'em an atomic

flare, so that's what it's got to be. It doesn't have to be 9, though. We can get away easy enough with killing a few people, so I'd say somebody in the outskirts—53 would be as good as any. So tell 53 his place gets it at midnight tomorrow night, and the fewer people in it the more will stay alive."

"Check. And I'll take care of 92?"

"Of course. You don't have to be told *every* move to make."

"Just wanted to make sure, is all. What do I do in the big fireworks?" It was clear that the underling was intensely curious about the phenomenon, but his curiosity was not to be satisfied.

"Nothing," his chief informed him flatly. "That isn't your dish. Now we'll eat."

Number One stopped talking, but he did not stop thinking; and Nadine could read, and Vesta could transcribe, thoughts as well as words.

"Besides, it's about time for 31 to earn some of the credits we're paying him," was the grimly savage thought.

This thought was accompanied by a picture, which Nadine spread in full in Cloud's mind. A tall, lean, gray Tellurian was aiming a mechanism—the details of which were so vague that it could have been anything from a vest-pocket flash-pencil up to a half-track mobile projector —at a power-plant, which immediately and enthusiastically went out of control in a blindingly incandescent flare of raw energy.

Fairchild!

Cloud's mind raced. That vortex on Deka *hadn't* been accidental, then, even though there had been no evidence— no suspicion—even the Lensmen hadn't guessed that the radiationist had been anything other than a very minor cog in Graves' thionite-producing machine! Nobody except Fairchild knew what he did or how he did it—the mob must have tried to find out, too, but he wouldn't give—but this stuff was very definitely for the future; not for now.

"QX, girls. A nice job—thanks," he said. "Now, Vesta, please tape the actual facts and the actual words of the interview—none of the pictures or guesses—in Middle Plateau Tomingan. Wherever possible, bracket real names

addresses with the code numbers. Tommie and Jim
can help you on that."

She did so.

When they came to that part of the transcription
dealing with Number Ninety Two, Jim stiffened and
swelled in rage.

"Ask him if that's an accurate report," Cloud directed.

"It's accurate enough as far as it goes," Jim boomed.
His voice, deeper and louder than Tommie's, and not
nearly as musical, almost shook the walls. "But he left out
half of it. What I really told him would have burned all
the tape off of that recorder."

"But they left in that . . . that awful one, three times."
Tommie, tough as she was, was shocked. "You ought to
be ashamed of yourself."

"Srizonified?" Cloud whispered to Vesta. "It sounded
bad, but not *that* hot. Is it?"

"Yes, the hottest in the language. I never saw it in
print, and heard it only once, and that was by accident.
Like most such things, though, it doesn't translate—
'descended from countless generations of dwellers in stinking, unflowering mud' is as close as I can come to it in
Spanish."

"QX. Finish up the tape and make two copies of it."

When the copies were ready Cloud handed them to
Tommie.

"Tell him to take one of these down to the Tomingan
equivalent of the D. A.'s office the first thing in the
morning," he instructed Vesta. "The other ought to go to
a big law firm—an honest one, if she knows of any. Now
ask Jim what he thinks he's going to do."

"I'm going to get a pair of blasters and . . ."

"Yeah?" Cloud's biting monosyllable, so ably translated
by the Vegian, stopped him in mid-sentence. "What
chance do you think you stand of getting home tonight in
one piece? Your copter is probably mined right now, and
they've undoubtedly made arrangements to blast you if
you leave here any other way, even on foot. If you want
to stay alive, though, I've got a suggestion to make."

"You may be right, sir." Jim's bluster died away as he
began really to think. "Do you see a way out?"

"Yes. Ordinary citizens don't wear armor here, any
more than anywhere else, so ordinary gangsters don't use

semi-portables. So, when you leave here, go to Tommie's room instead of out. They'll lay for you, of course, but while they're waiting Tommie will go out to our ship and bring back my G-P armor. You put it on, walk out openly, and take a ground-car—*not* a copter—to the ship. If they know armor they won't shoot at you, because you could shoot back. When you get to the ship go in, lock the port behind you, and stay there until I tell you to come out."

Jim, influenced visibly by the pleasant possibility of shooting back, accepted the plan joyously; and, after making sure that there were no spies or spy-rays on watch, the two Tomingans left the room.

A few minutes later, with the same precaution, Vesta and the Manarkan went to their own rooms; but they were on hand again after breakfast next morning.

"You know, of course, that you have no evidence admissible in even an honest court," Nadine began. "You knew it when you changed your mind about having a Tomingan voice, not Vesta's, on those tapes."

"Yes. Communicator-taps are out—violation of privacy."

"Exactly. And telepathy is worse. Any attempt to introduce telepathic testimony, on almost any non-telepathic world, does more harm than good. So, beyond establishing the fact of guilt in your own mind—a fact already self-evident, since such outrages can happen only when both courts and police are corrupt from top to bottom—I fail to see what you hope to gain."

"Wouldn't a Tomingan Lensman be interested?"

"There are none. There never have been any."

"Well, then, I'll take it up myself, with . . . ."

Cloud stopped in mid-thought. With whom? He could talk to Phil Strong, certainly, but he wouldn't get anywhere. He knew, as well as Nadine did, that the Galactic Patrol would not interfere with purely local politics unless something of inter-systemic scope was involved. The Galactic Council held, and probably rightly, that any people got the kind of local government they deserved. He certainly couldn't expect the Patrol to over-ride planetary sovereignty in regard to a thing that hadn't happened yet! He wrenched his mind away.

"Having any trouble following her, Nadine?" he asked.

"No. She's just leaving the fast-way now; going into his office."

Thus, through Nadine, Cloud accompanied Tommie into the office of the District Attorney, saw her tender the spool of tape, heard her explain in stormy language what it was.

"How did you get hold of it?" the D. A. demanded.

"How do you suppose?" Tommie shot back. "Do we have to come down to City Hall and take out a license to hang an ear onto such a stinking crumb, such a notorious mobster and general all-round heel as Number One is? Public Enemy Number One, it ought to be!"

"No, I wouldn't say that you would," the politician soothed. He had been thinking fast. "I'll run this tape as soon as I can take a minute alone in my chambers, and I promise you full and fast action. They've gone too far, this time. Just what, specifically, do you want me to do?"

"I'm no lawyer, so I don't know who does what, but I want this Protective Association junked and I want those murderers arrested. Today."

"Some of these matters lie outside the province of this office, but I can and will take initiatory steps. No one will be harmed, I assure you."

Apparently satisfied, Tommie left the D. A.'s office, but Nadine did not leave the D. A.'s mind. This was what the Blaster was after!

Sure enough, as soon as Tommie was out of sight, the official dashed into his private office and called Number One.

"One, they hung an ear on you last night!" he exclaimed, as soon as connection was made. "How come you didn't . . ."

"Horsefeathers!" the gangster snarled. "Who d'ya think you're kidding?"

"But they did! I've got a copy of it right here."

"Play it!"

The tape was played, and it was very clear that it was in no Tomingan's voice.

"No, it wasn't an ear," the D. A. admitted.

"And I was blocked against spy-rays," said Number One, "so it must have been a snooper. A snooper with a voice. Manarkans are snoopers, but they can't talk. Most snoopers can't . . . except maybe Ordoviks. There were a couple of them around last night. Can Ordoviks talk? And Chickladorians—are they snoopers?"

"I don't know."

"I don't know either, but I'll find out, and when I do I'll go gunning."

Tommie came back to Cloud's room and her serenity, skin-deep at best, vanished completely as the new tape was played.

"Condemn and blast that lying, slimy, two-faced, double-crossing snake!" she roared. "I'll call out the . . ."

"You won't either—pipe down!" Cloud ordered, sharply. "Mob rule never settled anything. That's what you expected, isn't it?"

"Well . . . more or less, I suppose . . . yes."

"QX. We got *something* to work on now, but we need more, and we've got only today to get it. Who's the crookedest judge in town—the one most apt to be in on this kind of a deal?"

"Trellis. High Judge Rose Trellis of the Enchanting . . ."

"Skip the embellishments. Take both of these tapes to Judge Trellis and *insist* on seeing him at once."

"It isn't a him—she's a her."

"Her, then. Make it snappy. And don't blow up if she gives you the brush-off. We're after data. And on your way back, pick up that newspaper editor and bring him along."

Chapter 9

_____TROUBLE ON TOMINGA

TOMMIE LEFT, accompanied mentally by Nadine, and reached the judge's antechamber; with Vesta taping in Middle-Plateau Tomingan everything that occurred. The approach was difficult, and Tommie's temper grew shorter and shorter.

"Get out of my way!" she bellowed finally at the sergeant-at-arms barring her way to the judicial Presence, in a voice that rattled the windows and was audible above four blocks of city traffic. "Or shoot, if you want to get your-self and this building and half of Mingia blown clear up into the stratosphere! Jump! Before I take that blaster and shove it so far down your throat it'll hit day-before-yesterday's breakfast!"

The guard did not have quite enough nerve to shoot, and Tommie almost wrenched the door of the judge's inner office off its hinges as she went in.

"What's this, pray? Get out! Sergeant-at . . . ."

"Shut up, Rose Trellis of the Enchanting Vistas of Exotic Blooms—you're listening, not talking. Here's two tapes of what Number One and his misbegotten scum have been doing. Play 'em! And then *do something* about 'em! And listen, you lying, double-crossing, back-biting slime-lizard!" Tommie's prettily-made-up face was in shocking contrast to the venemous fury in Tommie's eyes as she leaned over the judge's massive desk until nose was a scant ten inches from nose. "If that atomic blast goes off tonight you and your whole Srizonified crew will wish to all your devils you'd never been born!"

Whirling around, Tommie strode out; nor did anyone attempt to stop her. No one knew what would happen if they did; and no one cared to find out.

Judge Trellis did not play the tapes. In panic fashion she called the District Attorney, who promptly made it a three-way with Number One. The three talked busily for minutes, then met in person, together with several lesser lights, in a heavily-guarded room. This conference, the subject matter of which was so obvious as to require no detailing here, went on for a long time.

So long, in fact, that Tommie and the newspaper man got back to Cloud's hotel room while Vesta was still taping a word-by-word report of the proceedings. Tommie was subdued, almost apologetic.

"I know you told me not to blow up, Captain Cloud, but they made me so mad I couldn't help it."

"In this case just as well you did; maybe better. You scared her into calling a meeting, and they've spilled every bean in the pot. We've got exactly what we wanted—enough to stop that gang right in its tracks. Now, as soon as the girls get the last of it, we'll let your editor in on it."

It was soon over, and Cloud, after a quick run-down of

the situation and a play-back of parts of the tapes for the newshawk's benefit, concluded:—

"So, over the long pull, the issue isn't—can't be—in doubt. Public opinion will be aroused. There are honest judges, there are a lot of honest cops. At the next election this corrupt regime will be thrown out of office. However, that election is a year away, the present powers-that-be are all in the syndicate, and we must do something *today* to stop the destruction scheduled for tonight. Little Flower-and-so-on tells me that you're a crusading type, fighting a losing battle against this mob—that they've got you just about whipped—so I thought you would be interested in taking a slug at 'em by getting out an extra—strong enough to stir up enough public sentiment so they wouldn't dare go ahead. Would you like to do that?"

"Would I?" The newsman grinned wolfishly. "I'll get out the extra, yes; but I'll do a lot more than that. I'll print a hundred thousand dodgers and drop 'em from copters. I'll have blimps dragging streamers all over the sky. I'll buy time on every radio and tri-di station in town—have the juiciest bits of these tapes broadcast, every hour on the hour. Mister, I'll tear this town wide open before sundown tonight!"

He left, breathing fire and sulphurous smoke, and Cloud made motions to attract the Manarkan's attention.

"Nadine? These Tomingans take things big, don't they? All to the good, with one exception—will any repercussions—flarebacks—hit you? Those characters are tough, and will be desperate, and I wouldn't want to put you in line with a blaster."

"No . . . almost certainly not," Nadine replied, after a minute of thought. "They are looking for a telepath with a voice, which they won't find on Tominga. They know Manarkans well—many of us live here permanently—and I'm quite sure that none of the gang would suspect such an unheard-of thing as Vesta and I have been doing. They are not imaginative, and such a thing never happened before—not here, at least."

"No? Why not? What's strange about it?"

"The whole situation is new—unique. This is probably the first time in history that these exact circumstances—especially in regard to personnel—have come together. Consider, please, the ingredients: a real and bitter grievance, victims willing and anxious to take drastic action, a sympathetic telepath who is also an expert in shorthand, a master linguist, and, above all, a director or programmer —you—both able and willing to fit the parts together so that they work."

"Um . . . m . . .m. Never thought of it in that way. Could be, I guess. Well, all we can do now is wait and see what happens."

They waited, and saw. The crusading editor did everything he had promised. The extra hit the streets, its headlines screaming "CORRUPTION!" in the biggest type possible to use. The taped conversations, with names, amounts, times, and places, were printed in full. The accompanying editorial should have been written with sulphuric acid on asbestos paper. The leaflets, gaily littering the city, were even more vitriolic. Every hour, on the hour, speakers gave out what sound-trucks were blaring continuously—irrefutable proof that the city of Mingia was being run by a corrupt, rotten, vicious machine.

Mingia's citizens responded, but not quite as enthusiastically as the Blaster, from his limited acquaintance with the breed, had expected. There was some organizing, some demonstrating; but there was also quite a lot of "So what? If they don't, some other gang of politicians will."

Cloud, however, when he went to his rooms after supper, was well pleased with what he had seen. They *couldn't* blast 53, not after the events of the afternoon. The Chickladorians and Vesta and Nadine, when they came in, agreed with him. The situation was under control. They were tired, they said. It had been a long, hard day, and they were going to hit the sack. They left.

Cloud intended to stay awake until midnight, just to see what would happen, but he didn't. He was tired, too, and within a couple of minutes after he relaxed, alone, he was sound asleep in his chair.

Thus he did not hear the vicious thunder-clap of the atomic explosion at midnight; did not see the reflected brilliance of its glare. Nor did he hear the hurrying footsteps in the hotel's corridors. What woke him up was the concussion that jarred the whole neighborhood when a half-ton bomb demolished the building which had been Number One's headquarters.

Cloud jumped up, then, and ran out into the hall and

along it to Vesta's room. He pounded. No answer. The door was unlocked. He opened it. Vesta was not there!

Nadine was gone, too. So were the Chickladorians.

He rushed up to the lobby, only to encounter again the difficulty that had stopped him short before. *He could not make himself understood!* He didn't know three words of Upper Plateau, and nobody he could find knew even one word of English, Spanish, Spaceal, or any other language at his command.

He took an elevator down to the street level and flagged a cruising cab. He handed the driver the largest Tomingan bill he had; then, pointing straight ahead and making furious pushing motions, he made it plain that he knew where he wanted to go, and wanted to get there in a hurry. The hacker, stimulated by more cash than he had seen for a week, drove wherever Cloud pointed; and broke—or at least bent—most of Mingia's speed-laws in his eagerness to oblige.

Cloud's destination, of course, was the space-port; but when he got to the *Vortex Blaster I,* Jim wasn't there any more. None of his crew was aboard, either. The lifeboats were all in place, but the flitter was gone. So were both suits of armor—and the semi-portables—and the spare DeLameters—and both needles—even his space-hatchet!

He went up to the control room and glanced over the board. Everything was on zero except one meter, which was grazing the red. All four semis and both needles were running wide open—pulling every watt they could possibly draw!

Angry as he was, Cloud did not think of cutting the circuit. If he had thought of it he wouldn't have done it. He didn't know exactly what his officers were doing, of course, but he could do a shrewd job of guessing. If he had known what they were up to he wouldn't have permitted it, but it was too late to do anything about it now. With those terrific weapons in operation they *might* get back alive—without them, they certainly would not. *What* a land-office business those semis were doing!

They were.

Tommie and her brother, wearing Cloud's two suits of armor, were each *carrying* a semi-portable; wielding it, if not as easily as an Earthly gunner wields a sub-machine-gun, much more effectively. They were burning down a thick steel door. Well behind them, the third semi was bathing the whole front of the building in a blinding glare of radiance. In back, the fourth was doing the same to the rear wall. On the sides, the two needlebeams were darting from window to window, burning to a crisp any gangster gunner daring to show his head to aim.

For the Tomingans had not been nearly as optimistic as had Cloud, and they had made complete preparation for reprisal in case Number One should make good his threat. The Manarkan had been willing to cooperate. Thlaskin, ditto. Vesta had been quiveringly eager. Maluleme had gone along. They had not mutinied—they simply did not tell Cloud a thing about what they were going to do.

Number One had not been in his headquarters, of course, when that thousand-pound bomb let go. He thought himself safe—but he wasn't. Nadine the telepath knew exactly where he was and exactly what he was doing. Vesta the linguist poured the information along, via the flitter's broadcaster, to the receivers of hundreds of ground-cars and copters far below. Thlaskin the Master Pilot kept the flitter close enough to the fleeing Number One so that Nadine could read him—fully, she thought— but far enough away to avoid detection. Thus, wherever he went, Number One was pursued relentlessly, and his merciless pursuers closed in faster and faster.

Number One's flight, however, was not aimless. He knew that a snooper was on him, and had enough power of mind to shield a few highly important thoughts. He wasn't really THE Big Shot. He had called Yellow Castle, though, and they had told him that he could come in in one hour—the army would be ready. But did he have an hour, or not?

He did; just barely. The saps were snapping at his heels when he switched to a jet job and took off in a screaming straight line for the Castle.

Vesta wanted to ram him to drop a life-boat on him, to wreck him in any way possible; but Thlaskin refused. Captain Cloud would be mad enough at what they'd done already—any such rough stuff as *that* would be altogether too damn much! And, since the rebels' jets were still on the ground, Number One had reached sanctuary unharmed.

Yellow Castle, however, was not as impregnable as the

gangsters had supposed. They had armor, true, but it was not at all like Cloud's. They had weapons, true, but nothing even faintly resembling the frightful semi-portable projectors of the Galactic Patrol—nothing even remotely approaching the Patrol's beam-fed needle beams.

Thus the Tomingans, Tommie and Jim, stood in armor of proof scarcely an arm's length from Yellow Castle's heavy steel door and burned it down into a brooklet of molten metal. Then on in; blasting down everything that resisted and, finally, everything that moved. Nor did any gangster escape. Those who managed to avoid the armored pair were blasted by one of the other semis or speared by one of the needles.

Yellow Castle, already furiously ablaze, was left to burn. Jim, after giving instructions as to how his lieutenants were to dispose of such small fry as might be left alive in the city proper, helped his sister load the Blaster's weapons and armor into a ground-car. They drove out into the middle of a great open field. The flitter landed; Cloud's borrowed equipment was hauled aboard. Tommie and Jim followed it.

"If you were really smart, I think you'd flit right now," Vesta said to Tommie. "Captain Cloud isn't going to like this a little bit."

"I know it. I'm not smart. This was worth anything he cares to do about it. Besides, I want to thank him myself and tell him goodbye in person."

The flitter took off and returned to her mother-ship. Tommie and Thlaskin put her away, then the peculiarly assorted six went up to the control room and faced the quietly seething Tellurian.

Not boldly—only Tommie and Nadine were really at ease. Jim was defiant. Thlaskin was nervous and apprehensive; Maluleme was just plain scared. So was Vesta—her tail drooped to the floor; she seemed to have shrunk to four-fifths her normal size; her usual free-swinging, buoyant gait had changed almost to a slink.

Cloud stared at Nadine—chill, stern, aloof; an up-to-date Joan of Arc or a veritable destroying angel—nodded at her to synchronize with his mind. She did so, and her mind bore out everything implied by her attitude and expression. She was outraged to her innermost fiber by the conditions she had just helped to correct.

"You were the prime operator in this thing," he thought, flatly. "With your knowledge of law and your supposed respect for it, how could you take it into your own hands? Become part of a law-breaking mob?"

"It was necessary. Law in Mingia was shackled—completely inoperative. We freed it."

"By murder?"

"It was not murder. The lives of all who were killed were already forfeit. The corrupt judges, officials, and police officers will be dealt with by Mingian law, now again operative. Of all your crew, only Tommie could by any chance have been taken or recognized. If our coup had failed, she and Jim would have been shot without trial. Since we succeeded, however, Tommie was not recognized, being in your armor, and Jim is now Mingia's hero. He is also the new Commissioner of Police. Hence, aside from breaking local laws—which, as I have explained, do not count—we are guilty only of unauthorized use of Patrol equipment."

"Huh? How about interfering in planetary affairs, the worst in the book? And revealing Stage Ten stuff to a Stage Eight planet?"

"You are wrong on both counts," Nadine informed him. "We were on shore leave—that fact is in the log. We volunteered, purely as individuals, for one day of service in the Underground. This procedure, while of course forbidden to armed personnel of the Patrol, is perfectly legal to its civilian employees. A special ruling would have to be made to cover this particular incident, and no *ex post facto* penalties could be imposed."

"That's quibbling if I ever heard any, but you're probably right—legally—at that. But how do you wiggle out of the 'revealing' charge?"

"In the specific meaning of the word, as defined by the highest courts, nothing was revealed. Weapons and armor were seen, of course; but they have been seen on Tominga before. Nothing new was learned; hence there was no revealment. And as for Jim's leaving the ship against your orders, you had no right to issue such orders in the first place."

Still seething, but on a considerably lower level, Cloud pondered. It *wasn't* murder—nobody would or could call it that. "Extermination" would be more like it—or "justifi-

When the job was done, Nadine's mind and Cloud's met briefly. No direct reference was made to the unpleasantness on Tominga, nor to their somewhat variant ideas concerning it. Nadine wanted to stay on. She liked the job and she liked Cloud. He was somewhat impractical and visionary, a bit too idealistic in his outlook at times; but a strong and able man and a top-bracket commander, nevertheless.

And the Manarkan, in Cloud's mind, was not only a top-bracket medico, but also a *very* handy hand to have around.

On the fourteenth of Sol, then, the good ship *Vortex Blaster I* took off for Tellus, with Cloud wondering more than a little as to what was in the wind. He wasn't the type to be unduly perturbed about being called up on the carpet *per se;* but Phil didn't go in for mystery much—he explained things ... He couldn't possibly know anything about that Mingian business so soon ... and he was going to tell him all about it anyway ....

There was plenty of Laboratory business that shouldn't be relayed all over space, and this was undoubtedly some of it. Whatever it was, it'd have to keep until he got to Tellus, anyway, so he'd forget it until then.

But he didn't.

Chapter 10

JANOWICK

BACK ON TELLUS, Cloud took a fast 'copter to the Vortex Control Laboratory, still wondering what it was all about.

"Go right in, Dr. Cloud," Strong's secretary told him, even before he stopped at her desk. "He's been gnawing his nails ever since you landed."

Cloud went in. The Lensman was not alone; a woman who had been seated beside the desk was now standing, studying him eagerly.

"Hi, Phil," the Blaster said. "Why all the haste, and why

so cryptic? I've been wondering if you found where I hid the body—and which body it was."

"Hi, Storm. Nothing like that!" Strong laughed. "Doctor Janowick, Doctor Cloud—or rather, Joan, this is Storm. You know all about him that anybody does."

They shook hands, Cloud wondering all the more, and as he wondered he studied the woman, just as she was studying him

Janowick? *Janowick!* He'd never heard of any female Janowick, so she couldn't be anybody much in nucleonics. Not exactly fat, but definitely on the plump side. About a hundred and thirty five pounds, he guessed; and about five feet two. About his own age—no, a bit younger, thirty-some, probably. Brown hair, with a few white ones showing; wide-spaced gray eyes—slightly myopic, by the looks of her pixeyish, you-be-damned spectacles. Smart and keen—all in all, a prime number.

"This is why I pulled you in, Storm," the Lensman went on "As you know, we've been combing all Civilization, trying to find somebody—anybody—with enough of the right qualities. She's it. Head of the Department of Semantics at the Galactic Institute for Advanced Study. Doctor of Semantics, Ph.D. in cybernetics, D.Sc. in symbolic logic, and so on for half the alphabet. She is also a very good self-made telepath, and the only self-made perceiver I ever heard of. She's very good at that, too—she can outrange a Rigellian. And besides all that, she's a Past Grand Master at chess."

"*Past* Grand Master? Oh, I see— I don't suppose it *would* be quite *de rigueur* for a top-bracket telepath to win all the Grand Masters' championships. Also, in view of the perception business, I imagine all this is more than somewhat hush-hush?"

"Very much so. A few Lensmen and now you are all who are in on it. It'll have to stay top secret until we find out whether an ordinary mind can be developed into one like yours, or whether her brain, like yours, is something out of the ordinary."

"Yes, it'd be very bad to have billions of people screaming for a treatment that can't be given."

"Check. But to get back to Joan. She's done some almost unbelievable work and we think she'll do. You know what we're after, of course."

"All I'm afraid of is that you haven't looked far enough," the woman said, shaking her head dubiously. "You know, though, what an appalling job it was bound to be. I'll do whatever I can."

She did not state the problem, either. They all knew, too well, what it was. As matters then stood, the life of one man—Neal Cloud—was all-that stood between Civilization and loose atomic vortices; and it was starkly unthinkable that the Galactic Patrol would leave, for a second longer than was absolutely necessary, that situation unremedied.

"I see." Cloud broke the short silence. "Assuming that you haven't been sitting still doing nothing while I've been gone, brief me."

"Smart boy!" Strong applauded. "The first thing Joan did was to figure out that a nine-second prediction was out of the question for any computer, digital or analogue, possible to build with today's knowledge. Asked us what we could do to cut the time and how far we could cut it. With your little bombing flitter you have to have about nine seconds because you have to build up your speed to the required initial velocity of the bomb. That could be done away with, of course, by firing the bomb out of a ·Q-gun or something . . . ."

"But you'd have to have a special ship, much bigger than a flitter!" Cloud protested. "And special guns . . . . and the special pointers for those guns—or for the ship, if the guns were fixed-aligned—would be ver*ee* unsimple, believe me!"

"How right you are, Buster! Other things, too, that you haven't thought of yet, such as automatic compensation for air conditions and so on. Very much worth while, however, and all done—we've had a lot of people on this project. But to cut this short, the necessary ship turned out to be a scout cruiser; the minimum safe distance—assuming worst possible conditions and heaviest possible screening—is thirty two hundred meters . . . ."

"Wait a minute!" Cloud broke in. "I've worked closer than that!"

"You got badly burned once, too, remember; and, according to the medics, you've been taking some damage since. You won't from here on. But to resume: since the muzzle velocity we can use is limited, by the danger of prematuring on impact, to nine hundred sixteen meters per second, the time from circuit-closing to detonation is something over three and a half seconds—how much over depending on atmospheric conditions. That's absolutely the best we can do, so we gave Joan a minimum of three point six seconds of prediction to shoot at with her mechanical brains. She isn't quite there yet, but she's far enough along so that she has to work with you, on actual blasting, the rest of the way."

"Why?" Cloud argued. "If she stayed on the high side there'd be no danger of scattering; only of intensification, which wouldn't do any harm out in the badlands."

"Too chancy." The Lensman swept Cloud's argument aside with a wave of his hand. "So the quicker you get moved into your new ship, the *Vortex Blaster Two*, and get your practicing done, the sooner the two of you can be on your way to Chickladoria. Flit!"

"Just as you say, chief. Here's my report in full. Some of the stuff will jar you to the teeth; particularly Fairchild and the fact that every blow-up that has ever happened has been deliberate, not accidental."

"Huh? *Deliberate!* Have you blown your stack completely, Storm?"

"Uh-uh; but the proof is too long and involved to go into offhand. You'll have to get it from the tapes and it'll take you at least a week to check my math. Besides, you told us to flit. So come on, Joan—clear ether, Phil!"

The Blaster and his new assistant left the laboratory; and in the copter, en route to the field, Cloud wondered momentarily what it was about the Lensman's explanation that had not rung quite true. The first sight of his new vessel's control room, however, banished the unformed thought from his mind before it had taken any real root.

* * * * *

The transformed scout cruiser *Vortex Blaster II* hung poised and motionless over the badlands. The optical systems and beam-antennae and receptors of dozens of instruments, many of which were only months old, were focused sharply upon the loose atomic vortex a scant two miles distant.

A few of these instruments reported only to a small and

comparatively simple integrator which, after classifying and combining the incoming signals, put out as end-product the thin, black, violently-fluctuating line which was the sigma curve. Some others reported only to a massive mechanism, too heavy for any smaller vessel to carry, upon whose electronic complexities there is no need to dwell. Most of the information-gathering instruments, however, reported to both integrator and computer.

Not strapped down into a shock-absorber, but sitting easily in an ordinary pilot's bucket, quietly but supremely intent, "Storm" Cloud concentrated upon his sigma curve; practically oblivious to everything else. Without knowing how he did it he was solving continuously the simultaneous differential equations of the calculus of warped surfaces; extrapolating the sigma curve to an ever-moving instant of time three and nine-tenths seconds—the flight-time of the bombs plus his own reaction time—ahead of the frantic pen-point of the chart.

In his flitter, where he had required a nine- or ten-second prediction, he had always seized the first accept-able match that appeared. Now, however, needing only to extrapolate to less than four seconds, his technique was entirely different. He was now matching, from instant to instant, the predicted value of the curve against one or another of the twelve bombs lying in the firing chambers of heavy guns whose muzzles ringed the cruiser's needle-sharp nose.

And, as he had been doing ever since beginning to work with Joan and her mechanical brains, he was passing up match after match, waiting to see whether or not the current brain could deliver the goods. There had been a long succession of them—Alice, Betty, Candace, Deirdre, and so on. This one was Lulu, and it didn't look as though she was any good, either. He waited a while longer, however; then fined down his figures and got ready to blast.

The flight-time of the bomb, under present atmospheric conditions, would be three point five nine eight seconds, plus or minus point zero zero one. His reaction time was point zero eight nine. . . .

"Storm!" Joan broke in sharply, "Can you hold up a minute."

"Sure."

"That reaction time. I never spotted that before. Why didn't I?"

"I don't know. Never thought of it. Lumped it in, you know. Separated it now, I suppose, because I'm working so slowly, to give Lulu more of a chance. Why?"

"Because I've *got* to know all the odd things about you, and that isn't merely odd; it's superhuman."

"Oh, I wouldn't say that. Chickladorians average about point zero eight, and Vegians are still faster, about point zero seven. I checked up on that because they always test me three times when I renew my driver's license and aways pull a wise crack about me having a lot of cat blood in me. S'pose I could have?"

"Um...m...m. Probably not...I don't know for sure, but I don't believe that a Tellurian-Vegian cross would be possible; and even if possible, such a hybrid couldn't very well be fertile. But the more I find out about you, my friend, the more convinced I become that you're either a mutant or else have some ancestors who were most decidedly *not* Tellurians. But excuse this interruption, please—go ahead."

Cloud went. The flight time of the bomb, under present atmospheric conditions, would be three point five nine two seconds, plus or minus point zero zero two. His reaction time was point zero eight nine. In three point six eight one seconds the activity of the vortex would match bomb number eleven to within one-tenth of one percent.

His left hand flashed out, number eleven firing stud snapped down. The vessel shuddered as though struck by a trip-hammer as the precisely-weighed charge of propellant heptadetonite went off. The bomb sped truly, in both space and time. There was a detonation that jarred the planet to its core, a flare of light many times brighter than the sun at noon, a shock-wave that wrought havoc for miles.

But the scout cruiser and her occupants were unharmed. Completely inertialess, invulnerable, the vessel rode effortlessly away.

Neal Cloud glanced into his plate; turned his head.

"Out," he said, seemingly unnecessarily. "How'd Lulu work, Joan?"

"Better, but not good enough. She was on track all the way, but three point three was the best she could get ...

and I was *sure* we had it licked this time ... oh, *damn!*" The voice broke, ending almost in a wail.

"Steady, Joan!" Cloud was surprised at his companion's funk. "Only three tenths of a second to get yet, is all."

"*Only* three tenths—what d'you mean, *only?*" the woman snapped. "Don't you know that those three tenths of a second are just about in the same class as the three thousandths of a degree just above zero absolute?"

"Sure I do, but I know you, too. You're really blasting, little chum. Both Jane and Katy, you remember, were just as apt to be off track as on. You'll get it, Joan. As Vesta says, 'Tail high sister!' "

"Thanks, Storm. I needed that. You see, to keep her on track we had to put in more internal memory banks and that slowed her down ... we'll have to dream up some way of getting the information out of those banks faster ...."

"Can you tinker her—what'll the next version be? Margie?—up en route, or do you want to keep this ship near Sol while you work on it? Phil tells me I've got to flit for Chickladoria—and chop-chop, like quick."

"Oh ... Thlaskin and Maluleme have been crying in his beer, too, as well as yours?"

"I guess so, but that wasn't it. It's next on the list, an urgent—they've been screaming bloody murder for months. So, with or without a brain, I've got to blast off."

"Start blasting as soon as you like, just as we are," she decided instantly. "Much more important, at this stage, to work with you than to have Earth's resources close by. Besides, I think everything we're apt to need is already aboard—machine shop, electronics labs, materials, and experts."

"QX." He gave orders. Then:

"As for me, I'm going to hit the sack. I'm just about pooped."

"I don't wonder. That kind of stuff takes a lot of doing. 'Night, Storm."

Chapter 11

JOAN THE TELEPATH

THE FOLLOWING MORNING, en route to the planet of the pink humanoids, Cloud was studying a scratch-chart of the First Galaxy. He had been working on the thing for weeks; had placed several hundred crossed circles, each representing a loose atomic vortex. He was scrawling weird-looking symbols and drawing freehand connecting lines when Joan came swishing into the "office."

"Good morning, Effendi of Esoterica!" she greeted him gaily. "How's the massive intellect? Firing on all forty barrels, I hope and trust?"

"Missing on all forty is more like it. Ideas are avoiding me in droves." He looked her over amiably, in what he hoped she would think was a casual way.

He'd found himself doing quite a lot of that, lately . . . but she was *such* a swell egg! Why hadn't she ever married? What a waste *that* was! Face a bit on the strong side for vapid calendar-girl prettiness, but . . . .

"But kind of attractive, at that, in her own gruesome way, eh?" she finished the thought for him.

"Huh?" Cloud gulped, and, for the first time in years, blushed scarlet; flushed to the tips of his ears.

"I'm sorry, Storm, believe me. I don't think I was supposed to tell you—in fact, I know very well I wasn't—but I've simply got to. It isn't fair not to; besides, I've thought all along that Lensman Strong was wrong—that we'd go faster and farther if you knew than if you didn't."

"Oh—*that's* what Phil was holding out on me back there? I thought there was something fishy, but couldn't spot it."

"I was sure you did. So was Phil. You told me what the Tomingans call telepaths—snoopers? I *like* that word; it's so beautifully appropriate. Well, I'm snooping all the time. Not only while we're working, as you thought, but *all* the time, especially when you're relaxed and . . . and off-guard, so to speak. I've been doing it ever since I first met you."

Cloud blushed again. "So you knew exactly what I was thinking just then? You gave me a remarkably poor play-back"

"The portrait was much too flattering. But we'll skip that. Part of my job is to make a telepath out of you, so that you can show me with your mind—it can't be done in words or symbols—what it is that makes a mathematical prodigy tick."

"How are you figuring on going about it?"

"I don't know—yet."

"Phil tried, and so did a couple of Gray Lensmen, and I wasn't holding back a thing . . . oh, he emphasized that you're a *self-made* telepath. A different angle of approach? How did you operate on yourself?"

"I don't know that, either; but I hope to find out through you. I read, and studied, and tried, and all of a sudden—bang!—there it was. But words are useless; I'm coming into your mind. Now watch me closely, concentrate: *really* concentrate, as hard as you possibly can. Ready? It goes like this . . . . did you get it?"

"No. I couldn't follow the details—it seemed like an instantaneous transition. Didn't you have more to begin with than I've got?"

"I don't think so . . . pretty sure I didn't. I could receive—I think it's impossible for anyone to become a telepath who can't—but I couldn't send a lick. My psi rating was a flat zero zero zero. Now try it again. Take a good, solid grip on a thought and *throw* it at me."

"QX. I'll try." Cloud's forehead furrowed, his muscles tensed in effort. "Since you already know I've been wondering why you never married—why? Standards too high?"

"You might call it that." It was the woman's turn to blush, but her thought was clear and steady. Cloud was working with her better than he had ever worked with either Luda or Nadine. "Since the days of my teen-age crushes on tri-di idols I simply haven't been able to develop any interest in a man who didn't have as much of a brain as I have, and the only such I met were either already married or didn't have anything *except* a brain—which wouldn't do, either, of course."

"Of course not." Cloud felt something stirring inside him that he thought completely dead, and tried, in near-panic fashion, to kill it again. He changed the subject abruptly. "No luck—I'm not getting through to you at all. We'd better start all over, at the bottom. What's the first thing I've got to do to learn to be a snooper?"

"You must learn how to concentrate—intensively and in a very special way. You're very good at ordinary concentration—especially mathematical stuff—now; but this kind is different—so much so as to be a difference in kind, not merely of degree."

"Check. Point one, a new kind of concentration. Next?"

"No next. That's all. When you get so you can concentrate correctly—I'll coach you mind to mind on that, of course—we'll concentrate together, first on one gateway, then another. Something will click into place, and there you'll be."

"I hope. But suppose it doesn't? Can't it be worked out? You're on record as saying that the mind is simply a machine."

"No, it can't. The mind *is* a machine; just as much a machine as one of your automatic pilots or one of my computers. The troubles are that it is almost infinitely more complex and that we do not understand its basic principles—the fundamental laws upon which it operates. We may *never* understand them ... the mind may very well be so tied in with the life-principle—or soul; call it whatever you please—as to be knowable only to God."

"I'm glad you said that, Joan. I'm not formally religious, I suppose, but I do believe in a First Cause."

"One must, who knows as much about the Macrocosmic All as you do. But it's too early in the morning for very much of that sort of thing. What are you doing to that chart besides doodling all over it?"

"Those aren't doodles, woman!" he protested. "They're equations. In short-hand."

"Equations, I apologize. Doctor Cloud, elucidate."

"Doctor Janowick, I can't. This is where you came in. I had just pursued an elusive wisp of thought into what turned out to be a cul de sac. I whammed my head against a solid concrete wall." His light mood vanished as he went on:

"In spite of what everybody has always believed, I've

proved that loose atomic vortices are not accidental. They're deliberate, every one of them, and . . . ."

"Yes, I heard you tell Phil so," she interrupted. "I wanted to start screaming about your hypothesis then, and it's taken superhuman self-control to keep me from screaming about it ever since. That kind of math, though, of course is 'way over my head . . . For a long time I expected Phil to call up and blast you to a cinder, but he didn't . . . you may be—*must* be, I suppose—right."

"I am right," Cloud said, quietly. "Unless all the mathematics I know is basically, fundamentally fallacious, they've *got* to be deliberate; they simply *can't* be accidental. On the other hand, except for a few we know about which don't change the general picture in the least, I can't see any more than you can how they can possibly be deliberate, either."

"Are you trying to set up a paradox?"

"No. It's already set up. I'm trying to knock it down." Cloud's thought died away; his mind became a mathematical wilderness of such complexity that the woman, able mathematician that she was and scan as she would, was lost in seconds.

He finally shrugged himself out of it. "Another blind alley," he reported, sourly.

"With sufficient knowledge, any possible so-called paradox can be resolved," Joan mused, her mind harking back to the, to her, starkly unbelievable hypothesis Cloud had stated so baldly. "But I simply *can't* believe it, Storm!"

"I can't, either, hardly. However, it's easier for me to believe that than that all our basics are false. So that makes it another part of our job to find out what, or who, or why."

"Ouch! With a job of that magnitude on your mind, I'll make myself scarce. When you come up for air sometime give me a call on the squawk-box and we'll study concentration. 'Bye." She turned, started for the door.

"Wait a minute, Joan—why not start the ground-work now?"

"That's a thought—why not? But get away from that big table." She placed two chairs and they sat down knee to knee; almost eye to eye. "Now, Storm, come in. *Really* come in, this time; the first time you didn't really even half try."

"I did so!" he protested. "I tried then and I'm trying now. Just *how* do I go about it?"

"I can't tell you that, Storm; *nobody* can tell you that." She was thinking now, not talking. "There are no words, no symbology, even in the provinces of thought. And I can't do it for you: you *must* do it yourself. But if you can't—and you really can't be expected to, so soon—I'll come into your mind and try to *show* you what I mean."

She did so. There was a moment of fitting; of snuggling . . . there was a warmly intimate contact, much warmer and much more intimate than anything telepathic that either had ever experienced before; but it was not what they were after. Joan tried a different approach.

"Well, if that won't work, let's try this. Just imagine, Storm, that every cell of my brain—no, let's keep it on the immaterial level; every individual ultimate element of my mind—is a lock, but you can see exactly what the key must be like. You must make every corresponding unit of your mind into the appropriate key . . . No? We'll try again. Imagine that each element of my mind is half of a jigsaw puzzle—make yours fill out each picture . . ."

"I can't. Don't you know, Joan, how many thousands of millions of . . . ."

"What of it?" she flared. "You do things fully as complex every time you blast a vortex . . . Oh, that's it! Treat it as though it were a problem in n-dimensional differential equations, but don't let your subconscious do it alone—get right down there and work with it—do that and you'll have it all!" She seized his hands, squeezed them hard, and spoke aloud, the better to drive home the intensity of her convictions. "Buckle down, Storm, and dig . . . you can do it, I know you can do it. I *know* you can . . . dig in, big fellow . . . you don't have to pay *too* much attention to detail; get a chain started, like a zipper, and it'll finish itself . . . dig, Storm, DIG!"

Storm dug. His jaw-muscles tightened into lumps. Sweat beaded his face and trickled down his chest under his shirt. And suddenly something happened. Not very much of anything, but something. Something more than mere contact, but not a penetration—more like a fusion—a fusion which, however instead of spreading rapidly to completion, as Joan had said it would, existed for the merest perceptible instant of time in an almost infinitesi-

mal area and then vanished as instantaneously as it had
come. But there was no doubt whatever that he had read,
for an instant, a tiny portion of Joan's mind; there was no
chance whatever that she had sent him *that* thought—in
fact, she had been thinking at herself, not at him. And as
he perceived the tenor of that thought he let go all his
mental holds; tried frantically to bury the stolen thought
so deeply that Joan would never, *never* find out what it
had been . . .

No, not bury it, either. Flesh, rock, metal—any material substance was perfectly transparent to thought. What
wasn't? A thought-screen. He didn't have one, of course,
but he knew the formula, and if he thought about that
formula hard enough it might create interference enough.
The catch would be whether he could talk at the same
time . . . he probably could, if the subject matter didn't
require concentration.

Joan, of course, knew instantly when Cloud pulled his
mind away from hers; and, not waiting to ask why in
words, drove in a probe to find out. Much to her surprise,
however, her beam of mental force was stopped cold; she
could not touch Cloud's mind at all!

"A block!" she exclaimed unbelievingly. "A real dilly,
too—as hard and tight as a D7M29Z screen! What did
you do, anyway, Storm, and how? I didn't feel you get
in!"

He did not reply immediately. He was too busy; for,
besides holding the screen-thought, he was also analyzing
and studying the thought he had stolen from Joan: separat-
ing it out and arranging it into meaningful English words.
It was amazing, how many words could be contained in
one flashing, fleeting burst of thought.

"Joanie, my not-so-bright old friend," she had been
thinking, "you've simply got to cut out this silly damn
foolishness and act your age. You *must not* fall in love
with him; there'd be nothing in it for either of you. You
are thirty-four years old and he has had his Jo."

"Storm!" she snapped. "Answer me! Or did . . ." Her
tone changed remarkably: ". . . did something . . . happen
to you?"

"No, Joanie." He shook his head and wrenched his
attention back to reality. "But first, is whatever I'm doing
really a mind-block, and is it really holding?"

"Yes—to both—curse it! And 'Joanie', eh? You *did* get in. How did it go?"

"Not so good. Barely a touch. It didn't spread after we got it started. Just one flash and it went out."

"Hm ... m ... m. That's funny ... Not the way it worked with me at all. However, I don't see that it makes any difference whether you get it by drips and driblets or all at once, just so you get the full ability eventually. What was it you picked up the first time, Storm?"

"That's one thing you'll never know, if I have to hold this block forever."

"Oh." Joan blushed, vividly. "I know what it was, then, I think. But don't you see ... ?"

"No, I don't see," Cloud interrupted. "All I see is that it's worse than being a Peeping Tom in a girls' dormitory. I don't like it. I don't like any part of it."

"You wouldn't, of course—at first. Nevertheless, Storm, you and I have *got* to work together, whether either of us likes what happens or not. So let's get at it. Bring it out and look at it—let's see if it's so bad, really. It was just that I was afraid maybe I was going to fall in love with you and get burned to a crisp around the edges, wasn't it?"

"That was part of it. You were wrong in two things, though. No matter how much I loved Jo—and I really did love her, you know ..."

"I know, Storm." Her voice was very gentle. "Everybody knows you did. Not only did—you still do."

"Yes. So much so that I thought I'd never be able to talk about her without going off the deep end. But I can, now. I'm beginning to think that perhaps Phil Strong was right. Perhaps a man can love twice in his life, in exactly the same way."

The woman caught her breath and started to say something, then changed her mind. The man went on:

"The second point in error is that a woman at age thirty-four is not necessarily a doddering wreck with one foot in the grave and the other on a banana peel."

"Oh . . . I'm *so* glad, Storm!" she breathed; then changed mood with an almost audible snap. "There! It's done and your guard is down. It wasn't too bad, was it?"

"Not a bit." Cloud was surprised at how easily the thing had been ironed out. "You're a prime number, Joanie—a slick, smooth operator. As smooth as five feet and two inches of tan velvet."

"Uh-uh. Not me, so much; it's just that we're a very nicely-matched pair. But I think we'd better lay off a while before trying it again, don't you?"

"Check. Let our minds—mine, anyway—get over the jitters and collywobbles."

"Mine, too, brother; and I've got a sort of feeling that what that mind of yours is going to develop into, little by little, is something slightly different from ordinary telepathy. But in the meantime, you'd better get back to work."

"I don't know whether I can work up much enthusiasm for work right now or not."

"Sure you can, if you try. What were you doing to that chart when I came in? What have you got there, anyway?"

"Come on over and I'll show you." They bent over the work-table, heads almost touching. "The pink area is the explored part of the First Galaxy. The marks represent all the loose vortices I know of. I've been applying all the criteria I can think of to give me some kind of a toe-hold, but up to the present moment I'm completely baffled."

"Have you tried chronology yet? Peeling 'em off in layers—by centuries, say?"

"Not exactly, although I did run a correlation against time. Mostly been studying 'em either singly or en masse up to now. Might be worth a fling, though. Why? Got a hunch?"

"No. And no particular reason; just groping for more detailed data. Before you can solve any problem, you know, you must know exactly what the problem is—must be able to state it clearly. You can't do that yet, can you?"

"You know I can't. I've got some colored pins here somewhere . . . here they are. Read me the dates and I'll stick colors accordingly."

They soon ran out of colors; then continued with numbered-head thumb-tacks.

The job finished, they stood back and examined the results.

"See anything, Joan?"

"I see *something,* but before I mention it, give me a quick briefing on what you know already."

Cloud thought for a minute. "Well, the distribution in space is not random, but there is no significant correlation with location, age, size, power, load-factor, or actual number of power-plants. Nor with nature, condition, or age of the civilization of any planet. Nor with anything else I've been able to dream up.

"They aren't random in time, either; but there again there's no correlation with the age of the power-plant affected, the age-status of atomic power of any particular planet, or any other thing except one—there is an extremely high correlation—practically unity—with time itself."

"I thought so." Joan nodded. "That was what I noticed. The older, the fewer."

"Exactly. But with your new classification, Joan, I think I see something else." Cloud's mathematical-prodigy's mind pounced. "And *how!* Until very recently, Joan, the data will plot exactly on the ideal-growth-of-population curve."

"Oh, they breed, some way or other. Nice—that gives us a . . ."

"You said that, woman, I didn't. I stated a fact; if you wish to extrapolate it, that's your privilege—but it's also your responsibility."

"Huh! Don't go pedantic on me. Haven't you got any guesses?"

"Except for this recent jump, which we can probably ascribe to Fairchild and explosives, nary a guess. I can't see any possible point of application."

"Neither can I. But if that's the only positive correlation you can find, and it's just about unity, it must mean *something.*"

"Check. It's *got* to mean something. All we have to do is find out what . . . I think maybe I see something else." Bending over, he sighted across the chart from various angles. "Too many pins. Let's clear a belt through here." They did so. "Will you read 'em to me in order, beginning with the oldest?"

"At your service, sir. Sol."

Cloud stuck a pin in Sol.

"Galien— Salvador— DuPont— Eastman— Mercator— Centralia Tressilia—Chickladoria—Crevenia—DeSilva— Wynor—Aldebaran . . . ."

"Hold it! Don't want Aldebaran—can't use it. Take a look at this!" For this first time Cloud's voice showed excitement.

She looked, and saw a gently curving line of pins running three-quarters of the way across the chart. "Why—that's a smooth curve—looks as though it could be the arc of a circle—clear across all explored space!" she exclaimed.

Cloud's mind pounced again. "It is a circle—pretty close, that is, according to these rough figures. Will you read me the exact coordinates—spatial—from the book?"

She did so, and through Cloud's mind there raced the appropriate equations of solid analytic geometry.

"Even closer. Now let's apply a final refinement. From their proper motions we can put each star back to where it was at the vortex date. It'll take little time, but it may be worth it."

It was. Cloud's mien was solemn as he announced his final figures. "Those twelve suns all lay on the surface of a sphere. Radius, 53,327 parsecs, with a probable error of one point three zero parsecs—which, since the average density of the stars along that line is about point zero four five per cubic parsec, makes it as perfect a spherical surface as it is physically possible for it to be. The center of that sphere is almost exactly on the ecliptic; its coordinates are: Theta, 225°—12'—31.2647''; distance, 107.2259."

"Good heavens! It's *that* exact? And *that* far outside the Rim? That spoils my original idea of radiation from a center. But all of the twelve oldest vortices are on that surface, and *none* of them are anywhere else!"

"So they are. Which gets us where, lady?"

"Nowhere that I can see, with a stupendous velocity."

"You and me both. Another thing, why that particular time-space relationship in the first twelve? I can accept Tellus being first, because we had atomics first, but that logic doesn't follow through. Instead, the time order goes from Sol through Galien and so on to Eastman—to the very edge of unexplored territory along that arc—then, jumping back to the other side of Sol, goes straight on to the edge of Civilization in the opposite direction. Can you play *that* on any one of your brains, from Alice to Margie?"

"I don't see how."

"I don't, either. That relationship certainly means something, too, but I'm damned if I can make any sense out of it. And what sense is there in a spherical surface that big? And why so ungodly accurate? Alphacent, there, is less than one parsec outside the surface, but it didn't have a blow-up for over seven hundred years. How come? Anybody or anything capable of traveling that far could certainly travel half a parsec farther if he wanted to. And look at the time involved—over a thousand years! Assuming some purpose, what could it be? Human operations, or any other kind I know anything about, simply are not geared up to that kind of scope, either in space or in time. None of it makes any kind of sense."

"So you consider it purely fortuitous that this surface is as truly spherical as the texture of the medium will permit?" she asked, loftily.

"No, I don't, and you know I don't—and don't misquote me, woman! It's too fantastically accurate to be accidental. And that ties right in with the previous paradox—that vortices can't possibly be either accidental or deliberate."

"From a semantic viewpoint, your phraseology is deplorable. The term 'paradox' is inadmissible—meaningless. We simply haven't enough data. I simply *can't* believe, Storm, that those horrible things were set off on purpose."

"Deplorable phraseology or not, I've got enough data to put the probability out beyond the nine-sigma point—the same probability as that an automatic screw-machine running six-thirty-two brass hex nuts would accidentally turn out a thirty-six-inch jet-ring made of pure titanite, diamond-ground, finished, and fitted. We're getting nowhere faster and faster—with an acceleration of about 12 G's instead of any simple velocity."

He fell silent; remained silent so long that the woman spoke. "Well . . . what do you think we'd better do next?"

"All I can think of is to find out what's out there at the center of that sphere . . . and then to see if we can find any other leads in this mess on the chart. I'll call Phil."

Chapter 12

_____VESTA PRACTICES SPACEAL

THE CONNECTION was made and he brought Lensman Strong up to date, concluding: "So will you please get hold of Planetography with a crash priority on anything they know about that point?"

"I'll do that, Storm. I'll call you back."

Since Lensmen are potent beings, the call came soon.

"There's one sun there," Strong reported, "but it doesn't amount to much. A red dwarf—it may or may not be a single. Unexplored. Astronomical data only."

"How close did I come to it?"

"Allowing for proper motion, you speared it. Less than two hundredths of a parsec off. And there's nothing else within twelve parsecs—stars are mighty thin out beyond the Rim, you know."

"I know. That nails it, Phil. They don't know, of course, whether it has any planets or not?"

"No ... I see what you mean ... shall I get a special on it for you?"

"I wish you would. It'd be worth while, I think."

"So do I. I'll call Haynes and ask him to rush a ship out there to get us a fine-tooth on it."

"Thanks, Phil."

"And there was something else ... Oh yes, your friend Fairchild. Narcotics wants him, badly."

"I'm not surprised. Alive? That might take some doing."

"Or dead. No difference, as long as they have his head for positive identification," and at Cloud's surprised expression Strong went on: "They don't want him planting any more Trenconian broadleaf, is all, which he'll keep on doing as long as he's alive and loose."

"I see. Wish I'd known sooner; we probably could have caught him on Tominga."

"I doubt it. They've been checking back on him, and he's a very, _very_ sharp operator. He makes long flits, fast

. . . in peculiar directions. But if you stumble across him again, grab him or blast . . ."

"Just a minute, chief. You mean to say the *Patrol* can't *find* him?"

"Just that. He's in with a big, strong mob; probably heads it. They've been looking for him ever since you found out that he wasn't killed on Deka."

"I'm . . . I'm speechless. But Graves . . . but Graves was dead, of course . . . didn't *anybody* know Fairchild's personal pattern?"

"That's exactly it; nobody that they could get hold of knows his *real* pattern at all. All we've got that we can depend on are his retinals. That shows the kind of operator he is. So if you get a chance, blast him, but leave at least one eye whole and bring it in, in deep-freeze. Nothing else at the moment, is there?"

"Not that I know of. Clear ether, Phil!"

"Clear ether, Storm!"

The plate went black and Cloud turned soberly to Joan.

"Well, that clears Fairchild up, but doesn't help with the real mystery. So, unless we can dig some more dope out of this stuff on the chart, we can't do much until we get that finetooth."

Joan left the room, and Cloud, after racking his brain for an hour, got up, shook himself, and went down the corridor to his "private" office—which had long since ceased to be private, as far as his friends were concerned—where he found Vesta and Thlaskin talking busily in spaceal. Or, rather, the Vegian was talking; the pilot was listening attentively.

". . . think *I'm* built, you ought to've seen *this* tomato," Vesta was narrating blithely. "What I mean, she's a *dish!*" She went into a wrigglesome rhythm which, starting at the neck, flowed smoothly down her splendidly-modeled body to the ankles. "*Stacked?* She's stacked like Gilroy's Tower, Buster—an honest-to-god DISH, believe me, and raring to go. We were on one of those long-week-end jaunts around the system—you know, one of those deals where things are pretty apt to get just a hair off the green at times . . ."

"But hey!" Thlaskin protested. "You said yourself a while back you wasn't old enough for that kind of monkey-business!"

"Oh, I wasn't," Vesta agreed, candidly enough. "I still ain't. I just went along for the ride."

"And your folks *let* you?" Thlaskin was shocked.

"Natch." Vesta was surprised. "Why not? If a tomato don't learn the facts of life while she's young how's she going to decide what's good for her when she grows up?"

"With or without a license, I got to butt into this," Cloud announced, also in spaceal; seating himself on a couch and crossing his legs. He, too, was shocked; but he was also intensely curious. "Did you decide, Vesta?"

Before the girl could answer, however, Joan Janowick came strolling in.

"Is this a private brawl, or can anybody get in on it?" she asked, gaily.

"I invited myself in, so I'll invite you, too. Come in and sit down." He made room for her beside him and went on in English, speaking for her ear alone: "Just as well you don't know spaceal. This story Vesta is telling would curl your hair."

"Wake up, Junior." Joan did not speak, but poured the thought directly into his mind. "D'you think that cat-girl—that *kitten*—can block *me* out of her mind?"

"Oick! What a whiff! 'Scuse, please; my brain was out to lunch. But you'll get an earful, sister Janowick."

"It'll be interesting in a way you haven't thought of, too," Joan went on. "Vegians are essentially feline, you know, and cats as a race are both fastidious and promiscuous. Thus, conflict. Is that what this is about?"

"Could be—I haven't tried to read her." Then, aloud:

"Go ahead, Vesta. Did the experience help you decide?"

"Oh, yes. I'm too finicky to be a very good mixer. There's just too damn many people I simply can't stand the smell of."

"There's that *smell* thing again," Thlaskin said. "You've harped on it before. You mean to say you people's noses are *that* sensitive?"

"Absolutely. No two people smell alike, you know. Some smell nice and some just plain stink. F'rinstance, the boss here smells just wonderful—I could hug him all day and love it. Doctor Janowick, too, she smells almost like the skipper. You're nice, too, Thlaskin, and so is Maluleme, and Nadine. And Tommie ain't bad; but a lot of the others are just too srizonified much for my stomach."

"I see," Cloud said. "You *do* give some people a lot of room around here."

"Yeah, and that's what got this chick I was telling Thlaskin here about in such a jam. She's been bending her elbow pretty free, and taking a jab or so of this and that between drinks. But she ain't sozzled, y'understand, not by many a far piece; just lit up like Nyok spaceport. She's maybe been a bit on the friendly side with a few of her friends, so this big bruiser—not a Vegian; no tail, even; an Aldebaranian or some-such-like and a Class A-Triple-Prime stinker—gets interested in a big way. Well, he smells just like a Tellurian skunk, so she brushes him off, kind of private-like, a few times, but it don't take, so she finally has to give him the old heave-ho right out in front of everybody.

" 'You slimy stinker, I've told you a dozen times it's no dice—you stink!' she says, loud, clear, and plain. 'This ship ain't big enough to let me get far enough away from you to hold my breakfast down,' she says, and this burns the ape plenty.

" 'Lookit here, babe,' he says, coming to a boil, 'Bend an ear while I tell *you* something. No klevous Vegian chippie is going to play high and mighty with me, see? I'm fed up to the gozzle. So come down off your high horse right now, or I'll . . .'

" 'You'll what?' she snarls, and puts a hand behind her back. She's seeing red now, and fit to be tied. 'Make just one pass at me, you kedonolating slime-lizard,' she says, 'and I'll bust your pfztikated skull wide open!'

"He goes for her then, but, being a Vegian, her footwork's a lot better than his. She ducks, sidesteps, pulls her sap, and lets him have it, but good, right behind the ear. It takes the ship's croaker an hour to bring him to, and the skipper's so scared he blasts right back to Vegia and the croaker calls the hospital and tells 'em to have a meat-wagon standing by when we sit down."

"A very interesting and touching tale, Vesta," Cloud said then, in English, "but pretty rough language for a perfect lady, don't you think?"

"How the hell else . . ." Vesta started to reply in space-al, then switched effortlessly to English: "How else can a lady, however ladylike she may be, talk in a language which, except for its highly technical aspects, is basically and completely profane, obscene, vulgar, lewd, coarse, and foul? Not that that bothers me, of course . . ."

Nor did it, as Cloud well knew. When a Master of Languages studied a language he took it as a whole, no matter what that whole might be. Every nuance, every idiom, every possibility was mastered; and he used the language *as it was ordinarily used,* without prejudice or favor or motional bias.

". . . but it's so pitifully *inadequate*—there's *so* much that's completely missing! Thlaskin objected before, remember, that there wasn't any word in spaceal he could use—*would* use, I mean—to describe Maluleme as his wife. And my brother—Zambkptkn—I've mentioned him?"

"Once or twice," Cloud said, dryly. This was the understatement of the trip.

"He's a police officer. Not exactly like one of your Commissioners of Police, or Detective Inspector, but something like both. And in spaceal I can call him only one of four things, the English equivalents of which are 'cop,' 'lawman,' 'flatfoot,' and 'bull.' *What* a language! But I started to tell his story in spaceal and I'm going to finish it in spaceal. It'll be fun, in a way, to see how close I can come to saying what I want to say."

Then, switching back to the lingua franca of deep space;

"So that's how come my brother got into the act. The hospital called the cops, of course, so he was there with the meat wagon and climbed aboard. He was all set to pinch the jane and throw her in the can, but when he got the whole story, and especially when she says she's changed her mind about circulating around so much—it ain't worth it, she says, she'd rather be an out-and-out hermit than have to have even one more fight with anybody who smelled like that—of course he let her go."

"Let her *go!*" Cloud exclaimed. "How *could* he?"

"Why, sure, boss." Vesta, wide-eyed, gazed innocently at her captain. "The ape didn't *die*, you know, and she wasn't going to do it again, and he wasn't a Vegian, so didn't have any relatives or friends to go to the mat for him, and besides, anybody with one tenth of one percent of a brain would know better than to keep on making passes at a frail after she warned him how bad he stunk. What *else* could he do, chief?"

"What else, indeed?" Cloud said, in English. "I live; and—occasionally—I learn. Come on, Joan, let's go and devote the imponderable force of our massed intellects to the multifarious problems of loose atomic vortices."

On the way, Joan asked: "Our little Vesta surprised you, Storm?"

"Didn't she you? She had me gasping like a fish."

"Not so much. I know them pretty well and I used to breed cats. Scent: hearing—they can hear forty thousand cycles: the fact that they mature both mentally and physically long before they do sexually: some of their utterly barbarous customs: it's quite a shock to learn how—'queer,' shall I say?—some of the Vegian mores are to us of other worlds."

" 'Queer' is certainly the word—as queer as a nine-credit bill. But confound it, Joan, I *like* 'em!"

"So do I, Storm," she replied quietly. "They *aren't* human, you know, and by Galactic standards they qualify. And now we'll go and whack those vortices right on their center of impact."

"We'll do that, chum," he said. Then, in perfect silence he went on in thought: "Chum? Sweetheart, I meant ... My God, *what* a sweetheart you'd ..."

"Storm!" Joan half-shrieked, eyes wide in astonishment. "You're *sending!*"

"I'm not either!" he declared, blushing furiously. "I can't—you're *snooping!*"

"I'm not snooping—I haven't snooped a lick since I started talking. You *got* it back there, Storm!" She seized both his hands and squeezed. "You *did* it, and neither of us realized it 'til just this minute!"

Chapter 13

_____GAMES WITHIN GAMES

THE METHODS of operation of the *Vortex Blaster II* had long since been worked out in detail. Approaching any planet Captain Ross, through channels, would ask permission of the various governments to fly in atmosphere, permission to use high explosive, permission to land and be serviced, and permission—after standard precautions—to grant planetary leave to his ship's personnel. All this asking was not, of course, strictly necessary in his case, since every world having even one loose atomic vortex had been demanding long and insistently that Neal Cloud visit it next, but it was strictly according to protocol.

Astrogators had long since plotted the course through planetary atmosphere; not by the demands of the governments concerned and not by any ascending or descending order of violence of the vortices to be extinguished, but by the simple criterion of minimum flight-time ending at the pre-selected point of entry to the planet.

Thus neither Joan nor Cloud had anything much to do with planetary affairs until the chief pilot notified Joan that he was relinquishing control to her—which never happened until the vessel lay motionless with respect to the planet's surface and with the tip of her nose three two zero zero point zero meters distant from the center of activity of the vortex.

Approaching Chickladoria, the routine was followed precisely up to the point where Joan's mechanical brain took over. This time, however, the brain was not working, since Joan was in the throes of rebuilding "Lulu" into "Margie." On Chickladoria, then, the chief pilot did the piloting and "Storm" Cloud did the blasting, and everything ran like clockwork. The ship landed at Malthester spaceport and everyone who could possibly be spared disembarked.

Ready to leave the ship, Cloud went to the computer

room to make one last try. There, seated at desks, Joan
and her four top experts were each completely surrounded
by welters of reference books, pamphlets, wadded-up
scratch-paper, tapes, and punched cards.

"Hi, Joan—Hi, fellows and gals—why don't you break
down and come on out and get some fresh air?"

"Sorry, Storm, but the answer is still 'no'. We'll need all
this week, and probably more . . ." Joan looked up at him
and broke off. Her eyes widened and she whistled expres-
sively. "Myohmy, ain't he the *handsomest* thing, though? I
wish I *could* go along, Storm, if only to see you lay 'em
out in rows!"

For, since Chickladoria was a very warm planet—fully
as hot as Tominga had been—Cloud was dressed even
more lightly than he had been there; in sandals, breech-
clout, and DeLameter harness, the shoulder-strap of the
last-named bearing the three silver bars of a commander
of the Galactic Patrol. He was not muscled like a gladia-
tor, but his bearing was springily erect, his belly hard and
flat, his shoulders were wide, his hips were narrow, and his
skin was tanned to a smooth and even richness of brown.

"Wellwell! Not bad, Storm; not bad at all." One of the
men got up and looked him over carefully. "If I looked
like that, Joan, I'd play hookey for a couple of days
myself. But I wouldn't dare to—in that kind of a get-up
I'd look like something that had crawled out from under a
rock and I'd get sunburned from here to there."

"That's your own fault, Joe," a tall, lissom, brunette
lieutenant chipped in. "You *could* have the radiants on
while you do your daily dozens, you know. Me, I'm
mighty glad that *some* of the men, and not only us
women, like to look nice."

"Wait a minute, Helen!" Cloud protested, blushing.
"That's not it, and you know it. These fellows don't *have*
to mix socially with people who run around naked, and I
do."

"And how you hate it." The other man offered mock
sympathy, with a wide and cheerful grin. "*How* you
suffer—I don't think. But that holster-harness. It looks
regulation enough, but isn't there somehing a little different about it?"

"Yes. Two things." Cloud grinned back. "Left-handed,
and the holster's anchored so it can't flop around. Don't

know as I ever told you, but ever since that alleged pirate burned my arm off I've been practising the gun-slick's draw."

"Did you get it?" Joan asked impishly. "How good are you?"

"Not bad—in fact, I'm getting plenty good," Cloud admitted. "Come on up to the range sometime with a stop-watch and I'll show you."

"I'll do that. Right now—shall we?"

"Uh-uh. Can't. I'm due at the High Mayor's Reception in twenty minutes, and besides, I want to breathe some air that hasn't been rehabilitated, rejuvenated, recirculated, reprocessed, repurified, and rebreathed until it's all worn out. Happy landings, gang—I'll be thinking of you while I'm absorbing all that nice new oxygen and stuff."

"Particularly the stuff—and especially the *liquid* stuff!" Joe called after him just before he shut the door on his way out to join Thlaskin and Maluleme.

Going through customs was of course the merest formality, and an aircab whisked them into the city proper. Cloud really did enjoy himself as he strode along the walkway from the cabpark toward the Mayor's ... well, if not exactly a palace, it was close enough so as to make no difference. And he did attract plenty of attention. Not because of his dress or his build—most of the men on the street wore less than he did and many of them were just as trim and as fit—but because of the nature and variety of his bodily colors, which were literally astounding to these people, not one in twenty of whom had ever before seen a Tellurian in person.

For Chickladorians are pink; pink all over. Teeth, hair, skin, and nails; all pink. Not the pink of red blood showing through translucency, but that of opaque pigment. Most of their eyes, even—queerly triangular eyes with three lids instead of two—are of that same brick-reddish pink; although a few of the women have eyes of a dark and dusky green.

This visitor's skin, however, was of a color so monstrous it simply had to be seen to be believed. In fact, it wasn't the same color in any two places—it VARIED! His teeth were white; a horrible, dead-bone color. His lips, hair, and eyes—funny, round, flat opening things—were of still other sheerly unbelievable colors—there wasn't a *bit* of natural, healthy pink about him anywhere!

Thus the crowds of Chickladorians studied him much more intensively than he studied them; and Maluleme, strutting along at his side, basked visibly in the limelight. And thus, except for the two Chickladorians at his side and except for the unobtrusive but efficient secret-service men who kept the crowding throng in hand, Cloud could very well have been mobbed.

The walk was very short, and at its end:

"How long we got to stay, boss?" Thlaskin asked, in spaceal. "As soon as we can get away we want to join our folks and grab a jet for home."

"As far as I'm concerned you don't need to stay at all, or even come. Why?"

"Just checking, is all. His Nibs sent us a special bid, so we got to at least show up. But he don't know us from nothing, so after we tell him hello and dance a couple of rounds and slurp a couple of slugs we can scram and nobody'll know it unless you spill."

"No spill," Cloud assured him. "You dance with Maluleme first. I'll take the second—that'll drive it in that she's here. After that, flit as soon as you like. For the record, you'll be here until the last gilot is picked clean."

"Thanks, boss," and the three, entering the extravagantly-decorated Grand Ballroom, were escorted ceremoniously up to the Presence and the Notables and their surrounding V. I. P.'s.

They were welcomed effusively, Cloud being informed through several different interpreters that he was the third-most-important human being who had ever lived. He made—through two interpreter's, each checking the other's accuracy—his usual deprecatory speech concerning the extinguishment of loose atomic vortices. He led the Grand March with the president's wife, a lady whose name he did not quite catch and who, except for a pound or so of diamonds, rubies, emeralds, and other baubles, was just as bare as Maluleme was. So was the equally heavily bejeweled mayor's wife, with whom he had the first dance. She was neither young or slender, nor was she sexy. Then, as agreed, he danced with Maluleme, who was—but definitely!—all three.

However, as he circled the floor in time with the really

excellent music, he thought, not of the attractive package of femininity in his arms—who was one of his crew and Thlaskin's wife—but of Joan. She'd been training down, he'd noticed, and wearing more makeup, since those other girls had come aboard. She was getting to be a regular seven-sector callout—he'd *like* to dance with Joan this way!

There were other dances; some with girls like Maluleme, some with women like Madam Mayor, most with in-betweens. There was food, which he enjoyed thoroughly. There were drinks; which, except for ceremonial beakers of fayalin with the president and the mayor, he did not touch. And, finally, there was the very comfortable bed in his special suite at the hotel. Instead of sleep, however, there came a thing he expected least of any—a sharp, carefully-narrowed Lensed thought.

"This is Tivor Nordquist of Tellus, Commander Cloud, on my Lens," the thought flowed smoothly in. "I have waited until now so as not to startle you, not to make you show any sign of anything unusual going on. There must be no suspicion whatever that you even know there's a Lensman on the planet."

"I can take care of my part of that. One thing, though; I've got exactly one week to work with you. One week from today any possible excuse for me staying on Chickladoria goes p-f-f-t."

"I know. One day should button it up, two at most. Here's the print. I'm a narcotics man, really but . . ."

"Oh—Fairchild, eh?"

"Yes. Ellington told me you're quick on the uptake. Well, all leads to him via any drug channels fizzled out flat. So, since all these zwilnik mobs handle all kinds of corruption—racketeering, gambling, vice, and so on, as well as drugs—we decided to take the next-best line, which turned out to be gambling. After a lot of slow digging we found out that Fairchild's gang controls at least four planets; Tominga, Vegia, Chickladoria, and Palmer III."

"What? Why, those planets cover . . ."

"Check. That's what made the digging so tough, and thats why they did it that way. And you're scheduled for Vegia next, is why I'm meeting you here. But to get back to the story, we haven't got dope enough to find Fairchild himself except by pure luck. So we decided to make Fairchild's mob tell us where he is."

"That'll be a slick trick if we can do it."

"Here's how. *Somebody* on this planet knows how to call Fairchild in emergencies, so we'll create an emergency and he'll do it."

"My mind is open, but I'm a bit skeptical. What kind of an emergency have you got in mind?"

"Some of the details you'll have to ad lib as you go along, but it'll be, basically, bold-faced robbery without a blaster and with them jittery as glaidos because they can't figure it. I was going to try to do it myself, but I can't work without my Lens and I can't come near the hot spots without their spy-rays catching the Lens and blowing the whole show. Doctor Janowick told Phil Strong that she could, without using her sense of perception and after only a short practise run, beat any crooked card game any gambler could dream up—something about random and nonrandom numbers. Can she?"

"Um-m . . . never thought of it . . . *random* numbers . . . Oh, I see. Yes, she can. Especially the most-played one, that over-and-under-seven thing. And with a little telepathy thrown in, I can do the same with any crooked game they've got except a magnetically-controlled wheel; and I could do a fair job on that."

"Better and better. You and Miss Janowick, then; and be sure and bring Vesta the Vegian along."

"Vesta? Um . . . Maybe, at that. Adolescent Vegians not only can be, but are, interested in everything that goes on, everywhere. They're born gamblers, and she's already got a reputation for throwing money around regardless— and she's rich enough to afford it. And in a winning streak she'll stir up so much excitement that nobody will pay any attention to anybody else. However, things being what they are, I'll have to be mighty careful about letting her go on a gambling spree."

"Not too much so. Just hint that you won't fire her if she takes a fling or two at the tables and she'll be so happy about it and love you so much that she won't even think of wondering why."

And so it proved. After a long discussion of details with the Lensman, Cloud went to sleep. The following after- noon he went back to the ship and sought out Vesta, whom he found slinking dejectedly about with her tail almost dragging on the floor. Scarcely had he begun his suggestion, however, when:

"*Really*, chief?" Vesta's tail snapped aloft, her pointed ears quivered with eagerness. She hugged him ecstatically, burying her face in the curve of his neck and inhaling deeply. "You zmell *zo* wonderful, chief—but a wonderful man like you would *have* to smell zo, wouldn't he? I thought you'd smack me bow-legged if I even hinted at wanting to lay a ten-cento chip on the line. But I *know* I can beat the games they've got on *this* planet . . . and besides, I've been gone half a year and haven't spent a hundred credits and I've learned nine languages including your cursed English . . ."

She took out her book of Travelers Cheques and stared at it thoughtfully. "Maybe, though, just to be on the safe side, I'd better tear one of these out and hide it in my room. It'd be *awful* to have to call my mother for jet fare home from the 'port. She and dad both'd yowl to high heaven—they'd claw me ragged."

"Huh? But listen!" Cloud was puzzled. "If you shoot such a terrific wad as that, what possible difference would it make whether you had plane fare for a few hundred miles left or not?"

"Oh, lots," she assured him. "They don't expect me to have much of any of my allowance left when I get home, and I never intended to, anyway. But *anybody* with half a brain is expected to be able to get home from a party— *any* kind of a party—without crying for help, and without walking, either; so I'll go hide one of these slips."

"If *that's* all that's bothering you, no matter," Cloud said quickly. "You've got another pay day coming before we get to Vegia, you know."

"Oh, I never thought of that—I've never been on a payroll before, you know, and can't get used to being paid for doing nothing. But can we go now, Captain Nealcloud, please? I can't wait!"

"If Joan's ready we can. We'll go see."

But Joan was not ready. "Did you actually think she would be?" Helen asked. "Don't you know that the less a woman puts on the longer it takes her to do it?"

"Nope—I s'posed Doctor Joan Janowick would be above such frippery."

"You'd be surprised. But say, how'd you talk her into this vacation? Your manly charm, no doubt."

"Could be, but I doubt it. All she wanted was half an excuse and the promise I wouldn't get sore if we have to kill a couple of days in space before starting shooting on Vegia . . . Hot Dog!—just *look* who's here!"

Joan came in, pausing in embarrassment, at the burst of applause and whistles that greeted her. She was richly, deeply tanned; taut, trim, and dainty—she had trained down to a hundred and fifteen pounds—her bra was a triumph of the couturier's art. She, too, was armed; her DeLameter harness sported the two-and-a-half silver bars of a lieutenant commander.

"Ouch—I'm bedazzled!" Cloud covered his eyes ostentatiously, then, gradually and equally ostentatiously recovering his sight: "Very nice, Joanie—you're a ver*ee* slick chick. With a dusting of powdered sugar and a dab of cream you'd make a right tasty snack. Just one thing—a bit overdressed, don't you think?"

"*Overdressed!*" she exclaimed. "Listen, you—I've never worn a bathing suit *half* as skimpy as this in my whole life, and if you think I'm going to wear any *less* than this you're completely out of your mind!"

"Oh, it isn't *me!*" Cloud protested. "Patrol Regs are strict that way—when in Rome you've got to be a Roman candle, you know."

"I know, but I'm Roman candle enough right now—in fact, I feel like a flaming skyrocket. Why, this thing I've got on is scarcely more than a G-string!"

"QX—we'll let it pass—this time . . ."

"Hey, you know something?" Joe interrupted him before Joan did. "Vegia is a couple of degrees warmer than this, and they don't overdo the matter of clothes there, either. I *am* going to start basking under the radiants. If I get myself cooked to a nice, golden brown, Helen—like a slice of medium-done toast—will you do Vegiaton with me?"

"It's a date, brother!"

As Joe and Helen shook hands to seal the agreement, the two Patrol officers and Vesta strode out.

They took a copter to the Club Elysian, the plushiest and one of the biggest places on the planet. The resplendently decorated—in an undressed way, of course—doorman glanced at the DeLameters, but, knowing the side-arm to be the one indispensable item of the Patrol uniform wherever found, he greeted them cordially in impeccable Galactic Spanish and passed them along.

"The second floor, I presume, sir and mesdames?" The host, a very good rule-of-thumb psychologist, classified these visitors instantly and suggested the region where both class and stakes were high. Also, and as promptly, he decided to escort them personally. Two Patrol officers and a Vegian—especially the Vegian—rated special attention.

The second floor was really a place. The pile of the rug was over half an inch deep. The lighting was neither too garish nor too dim. The tastefully-placed paintings and tapestries adorning the walls were neither too large nor too small, each for its place; and each was a masterpiece.

"May we use Patrol currency, or would you rather we took chips?" Cloud asked.

"Either one, sir; just as you wish."

"We Tellurians are all set, then, but Miss Vesta here would like to cash a few Travelers' Cheques."

"Certainly, Miss Vesta. I'll be delighted to take care of it for you. How do you wish the money, please?"

"I'll want a little small stuff to get the feel of the house ... say a thousand in tens and twenties. The rest of it in fifties and hundreds, please—mostly hundreds."

Vesta peeled off and thumb-printed ten two-thousand credit cheques and the host, bowing gracefully, hurried away.

"One thing, Vesta," Cloud cautioned. "Don't throw it away too fast. Save some for next time."

"Oh, I always do, chief. This'll last me the week, easily. I run wild only when I'm in a winning streak."

The host came up with her money; and as Vesta made a beeline for the nearest wheel:

"What do you like, Joan?" Cloud asked. "A wheel?"

"I don't think so; not at first, anyway. I've had better luck with the under-and-overs. They're over there, aren't they, sir?"

"Yes, madame. But is there anything I can do first? Refreshments of any kind—an appetizer, perhaps?"

"Not at the moment, thanks."

"If you wish anything, at any time, just send a boy. I'll

look you up from time to time, to be sure you lack nothing. Thank you very much, sir and madame."

The host bowed himself away and the two officers strolled over to the bank of "under-and-over" tables, which were all filled. They stood at ease for a few minutes; chatting idly, enjoying their cigarettes, gazing with interest and appreciation around the huge, but wonderfully beautiful room. There was no indication whatever that either of the two Patrolmen was the least bit interested in the fall of the cards, or that two of the keenest mathematical minds in space knew exactly, before the man ahead of them got tired of losing fifty-credit chips, the denomination and the location of every card remaining in the rack.

Joan could, of course, have read either the cards, or the dealer's mind, or both; but she was not doing either—yet. This was a game—on the side, so to speak—between her and Storm. Nor was it at all unequal, for Cloud's uncanny ability to solve complex mathematical problems was of very little assistance here. This was a matter of more-or-less simple sequences; of series; of arrangements; and her years of cybernetic training more than made up for his advantage in speed.

"Your pleasure, madame or sir? Or are you together?"

"We're together, thanks. We'll take the next, for an M." Cloud placed a one-thousand-credit note in the velvet-lined box.

Two thin stacks of cards lay on the table at the dealer's right; one pile face up, the other, face down. He took the top card from the rack, turned it over, and added it to the face-up stack. "The ten of clubs," he droned, sliding a one-thousand-credit bill across the table to Cloud. "What is your pleasure, sir and madame?"

"Let it ride. Two M's in the box," Cloud said, tossing the new bill on top of its mate. "Throw one."

"Discard one." The dealer removed the next card and, holding it so that neither he nor the players could see its face, added it to the face-down pile. "What is your pleasure, sir and madame?"

"Throw one."

"Discard one."

"We'll take this one," and there were four thousand credits in the box.

Throw one take one, and there were eight thousand.

The eight became sixteen; then thirty-two; and the dealer lost his urbanity completely. He looked just plain ugly.

"Maybe that's enough for now," Joan suggested. "After all, we don't want to take *all* the man's money."

"Tightwad's trick, huh? Quit while yer ahead?" the dealer sneered. "Why'n'cha let 'er ride just once more?"

"If you insist, we will," Cloud said, "but I'm warning you it'll cost you thirty two more M's."

"That's what *you* think, Buster—I think different. Call your play!"

"We'll take it!" Cloud snapped. "But listen, you clever-fingered jerk—I know just as well as you do that the top card is the king of clubs, and the one below it is the trey of diamonds. So, if you want to stay healthy, move slowly and be damned sure to lift just one card, not two, and take it off the top and not the bottom!"

Glaring in baffled fury, the dealer turned up the king of clubs and paid his loss.

At the next table the results were pretty much the same, and at the third. At the fourth table, however, instead of pyramiding, they played only single M-bills. They lost—won—lost—lost—won—lost—won—lost. In twenty plays they were only two thousand credits ahead.

"I think I've got it, Joan," Cloud said then. "Coming up—eight, six, jack, five, deuce?"

"Uh-uh. I don't think so. Eight, six, jack, three, one, I think. The trey of spades and the ace of hearts. A two-and-one shift with each full cycle."

"Um ... m. Could be ... but do you think the guy's that smart?"

"I'm pretty sure of it, Storm. He's the best dealer they have. He's been dealing a long time. He knows cards."

"Well, if you're done passing out compliments, how about calling a play?" the dealer suggested.

"QX. We'll take the eight for one M ... and it *is* the eight, you notice ... let it ride ... throw the six—without looking, of course ... we'll take the jack for two M's ..."

The host, accompanied by no less a personage than the manager himself, had come up. They stood quietly and listened as Cloud took three bills out of the box, leaving one, and went on:

"The next card is either a five or a trey. That M there is to find out which it is."

"Are you sure of that?" the manager asked.

"Not absolutely, of course," Cloud admitted. "There's one chance in approximately fourteen million that both my partner and I are wrong."

"Very good odds. But since you lose in either case, why bet?"

"Because if it's a trey, she solved your system first. If it's a five, I beat her to it."

"I see, but that isn't necessary." The manager took the remaining cards out of the rack, and, holding them carefully and firmly, wrapped the M-note tightly around them. Then, picking up the two small stacks of played cards, he handed the whole collection to Cloud, at the same time signalling the dealer to go ahead with his game. "We'll be smothered in a crowd very shortly, and I would like very much to play with you myself. Will you, sir and madame, be gracious enough to continue play in private?"

"Gladly, sir," Joan assented, at Cloud's questioning glance. "If it would not put you out too much."

"I am delighted," and, beckoning to a hovering waiter, he went on: "We will have refreshments, of course. In uniform, you might possibly prefer soft drinks? We have some very good Tellurian ginger ale."

"That'd be fine," Cloud said, even while he was thinking at the Lensman in contact with his mind: "Safe enough, don't you think? He couldn't be thinking of any rough stuff yet."

"Perfectly safe," Nordquist agreed. "He's just curious. Besides, he's in no shape to handle even the *Vortex Blaster* alone, to say nothing of the task force he knows would be here two hours after anything happened to either of you."

The four strolled in friendly fashion to the suggested private room. As soon as they were settled:

"You said the top card would be either a five or a trey," the manager said. "Shall we look?"

It was the trey of spades. "Congratulations, Joanie, a mighty swell job. You really clobbered me on that one." He shook her hand vigorously, then handed the bill to the manager. "Here's your M-note, sir."

"I couldn't think of it, sir. No tipping, you know . . ."

"I know. Not a tip, but your winnings. I called the play, remember. Hence, I insist."

"Very well, if you insist. But don't you want to look at the next one?"

"No. It's the ace of hearts—can't be anything else."

"To satisfy my own curiosity, then." The manager flipped the top card delicately. It was the ace of hearts. "No compulsion, of course, but would mind telling me how you can *possibly* do what you have just done?"

"I'll be glad to," and this was the simple truth. Cloud had to explain, before the zwilniks began to suspect that they were being taken by an organized force of Lensmen and snoopers. "We aren't even semi-habitual gamblers. The lieutenant-commander is Doctor Joan Janowick, the Patrol's ace designer of big, high-speed electronic computers, and I am Neal Cloud, a mathematical analyst."

"You are 'Storm' Cloud, the Vortex Blaster," the manager corrected him. "A super-computer yourself. I begin to see, I think . . . but go ahead, please."

"You undoubtedly know that random numbers, which underlie all games of chance, must be just that—purely random, with nothing whatever of system or of orderliness in their distribution. Also that a stacked deck, by definition, is most decidedly *not* random. We were kicking that idea around, one day, and decided to study stacked decks, to see how systematic such distributions actually were. Well—here's the new part—we learned that any dealer who stacks a deck of cards does so in some definite pattern; and that pattern, whether conscious or unconscious, is always characteristic of that one individual. The more skilled the dealer, the more complex, precise, complete, and definite the pattern. Any pattern, however complex, can be solved; and, once solved, the cards might just as well be lying face up and all in sight.

"On the other hand, while it is virtually impossible for any dealer to shuffle a deck into a really random condition, it can approach randomness so nearly that the patterns are short and hence very difficult to solve. Also, there are no likenesses or similarities to help. Worst of all, there is the house leverage—the sevens of hearts, diamonds, and clubs, you know—of approximately five point seven seven percent. So it is mathematically certain that she and I would lose, not win, against any dealer who was not stacking his decks."

"I ... am ... surprised. I'm *amazed*," the manager said. He was, too; and so was the host. "Heretofore it has always been the guest who loses by manipulation, not the house." It is noteworthy that neither the manager nor host had at any time denied, even by implication, that their games of "chance" were loaded. "Thanks, immensely, for telling me ... By the way, you haven't done this very often before have you?" the manager smiled ruefully.

"No." Cloud smiled back. "This is the first time. Why?"

"I thought I would have heard of it if you had. This of course changes my mind about wanting to deal to you myself. In fact, I'll go farther—any dealer you play with here will be doing his level best to give you a completely random distribution."

"Fair enough. But we proved our point, which was what we were primarily interested in, anyway. What'll we do with the rest of the day, Joan—go back to the ship?"

"Uh-uh. This is the most comfortable place I've found since we left Tellus, and if I don't see the ship again for a week it'll be at least a week too soon. Why don't you send a boy out with enough money to get us a chess kit? We can engage this room for the rest of the day and work on our game."

"No need for that—we have all such things here," the host said quickly. "I'll send for them at once."

"No no—no money, please," the manager said. "I am still in your debt, and as long as you will stay you are my guests ..." he paused, then went on in a strangely altered tone: "But chess ... and Janowick ... Joan Janowick, not at all a common name ... surely not Past Grand Master Janowick? She—retired—would be a much older woman."

"The same—I retired for lack of time, but I still play as much as I can. I'm flattered that you have heard of me." Joan smiled as though she were making a new and charming acquaintance. "And you? I'm sorry we didn't introduce ourselves earlier."

"Permit me to introduce Host Althagar, assistant manager. I am called Thlasoval."

"Oh, I know of you, Master Thlasoval. I followed your

game with Rengodon of Centralia. Your knight-and-bishop end game was a really beautiful thing."

"Thank you. *I* am *really* flattered that you have heard of *me*. But Commander Cloud . . .?"

"No, you haven't heard of him. Perhaps you never will, but believe me, if he had time for tournament play he'd be high on the Grand Masters list. So far on this cruise he's won one game, I've won one, and we're on the eighty fourth move of the third."

The paraphernalia arrived and the Tellurians set the game up rapidly and unerringly, each knowing exactly where each piece and pawn belonged.

"You have each lost two pawns, one knight, and one bishop—in eighty three moves?" Thlasoval marveled.

"Right," Cloud said. "We're playing for blood. Across this board friendship ceases; and, when dealing with such a pure unadulterated tiger as she is, so does chivalry."

"If I'm a tiger, I'd hate to say what *he* is." Joan glanced up with a grin. "Just study the board, Master Thlosoval, and see for yourself who is doing what to whom. I'm just barely holding him: he's had me on the defensive for the last forty moves. Attacking him is just like trying to beat in the side of a battleship with your bare fist. Do you see his strategy? Perhaps not, on such short notice."

Joan was very willing to talk chess at length, because the fact that Fairchild's Chickladorian manager was a chess Master was an essential part of the Patrol's plan.

"No . . . I can't say that I do."

"You notice he's concentrating everything he can bring to bear on my left flank. Fifteen moves from now he'd've been focussed on my King's Knight's Third. Three moves after that he was going to exchange his knight for my queen and then mate in four. But, finding out what he was up to, I've just derailed his train of operations and he has to revise his whole campaign."

"No wonder I didn't see . . . I'm simply not in your class. But would you mind if I stay and look on?"

"We'll be glad to have you, but it won't be fast. We're playing strict tournament rules and taking the full four minutes for each move."

"That's quite all right. I really *enjoy* watching Grand Masters at work."

Master though he was, Thlasoval had no idea at all of

what a terrific game he watched. For Joan Janowick and Neal Cloud were not playing it; they merely moved the pieces. The game had been played long since. Based upon the greatest games of the greatest masters of old, it had been worked out, move by move, by chess masters working with high-speed computers.

Thus, while Joan and Storm were really concentrating, it was not upon chess.

Chapter 14

————————————VESTA THE GAMBLER

JOAN WAS HANDLING the card games, Cloud the wheels. The suggestion that it would be smart to run honest games had been implanted in the zwilniks' minds, not because of the cards, but because of the wheels; for a loaded, braked, and magnetized wheel is a very tough device to beat.

Joan, then, would read a deck of cards, and a Lensman or a Rigellian would watch her do it. Then the observing telepath would, all imperceptibly, insert hunches into the mind of a player. And what gambler has ever questioned his hunches, especially when they pay off time after time after time? Thus more and more players began to win with greater or lesser regularity and the gambling fever— the most contagious and infectious disorder known to man—spread throughout the vast room like a conflagration in a box-factory.

And Storm Cloud was handling the wheels.

"Place your bets, ladies and gentlemen, before the ball enters Zone Green," the croupiers intoned. "The screens go up, no bets can be placed while the ball is in the Green."

If the wheels had not been rigged, Cloud could have computed with ease the exact number upon which each ball would come to rest. In such case the Patrol forces would not, of course, have given Vesta the Vegian complete or accurate information. With her temperament and her bank-roll, she would have put the place out of business

in an hour; and such a single-handed killing was not at all
what the Patrol desired.

But the wheels, of course, were rigged. Cloud was being
informed, however, of every pertinent fact. He knew the
exact point at which the ball crossed the green borderline.
He knew its exact velocity. He knew precisely the
strengths of the magnetic fields and the permeabilities,
reluctances, and so on, of all the materials involved. He
knew just about how much braking force could be applied
without tipping off the players and transforming them
instantly into a blood-thirsty mob. And finally, he was
backed by Lensmen who could at need interfere with the
physical processes of the croupiers without any knowledge
on the part of the victims.

Hence Cloud did well enough—and when a house is
paying thirty five to one on odds that have been cut down
to eight or ten to one, it is very, *very* bad for the house.

Vesta started playing conservatively enough. She went
from wheel to wheel, tail high in air and purring happily
to herself, slapping down ten-credit notes until she won.

"*This* is the wheel I like!" she exclaimed, and went to
twenties. Still unperturbed, still gay, she watched nine of
them move away under the croupier's rake. Then she won
again.

Then fifties. Then hundreds. She wasn't gay now, nor
purring. She wasn't exactly tense, yet, but she was warm-
ing up. As the tenth C-note disappeared, a Chickladorian
beside her said:

"Why don't you play the colors, miss? Or combinations?
You don't lose so much that way."

"No, and you don't win so much, either. When I'm
gambling I *gamble*, brother . . . and wait just a minute
. . ." the croupier paid her three M's and an L . . . "See
what I mean?"

The crowd was going not-so-slowly mad. Assistant
Manager Althagar did what he could. He ordered all
rigging and gimmicks off, and the house still lost. On
again, off again; and losses still skyrocketed. Then, hurrying over to the door of a private room, he knocked
lightly, opened the door, and beckoned to Thlasoval.

"All hell's out for noon!" he whispered intensely as the
manager reached the doorway. "The crowd's winning like
crazy—everybody's winning! D'you s'pose it's them damn

Patrolmen there crossing us up—and how in *hell* could it be?"

"Have you tried cutting out the gimmicks?"

"Yes. No difference."

"It can't be them, then. It couldn't be anyway, for two reasons. The kind of brains it takes to work that kind of problems in your head can't happen once in a hundred million times, and you say everybody's doing it. They *can't* be, dammit! Two, they're Grand Masters playing chess. You play chess yourself."

"You know I do. I'm not a Master, but I'm pretty good."

"Good enough to tell by looking at 'em that they don't give a damn about what's going on out there. Come on in."

"We'll disturb 'em and they'll be sore as hell."

"You *couldn't* disturb these two, short of yelling in their ear or joggling the board." The two walked toward the table. "See what I mean?"

The two players, forearms on table, were sitting rigidly still, staring as though entranced at the board, neither moving so much as an eye. As the two Chickladorians watched, Cloud's left forearm, pivoting on the elbow, swung out and he moved his knight.

"Oh, no ... no!" Shocked out of silence, Thlasoval muttered the words under his breath. "Your queen, man— your queen!"

But this opportunity, so evident to the observer, did not seem at all attractive to the woman, who sat motionless for minute after minute.

"But come on, boss, and look this mess over," the assistant urged. "You're on plus time now."

"I suppose so." They turned away from the enigma. "But *why* didn't she take his queen? I couldn't see a thing to keep her from doing it. I would have."

"So would I. However, almost all the pieces on that board are vulnerable, some way or other. Probably whichever one starts the shin-kicking will come out at the little end of the horn."

"Could be, but it won't be kicking shins. It'll be slaughter—and *how* I'd like to be there when the slaughter starts! And I *still* don't see why she didn't grab that queen ..."

"Well, you can ask her, maybe, when they leave. But right now you'd better forget chess and take a good, long gander at what that Vegian hell-cat is doing. She's wilder than a Radelgian cateagle and hotter than a DeLameter. She's gone just completely nuts."

Tense, strained, taut as a violin-string in every visible muscle, Vesta stood at a wheel; gripping the ledge of the table so fiercely that enamel was flaking off the metal and plastic under her stiff, sharp nails. Jaws hard set and eyes almost invisible slits, she growled deep in her throat at every bet she put down. And those bets were all alike— ten thousand credits each—and she was still playing the numbers straight. They watched her lose eighty thousand credits; then watched her collect three hundred and fifty thousand.

Thlasoval made the rounds, then; did everything he could to impede the outward flow of cash, finding that there wasn't much of anything he could do. He beckoned his assistant.

"This is bad, Althagar, believe me," he said. "And I simply can't figure any part of it . . . unless . . ." His voice died away.

"You said it. I can't, either. Unless it's them two chess-players in there, and I'll buy it that it ain't, I haven't even got a guess . . . unless there could be some Lensmen mixed up in it somewhere. They could do just about anything."

"*Lensmen?* Rocket-juice! There aren't any—we spy-ray everybody that comes in."

"Outside, maybe, peeking in. Or some other snoopers, maybe, somewhere?"

"I can't see it. We've had Lensmen in here dozens of times, for one reason or another, business and social both, and they've always shot straight pool. Besides, all they're getting is money, and what in all eleven hells of Telemanchia would the Patrol want of our *money?* If they wanted us for anything they'd come and get us, but they wouldn't give a cockeyed tinker's damn for our *money.* They've already got all the money there is!"

"That's so, too. Money . . .hm, money in gobs and slathers . . . Oh, you think . . . the Mob? D'ya s'pose it's got so big for its britches it thinks it can take *us* on?"

"I wouldn't think they could be *that* silly. It's a lot more reasonable, though, than that the Patrol would be horsing around this way."

"But how? Great Kalastho, *how?*"

"How do I know? Snoopers, as you said—or perceivers, or any other ringers they could ring in on us."

"Nuts!" the assistant retorted. "Just who do you figure as ringers? The Vegian isn't a snooper, she's just a gambling fool. No Chickladorian was ever a snooper, or a perceiver either, and these people are just about all regular customers. And *everybody's* winning. So just where does that put you?"

"Up the creek—I know. But dammit, there's *got* to be snoopery or some other funny stuff *somewhere* in this!"

"Uh-uh. Did you ever hear of a perceiver who could read a deck or spot a gimmick from half a block away?"

"No, but that doesn't mean there aren't any. But what stops me is what can we *do* about it? If the Mob *is* forted up in that hotel across the street or somewhere beside or behind us . . . there isn't a damn thing we can do. They'd have more gunnies than we could send in, even if we knew exactly where they were, and we can't send a young army barging around without anything but a flimsy suspicion to go on—the lawmen would throw us in the clink in nothing flat . . . Besides, this Mob idea isn't exactly solid, either. How'd they get their cut from all these people? Especially the Vegian?"

"The Vegian, probably not; the rest, probably so. They could have passed the word around that this is the big day. Anybody'd split fifty-fifty on a cold sure thing."

"Uh-uh. I won't buy that, either. I'd've known about it—somebody would have leaked. No matter how you figure it, it doesn't add up."

"Well, then?"

"Only one thing we can do. Close down. While you're doing that I'll go shoot in a Class A Double Prime Urgent to top brass."

Hence Vesta's croupier soon announced to his clientele that all betting was off, at least until the following day. All guests would please leave the building as soon as possible.

For a couple of minutes Vesta simply could not take in the import of the announcement. She was stunned. Then:

"Whee . . . yow . . . ow . . . erow!" she yowled, at the

top of her not inconsiderable voice. "I've won ... I've *won* ... I'VE WON!" She quieted down a little, still shell-shocked, then looked around and ran toward the nearest familiar face, which was that of the assistant manager. "Oh, senor Althagar, do you actually want me to quit while I'm *ahead?* Why, I never *heard* of such a thing—it certainly never happened to *me* before! And I'm going to stop gambling *entirely*—I'll *never* get such a thrill as this again if I live a million years!"

"You're *so* right, Miss Vesta—you never will." Althagar smiled—as though he had just eaten three lemons without sugar, to be sure, but it was still a smile. "It's not that we *want* you to quit, but simply that we can't pay any more losses. Right now I am most powerfully psychic, so take my advice, my dear, and stop."

"I'm going to—honestly, I am." Vesta straightened out the thick sheaf of bills she held in her right hand, noticing that they were all ten-thousands. She dug around in her bulging pouch; had to dig halfway to the bottom before she could find anything smaller. With a startled gasp she crammed the handful of bills in on top of the others and managed, just barely, to close and lock the pouch. "Oh, I've got to *fly*—I must find my boss and tell him all about this!"

"Would you like an armed escort to your hotel?"

"That won't be necessary, thanks. I'm going to take a copter direct to the ship."

And she did.

It was not until the crowd was almost all gone that either Thlasoval or Althagar even thought of the two chess-players. Then one signalled the other and they went together to the private room, into it, and up to the chess-table. To the casual eye, neither player had moved. The board, too, showed comparatively little change; at least, the carnage anticipated by Thlasoval had not materialized.

Althagar coughed discreetly; then again, a little louder. "Sir and madam, please ..." he began.

"I told you they'd be dead to the world," Thlasoval said; and, bending over, lifted one side of the board. Oh, very gently, and not nearly enough to dislodge any one of the pieces, but the tiny action produced disproportionately large results. Both players started as though a bomb had exploded beside them, and Joan uttered a half-stifled scream. With visible efforts, they brought themselves down from the heights to the there and the then. Cloud stretched prodigiously; and Joan, emulating him, had to bring one hand down to cover a jaw-cracking yawn.

"Excuse me, Grand Master Janowick and Commander Cloud, but the Club is being closed for repairs and we must ask you to leave the building."

"Closed?" Joan parroted, stupidly, and:

"For repairs?" Cloud added, with equal brilliance.

"Closed. For repairs." Thlasoval repeated, firmly. Then, seeing that his guests were coming back to life quite nicely, he offered Joan his arm and started for the door.

"Oh, yes, Grand Master Janowick," he said en route. "May I ask why you refused the Commander's queen?"

"He would have gained such an advantage in position as to mate in twelve moves."

"I see ... thanks." He didn't, at all, but he had to say something. "I wonder ... would it be possible for me to find out how this game comes out?"

"Why, I suppose so." Joan thought for a moment. "Certainly. If you'll give me your card I'll send you a tape of it after we finish."*

The two Patrolmen boarded a 'copter. Joan looked subdued, almost forlorn. Cloud took her hand and squeezed it gently.

"Don't take it so hard, Joan," he thought. He found it remarkably easy to send to her now; in fact, telepathy was easier and simpler and more natural than talking. "We had it to do."

"I suppose so; but it was a dirty, slimy, stinking, *filthy* trick, Storm. I'm ashamed ... I feel soiled."

"I know how you feel. I'm not so happy about the thing, either. But when you think of thionite, and what *that* stuff means ...?"

"That's true, of course ... and they stole the money in

---

* A few months later, Joan did send him the full game, which white of course won. Thlasoval studied it in secret for over five years; and then, deciding correctly that he never would be able to understand its terrifically complex strategy, he destroyed the tape. It is perhaps superfluous to all that this game was never published. E.E.S.

the first place ... Not that two wrongs, or even three or four, make a right ... but it does *help*."

She cheered up a little, but she was not yet her usual self when they boarded the *Vortex Blaster II*.

Vesta met them just inside the lock. "Oh, chief, I won—I won!" she shrieked, tail waving frantically in air. "Where'd you go after the club closed? I looked all *over* for you—do you know how much I won, Captain Neal-cloud?"

"Haven't any idea. How much?"

"One million seven hundred sixty two thousand eight hundred and ten credits! Yow-wow-yow!"

"Whew!" Cloud whistled in amazement. "And you're figuring on giving it all back to 'em tomorrow?"

"I ... I haven't quite decided." Vesta sobered instantly. "What do *you* think, chief?"

"Not being a gambler, I don't have hunches very often, but I've got one now. In fact, I know one thing for certain damn sure. There isn't one chance in seven thousand million of anything like this ever happening to you again. You'll lose your shirt—that is, if you had a shirt to lose," he added hastily.

"You know, I think you're right? I thought so myself, and you're the second smart man to tell me the same thing."

"Who was the first one?"

"That man at the club, Althagar, his name was. So, with three hunches on the same play, I'd be a fool not to play it that way. Besides, I'll *never* get another wallop like that ... my uncle's been wanting me to be linguist in his bank, and with a million and three-quarters of my own I could buy half his bank and be a linguist and a cashier both. Then I couldn't *ever* gamble again."

"Huh? Why not?"

"Because Vegians, especially young Vegians, like me, haven't got any sense when it comes to gambling," Vesta explained, gravely. "They can't tell the difference between their own money and the bank's. So everybody who amounts to anything in a bank makes a no-gambling declaration and if one ever slips the insurance company boots him out on his ear and he takes a blaster and burns his head off ..."

Cloud flashed a thought at Joan. "Is this another of your strictly Vegian customs?"

"Not mine; I never heard of it before," she flashed back. "Very much in character, though, and it explains why Vegian bankers are regarded as being very much the upper crust."

". . . so I *am* going to buy half of that bank. Thanks, chief, for helping me make up my mind. Good night, you two lovely people; I'm going to bed. I'm just about bushed." Vesta, tail high and with a completely new dignity in her bearing, strode away.

"Me, too, Storm; on both counts," Joan thought at Cloud. "You ought to hit the hammock, too, instead of working half the night yet."

"Maybe so, but I want to know how things came out, and besides they may want some quick figuring done. Good night, little chum." His parting thought, while commonplace enough in phraseology, was in fact sheer caress; and Joan's mind, warmly intimate, accepted it as such and returned it in kind.

Cloud left the ship and rode a scooter across the field to a very ordinary-looking freighter. In that vessel's control room, however, there were three Lensmen and five Rigellians, all clustered around a tank-chart of a considerable fraction of the First Galaxy.

"Hi, Cloud!" Nordquist greeted him with a Lensed thought and introduced him to the others. "All our thanks for a really beautiful job of work. We'll thank Miss Janowick tomorrow, when she'll have a better perspective. Want to look?"

"I certainly do. Thanks." Cloud joined the group at the chart and Nordquist poured knowledge into his mind.

Thlasoval, the boss of Chickladoria, had been under full mental surveillance every minute of every day. The scheme had worked perfectly. As the club closed, Thlasoval had sent the expected message; not by ordinary communications channels, of course, but via long-distance beamer. It was beamed three ways; to Tominga, Vegia, and Palmer III. That proved that Fairchild wasn't on Chickladoria; if he had been, Thlasoval would have used a broadcaster, not a beamer.

Shows had been staged simultaneously on all four of Fairchild's planets, and only on Vegia had the planetary manager's message been broadcast. Fairchild was on Vegia, and he wouldn't leave it: a screen had been thrown around the planet that a microbe couldn't squirm through and it wouldn't be relaxed until Fairchild was caught.

"*Simultaneous shows?*" Cloud interrupted the flow of information. "On four planets? He won't connect the *Vortex Blaster* with it, at all, then."

"We think he will," the Lensman thought, narrowing down. "We're dealing with a *very* shrewd operator. We hope he does, anyway, because a snooper put on you or any one of your key people would be manna from heaven for us."

"But how *could* he suspect us?" Cloud demanded. "We couldn't have been on four planets at once."

"You will have been on three of them, though; and I can tell you now that routing was not exactly coincidence."

"Oh . . . and I wasn't informed?"

"No. Top Brass didn't want to disturb you too much, especially since we hoped to catch him before things got this far along. But you're in it now, clear to the neck. You and your people will be under surveillance every second, from here on in, and you'll be covered as no chief of state was ever covered in all history."

Chapter 15

JOAN AND HER BRAINS

THE TRIP FROM Chickladoria to Vegia, while fairly long, was uneventful.

Joan spent her working hours, of course, at her regular job of rebuilding the giant computer. Cloud spent his at the galactic chart or in the control room staring into a tank; classifying, analyzing, building up and knocking down hypotheses and theories, wringing every possible drop of knowledge from all the data he could collect.

In their "spare" time, of which each had quite a great deal, they worked together at their telepathy; to such good purpose that, when so working, verbal communication between them became rarer and rarer. And, alone or in a crowd, within sight of each other or not, in any place or at any time, asleep or awake, each had only to think at the other and they were instantly in full mental rapport.

And oftener and oftener there came those instantaneously-fleeting touches of something infinitely more than mere telepathy; that fusion of minds which was so ultimately intimate that neither of the two could have said whether he longed for or dreaded its full coming the more. In fact, for several days before reaching Vegia, each knew that they could bring about that full fusion any time they chose to do so; but both shied away from its consummation, each as violently as the other.

Thus the trip did not seem nearly as long as it actually was.

The first order of business on Vegia, of course, was the extinguishment of its five loose atomic vortices—for which reason this was to be pretty much a planetary holiday, although that is of little concern here.

As the *Vortex Blaster II* began settling into position, the two scientists took their places. Cloud was apparently his usual self-controlled self, but Joan was white and strained—almost shaking. He sent her a steadying thought, but her block was up, solid.

"Don't take it so hard, Joanie," he said, soberly. "Margie'll take 'em, I hope—but even if she doesn't, there's a dozen things not tried yet."

"That's just the trouble—there *aren't!* We put just about everything we had into Lulu; Margie is only a few milliseconds better. *Perhaps* there are a dozen things not tried yet, but I haven't the faintest, foggiest smidgeon of an idea of what any of them could be. Margie is the last word, Storm—the best analogue computer it is possible to build with today's knowledge."

"And I haven't been a lick of help. I wish I could be, Joan."

"I don't see how you can be . . . Oh, excuse me, Storm, I didn't mean that half the way it sounds. Do you want to check the circuitry? I'll send for the prints."

"No, I couldn't even carry your water-bottle on that part of the job. I've got just a sort of a dim, half-baked idea that there's a possibility that maybe I haven't been giving you and your brains a square deal. By studying the graphs of the next three or four tests maybe I can find out whether . . ."

"Lieutenant-Commander Janowick, we are in position," a crisp voice came from the speaker. "You may take over when ready, madam."

"Thank you, sir." Joan flipped a switch and Margie took control of the ship and its armament—subject only to Cloud's overriding right to fire at will.

"Just a minute, Storm," Joan said then. "Unfinished business. Whether what?"

"Whether there's anything I can do—or fail to do—that might help; but I've got to have a lot more data."

Cloud turned to his chart, Joan to hers; and nothing happened until Cloud blew out the vortex himself.

The same lack of something happened in the case of the next vortex, and also the next. Then, as the instruments began working in earnest on the fourth, Cloud reviewed in his mind the figures of the three previous trials. On the first vortex, a big toughie, Margie had been two hundred fifty milliseconds short. On the second, a fairly small one, she had come up to seventy-five. On Number Three, middle-sized, the lag had been one twenty-five. That made sense. Lag was proportional to activity and it was just too bad for Margie. And just too *damn* bad for Joanie—the poor kid was just about to blow her stack . . .

But wait a minute! What's this? This number four's a little bit of a new one, about as small as they ever come. Margie ought to be taking it, if she's ever going to take anything . . . but she isn't! She's running damn near three hundred mils behind! Why? Oh—amplitudes—frequencies extreme instability . . . Lag isn't proportional *only* to activity, then, but jointly to activity and to instability.

That gives us a chance—but what in all nine of Palain's purple *hells* is that machine *doing* with that data?

He started to climb out of his bucket seat to go around to talk to Joan right then, but changed his mind at his first move. Even if Margie *could* handle this little one it wouldn't be a real test, and it'd be a crying shame to give Joan a success here and then kick her in the teeth with a flat failure next time. No, the next one, the only one left and Vegia's worst, would be the one. If Margie could handle *that*, she could snuff anything the galaxy had to offer.

Hence Cloud extinguished this one, too, himself. The *Vortex Blaster II* darted to its last Vegian objective and lined itself up for business. Joan put Margie to work as usual; but Storm, for the first time, did not take his own place. Instead, he came around and stood behind Joan's chair.

"How're we doing, little chum?" he asked.

"Rotten!" Joan's block was still up; her voice was choked with tears. "She's come *so* close half a dozen times today—why—*why* can't I get that last fraction of a second?"

"Maybe you can." As though it were the most natural thing in the world—which in fact it was—Cloud put his left arm around her shoulders and exerted a gentle pressure. "Bars down, chum—we can think a lot clearer than we can talk."

"That's better," as her guard went down. "Your differential 'scope looks like it's set at about one centimeter to the second. Can you give it enough vertical gain to make it about five?"

"Yes. Ten if you like, but the trace would keep jumping the screen on the down-swings."

"I wouldn't care about that—closest approach is all I want. Give it full gain."

"QX, but why?" Joan demanded, as she made the requested adjustment. "Did you find out something I can't dig deep enough in your mind to pry loose?"

"Don't know yet whether I did or not—I can tell you in a couple of minutes," and Cloud concentrated his full attention upon the chart and its adjacent oscilloscope screen.

One pen of the chart was drawing a thin, wildly-wavering red line. A few seconds behind it a second pen was tracing the red line in black; tracing it so exactly that not the tiniest touch of red was to be seen anywhere along the black. And on the screen of the differential oscilloscope the fine green saw-tooth wave-form of the electronic trace, which gave continuously the instantaneous value of the brain's shortage in time, flickered insanely and apparently reasonlessly up and down; occasionally falling clear off the bottom of the screen. If that needle-pointed trace should touch the zero line, however briefly, Margie the

Brain would act; but it was not coming within one fu
centimeter of touching.

"The feeling that these failures have been partly, or
even mostly, my fault is growing on me," Cloud thought,
tightening his arm a little: and Joan, if anything, yielded
to the pressure instead of fighting away from it. "Maybe I
haven't been waiting long enough to give your brains the
leeway they need. To check: I've been assuming all along
that they work in pretty much the same way I do; that
they handle all the data, out to the limit of validity of the
equations, but aren't fast enough to work out a three-
point-six-second prediction.

"But if I'm reading those curves right Margie simply
isn't working that way. She doesn't seem to be extrapolating *anything* more than three and a half seconds ahead—
'way short of the reliability limit—and sometimes a lot
less than that. She isn't *accepting* data far enough ahead.
She acts as though she can gulp down just so much
information without choking on it—so much and no
more."

"Exactly. An over-simplification, of course, since it isn't
the kind of choking that giving her a bigger throat would
cure, but very well put." Joan's right hand crept across her
body, rested on Cloud's wrist, and helped his squeeze,
while her face turned more directly toward the face so
close to hers. "That's inherent in the design of all really
fast machines . . . and we simply don't know any way of
getting away from it . . . Why? What has that to do with
the case?"

"A lot—I hope. When I was working in a flitter I had
to wait up to half an hour sometimes, for the sigma curve
to stabilize enough so that the equations would hold valid
will give a longer valid prediction."

"Stabilize? How? I've never seen a sigma curve flatten
out. Or does 'stabilize' have a special meaning for you
vortex experts?"

"Could be. It's what happens when a sigma becomes a
little more regular than usual, so that a simpler equation
will give a longer valid prediction."

"I see; and a difference in wave-form that would be
imperceptible to me might mean a lot to you."

"Right. It just occurred to me that a similar line of
reasoning may hold for this seemingly entirely different set

f conditions. The less unstable the curve, the less complicated the equations and the smaller the volume of actual
data . . ."

"Oh!" Joan's thought soared high. "So Margie may
work *yet*, if we wait a while?"

"Check. Browning can't take the ship away from you,
can he?"

"No. Nobody can do anything until the job is done or I
punch that red 'stop' button there. D'you suppose she *can*
do it? Storm? How long can we wait?"

"Half an hour, I'd say. No, to settle the point definitely,
let's wait until I can get a full ten-second prediction and
see what Margie's doing about the situation then."

"Wonderful! But in that case, it might be a good idea
for you to be looking at the chart, don't you think?" she
asked, pointedly. His eyes, at the moment, were looking
directly into hers, from a distance of approximately twelve
inches.

"I'll look at it later, but right now I'm . . ."

The ship quivered under the terrific, the unmistakable
trip-hammer blow of propellant heptadetonite. Unobserved
by either of the two scientists most concerned, the sigma
curve had, momentarily, become a trifle less irregular. The
point of the sawtooth wave had touched the zero line.
Margie had acted. The visiplate, from which the heavily-
filtered glare of the vortex had blazed so long, went
suddenly black.

"*She did it*, Storm!" Joan's thought was a mental shriek
of pure joy. "*She really worked!*"

Whether, when the ship went free, Joan pulled Storm
down to her merely to anchor him, or for some other
reason; whether Cloud grabbed her merely in lieu of a
safety-line or not; which of the two was first to put arms
around the other; these are moot points impossible of
decision at this date. The fact is, however, that the two
scientists held a remarkably unscientific pose for a good
two minutes before Joan thought that she ought to object
a little, just on general principles. Even then, she did not
object with her mind; instead she put up her block and
used her voice.

"But, after all, Storm," she began, only to be silenced as
beloved women have been silenced throughout the ages.

She cut her screen then, and her mind, tender and unafraid, reached out to his.

"This might be the perfect time, dear, to merge our minds? I've been scared to death of it all along, but no more . . . let's?"

"Uh-huh," he demurred. "I'm *still* afraid of it. I've been thinking about it a lot, and doing some drilling, and the more I play with it the more scared I get. It's dangerous. It's like playing with duodec. I've just about decided that we'd better let it drop."

"Afraid? For yourself, or for me? Don't try to lie with your mind, Storm; you can't do it. You're afraid only for me, and you needn't be. I've been thinking, too, and digging deep, and I know I'm ready." She looked up at him then, her quick, bright, impish grin very much in evidence. "Let's go."

"QX, Joanie, and thanks. I've been wanting this more than I ever wanted anything before in my life. But not holding hands, this time. Heart to heart and cheek to cheek."

"Check—the closer the better."

They embraced, and again mind flowed into mind; this time with no thought of withholding or reserve on either side. Smoothly, effortlessly, the two essential beings merged, each fitting its tiniest, remotest members into the deepest, ordinarily most inaccessible recesses of the other; fusing as quickly and as delicately and as thoroughly as two drops of water coalescing into one.

In that supremely intimate fusion, that ultimate union of line and plane and cellule, each mind was revealed completely to the other; a revealment which no outsider should expect to share.

Finally, after neither ever knew how long, they released each other and each put up, automatically, a solid block.

"I don't know about you, Storm," Joan said then, "but I've had just about all I can take. I'm going to bed and sleep for one solid week."

"You and me both," Storm agreed, ungrammatically, but feelingly. "Good night, sweetheart . . . and this had all better be strictly hush-hush, don't you think?"

"I *do* think," she assured him. "Can't you just imagine the field-day the psychs would have, taking us apart?"

In view of the above, it might be assumed that the

parting was immediate, positive, and undemonstrative; but such was not exactly the case. But they did finally separate, and each slept soundly and long.

And fairly early the next morning—before either of them got up, at least—Cloud sent Joan a thought.

"Awake, dear?"

"Uh-huh. Just. 'Morning, Storm."

"I've got some news for you, Joanie. My brain is firing on ten times as many barrels as I ever thought it had, and I don't know what half of 'em are doing. Among other things, you made what I think is probably a top-bracket perceiver out of me."

"So? Well, don't peek at me, please . . . but why should I say that, after having studied in Rigel Four for two years? Women are funny, I guess. But, for your information, I have just extracted the ninth root of an eighteen-digit number, in no time at all and to the last significant decimal place, and I *know* the answer is right. How do you like *them* potatoes, Buster?"

"Nice. We really absorbed each other's stuff, didn't we? But how about joining me in person for a soupcon of ham and eggs?"

"That's a thought, my thoughtful friend; a cogent and right knightly thought. I'll be with you in three jerks and a wiggle." And she was.

Just as they finished eating, Vesta breezed in. "Well, you two deep-sleepers finally crawled out of your sacks, did you? It is confusing, though, that ship's time never agrees with planetary time. But I live here, you know, in this city you call 'Vegiaton,' so I went to bed at noon yesterday and I've got over half a day's work done already. I saw my folks and bought half of my uncle's bank and made the no-gambling declaration and I want to ask you both something. After the Grand Uproar here at the 'port in your honor, will you two and Helen and Joe and Bob and Barbara come with me to a little dance some of my friends are having? You've been *zo* good to me, and I want to show you off a little."

"We'll be *glad* to, Vesta, and thanks a lot," Joan said, flashing a thought at Cloud to let her handle this thing her own way, "and I imagine the others would be, too, but . . . well, it's for *you*, you know, and we might be intruding . . ."

"Why, not at all!" Vesta waved the objection away with an airy flirt of her tail. "You're friends of mine! And everybody's real friends are always welcome, you know, everywhere. And it'll be small and quiet; only six or eight hundred are being asked, they say . . ." she paused for a moment: ". . . of course, after it gets around that we have *you* there, a couple of thousand or so strangers will come in too; but they'll all smell nice, so it'll be QX."

"How do you know what they'll smell like?" Cloud asked.

"Why, they'll smell like our crowd, of course. If they didn't they wouldn't *want* to come in. It's QX, then?"

"For us two, yes; but of course we can't speak for the others."

"Thanks, you wonderful people; I'll go ask them right now."

"Joan, have you blown your stack completely?" Cloud demanded. "Small—quiet—six or eight *hundred* invited—a couple of thousand *or so* gate-crashers—what do you want to go to a brawl like *that* for?"

"The chance is too good to miss—it's priceless . . ." She paused, then added, obliquely: "Storm, have you any idea at all of what Vesta thinks of you? You haven't snooped, I'm sure."

"No, and I don't intend to."

"Maybe you ought to," Joan snickered a little, "except that it would inflate your ego too much. It's hard to describe. It's not exactly love—and not exactly worship, either god-worship or hero-worship. It isn't exactly adoration, but it's very much stronger than mere admiration. A mixture of all these, perhaps, and half a dozen others, coupled with a simply unbelievable amount of *pride* that you are her friend. It's a peculiarly Vegian thing, that Tellurians simply do not feel. But here's why I'm so enthused. It has been over twenty years since any non-Vegian has attended one of these uniquely Vegian parties except as an outsider, and a Vegian party with outsiders looking on isn't a Vegian party at all. But we Storm, will be going as insiders!"

"Are you sure of that?"

"Positive. Oh, I know it isn't *us* she wants, but *you;* but that won't make any difference. As Vesta's friend—'friend' in this case having a very special meaning—you're in the center of the inner circle. As friends of yours, the rest of us are in, too. Not in the inner circle, perhaps, but well inside the outside circle, at least. See?"

"Dimly. 'A friend of a friend of a friend of a very good friend of mine,' eh? I've heard that ditty, but I never thought it meant anything."

"It does here. We're going to have a time. See you in about an hour?"

"Just about. I've got to check with Nordquist."

"Here I am, Storm," the Lensman's thought came in. Then, as Cloud went toward his quarters, it went on; "Just want to tell you we won't have anything for you to do here. This is going to be a straight combing job."

"That won't be too tough, will it? A Tellurian, sixty, tall, thin, grave, distinguished-looking . . . or maybe . . ."

"Exactly. You're getting the idea. Cosmeticians and plastic surgery. He could look like a Crevenian, or thirty years old and two hundred pounds and slouchy. He could look like anything. He undoubtedly has a background so perfectly established that fifteen thoroughly honest Vegians would swear by eleven of their gods that he hasn't left his home town for ten years. So every intelligent being on Vegia who hasn't got a live tail, with live blood circulating in it, is going under the Lens and through the wringer if we have to keep Vegia in quarantine for a solid year. He is *not* going to get away from us this time."

"I'm betting on you, Nordquist. Clear ether!"

The Lensman signed off and Cloud, at the end of the specified hour, undressed and redressed and went to the computer room. All the others except Joe were already there.

"Hi, peoples!" Cloud called; then did a double-take. "Wow! And likewise, Yipes! How come the tri-di outfits didn't all collapse, Joan, when those two spectaculars took up cybernetics?"

"I'll never know, Storm." Joan shook her head wonderingly, then went on via thought; and Cloud felt her pang of sheer jealousy. "Why is it that big girls are always so much more beautiful than little ones? And the more clothes they take off the better they look? It simply isn't *fair!*"

Cloud's mind reached out and meshed with hers. "Sure

it is, sweetheart. They're beauties; you can't take that away from them . . ."

And beauties they certainly were. Helen, as has been said, was lissom and dark. Her hair was black, her eyes a midnight blue, her skin a deep, golden brown. Barbara, not quite as tall—five feet seven, perhaps—was equally beautifully proportioned, and even more striking-looking. Her skin was tanned ivory, her eyes were gray, her hair was a shoulder-length, carefully-careless mass of gleaming, flowing, wavy silver.

". . . they've got a lot of stuff: but believe me, there are several grand lots of stuff they *haven't* got, too. I wouldn't trade half of you for either one of them—or both of them together."

"I believe that—at least, about *both* of them," Joan giggled mentally, "but how many men . . ."

"Well, how many men do you want?" Cloud interrupted.

"Touché, Storm . . . but do you really . . ."

What would have developed into a scene of purely mental lovemaking was put to an end by the arrival of Joe Mackay, who also paused and made appropriate noises of appreciation.

"But there's one thing I don't quite like about this deal," he said finally. "I'm not too easy in my mind about making love to a moll who is packing a Mark Twenty Eight DeLameter. The darn thing might go off."

"Keep your distance, then, Lieutenant Mackay!" Helen laughed. "Well, are we ready?"

They were. They left the ship and walked in a group through the throng of cheering Vegians toward the nearby, gaily-decorated stands in which the official greetings and thank-yous were to take place. Helen and Babs loved it; just as though they were parading as finalists in a beauty contest. Bob and Joe wished that they had stayed in the ship and kept their clothes on. Joan didn't quite know whether she liked this kind of thing or not. Of the six Tellurians, only Neal Cloud had had enough experience in public near-nudity so that it made no difference. And Vesta?

Vesta was fairly reveling—openly, unashamedly reveling—in the spotlight with her Tellurian friends. They reached the center stand, were ushered with many flourishes to a reserved section already partly filled by Captain Ross and the lesser officers and crewmen of the good-will-touring Patrol ship *Vortex Blaster II*. Not all of the officers, of course, since many had to stay aboard, and comparatively few of the crew; for many men insist on wearing Tellurian garmenture and refuse to tan their hides under ultra-violet radiation—and no untanned white Tellurian skin can take with impunity more than a few minutes of giant Vega's blue-white fury.

Of the ceremonies themselves, nothing need be said; such things being pretty much of a piece, wherever, whenever, or for whatever reason held. When they were over, Vesta gathered her six friends together and led them to the edge of the roped-off area. There she uttered a soundless (to Tellurian ears) whistle, whereupon a group of Vegian youths and girls formed a wedge around the seven and drove straight through the milling crowd to its edge. There, by an evidently pre-arranged miracle, they found enough 'copters to carry them all.

Chapter 16

VEGIAN JUSTICE

THE NEARER THEY got to their destination the more fidgety Vesta became. "Oh, I *hope* Zambkptkn could get away and be there by now—I haven't seen him for over half a year!"

"Who?" Helen asked.

"My brother. Zamke, you'd better call him, you can pronounce that. The police officer, you know."

"I thought you saw him this morning?" Joan said.

"I saw my other brothers and sisters, but not him—he was tied up on a job. He wasn't sure just when he could get away tonight."

The 'copter dropped sharply. Vesta seized Cloud's arm and pointed. "That's where we're going; that big building with the landing-field on the roof. The Caravanzerie. Zee?" In moments of emotion or excitement, most of Vesta's sibilants reverted to Z's.

"I see. And this is your Great White Way?"

It was, but it was not white. Instead, it was a blaze of red, blue, green, yellow—all the colors of the spectrum. And crowds! On foot, on bicycles, on scooters, motorbikes, and motortricycles, in cars and in 'copters, it seemed impossible that *anything* could move in such a press as that. And as the air-cab approached its destination Neal Cloud, space-hardened veteran and skillful flyer though he was, found himself twisting wheels, stepping on pedals, and cutting in braking jets, none of which were there.

How that jockey landed his heap and got it into the air again all in one piece without dismembering a single Vegian, Cloud never did quite understand. Blades were scant fractional inches from blades and rotors; people were actually shoved aside by the tapering bumpers of the cab as it hit the deck; but nothing happened. This, it seemed, was *normal!*

The group re-formed and in flying-wedge fashion as before, gained the elevators and finally the ground floor and the ballroom. Here Cloud drew his first full breath for what seemed like hours. The ball-room was tremendous—and it was less than three-quarters filled.

Just inside the doorway Vesta paused, sniffing delicately. "He *is* here—come on!" She beckoned the six to follow her and rushed ahead, to be met at the edge of the clear space in head-on collision. Brother and sister embraced fervently for about two seconds. Then, reaching down, the man broke his sister's grip and flipped her around sidewise, through half of a vertical circle, so that her feet pointed straight up. Then, with a sharp *"Blavzkt!"* he snapped into a back flip.

"Blavzkt—Zemp!" she shouted back, bending beautifully into such an arch that, as his feet left the floor, hers landed almost exactly where his had been an instant before. Then for a full minute and a half the joyous pair pinwheeled, without moving from the spot; while the dancers on the floor, standing still now, applauded enthusiastically with stamping, hand-clapping, whistles, cat-calls, and screams.

Vesta stopped the exhibition finally, and led her brother toward Cloud and Joan. The music resumed, but the dancers did not. Instead, they made a concerted rush for the visitors, surrounding them in circles a dozen deep.

Vesta, with both arms wrapped tightly around Cloud and her tail around Joan, shrieked a highly consonantal sentence—which Cloud knew meant "Lay off these two for a couple of minutes, you howling hyenas, they're mine"—then, switching to English: "Go ahead, you four, and have fun!"

The first two men to lay hands on the two tall Tellurian beauties were, by common consent and without argument, their first partners. Two of the Vegian girls, however, were not so polite. Both had hold of Joe, one by each arm, and stood there spitting insults at each other past his face until a man standing near by snapped a few words at them and flipped a coin. The two girls, each still maintaining her grip, leaned over eagerly to see for themselves the result of the toss. The loser promptly relinquished her hold on Joe and the winner danced away with him.

"Oh, this is *wonderful,* Storm!" Joan thought. "We've been *accepted*—we're the first group I ever actually *knew* of to really break through the crust."

The Vegians moved away. Vesta released her captives and turned to her brother.

"Captain Cloud, Doctor Janowick, I present to you my brother Zamke," she said. Then, to her brother: "They have been very good to me, Zambktpkn, both of them, but especially the captain. You know what he did for me."

"Yes, I know." The brother spoke the English "S" with barely a trace of hardness. He shook Cloud's hand firmly, then bent over the hand, spreading it out so that the palm covered his face, and inhaled deeply. Then, straightening up: "For what you have done for my sister, sir, I thank you. As she has said, your scent is pleasing and will be remembered long, enshrined in the Place of Pleasant Odors of our house."

Turning to Joan, and omitting the handshake, he repeated the performance and bowed—and when an adult male Vegian sets out to make a production of bowing, it is a production well worth seeing.

Then, with the suddenest and most complete change of manner either Cloud or Joan had ever seen he said: "Well, now that the formalities have been taken care of, Joan, how about us hopping a couple of skips around the floor?"

Joan was taken slightly aback, but rallied quickly. "Why, I'd love it ... but not knowing either the steps or the music, I'm afraid I couldn't follow you very well."

"Oh that won't make any ..." Zamke began, but Vesta drowned him out.

"Of *course* it won't make any difference, Joan!" she exclaimed. "Just go ahead and dance any way you want to. He'll match your steps—and if he so much as touches one of your slippers with his big, fat feet, I'll choke him to death with his own tail!"

"And I suppose it is irrefutable that you can and will dance with me with equal dexterity, aplomb, and insouciance?" Cloud asked Vesta, quizzically, after Joan and Zamke had glided smoothly out into the throng.

"You zaid it, little chum!" Vesta exclaimed, gleefully, "And I know what all those words mean, too, and if I ztep on either one of *your* feet I'll choke *my* zelf to death with my *own* tail, zo there!"

Snuggling up to him blissfully, Vesta let him lead her into the crowd. She of course was a superb dancer; so much so that she made him think himself a much better dancer than he really was. After a few minutes, when he was beginning to relax, he felt an itchy, tickling touch— something almost impalpable was creeping up his naked back—the fine, soft fur of the extreme tip of Vesta's ubiquitous tail!

He grabbed for it, but, fast as he was, Vesta was faster, and she shrieked with glee as he missed the snatch.

"See here, young lady," he said, with mock sternness, "if you don't keep your tail where it belongs I'm going to wrap it around your lovely neck and tie it into a bow-knot."

Vesta sobered instantly. "Oh ... do you *really* think I'm lovely, Captain Nealcloud—my neck, I mean?"

"No doubt about it," Cloud declared. "Not only your neck—all of you. You are most certainly one of the most beautiful things I ever saw."

"Oh, thanks ... I hadn't ..." she stared into his eyes for moments, as if trying to decide whether he really meant it or was merely being polite; then, deciding that he did mean it, she closed her eyes, let her head sink down onto his shoulder, and began to purr blissfully; still matching perfectly whatever motions he chose to make.

In a few minutes, however, they heard a partially-stifled shriek and a soprano voice, struggling with laughter, rang out.

"Vesta!"

"Yes, Babs?"

"What do you do about this tail-tickling business? I never had to cope with anything like *that* before!"

"Bite him!" Vesta called back, loudly enough for half the room to hear. "Bite him good and hard, on the end of the tail. If you can't catch the tail, bite his ear. Bite it good."

"Bite him? Why, I *couldn't*—not *possibly!"*

"Well, then give him the knee, or clout him a good, solid tunk on the nose. Or better yet; tell him you won't dance with him any more—he'll be good."

"Now you tell us what to do about tail-ticklers," Cloud said then. "S'pose I'd take a good bite at *your* ear?"

"I'd bite you right back," said Vesta, gleefully, "and I bet you'd taste just as nice as you smell."

The dance went on, and Cloud finally, by the aid of both Vesta and Zamke, did finally manage to get one dance with Joan. And, as he had known he would, he enjoyed it immensely. So did she.

"Having fun, chum? I never saw you looking so starry-eyed before."

"Oh, brother!" she breathed. "To say that I was never the belle of any ball in my schooldays is the understatement of the century, but here ... can you imagine it, Storm, *me* actually outshining Barbara Benton and Helen Worthington both at once?"

"Sure I can. I told you . . ."

"Of course it's probably because their own women are so big that I'm a sort of curiosity," she rushed on, "but whatever the reason, this dance is going down in my memory book in great big letters in the reddest ink I can find!"

"Good for you—hail the conquering heroine!" he applauded. "It'll do you good to have your ego inflated a little. But what do *you* do about this tail-tickling routine?"

"Oh, I grab their tails"—with her sense of perception, she could, of course—"and when they try to wiggle them free I wiggle back at them, like this," she demonstrated, "and we have a perfectly wonderful time."

"Wow! I'll bet you do—and when I get you home, you shameless . . ."

"Sorry, Storm, my friend," the big Vegian who cut in wasn't sorry at all, and he and Cloud both knew it. "You can dance with Joan any time and we can't. So loosen all clamps, friend. Grab him, Vzelkt!"

Vzelkt grabbed. So, in about a minute, did another Vegian girl; and then after a few more minutes, it was Vesta's turn again. No other girl could dance with him more than once, but Vesta, by some prearranged priority, could have him once every ten minutes.

"Where's your brother, Vesta?" he asked once. "I haven't seen him for an hour."

"Oh, he had to go back to the police station. They're all excited and working all hours. They're chasing Public Enemy Number One—a Tellurian, they think he is, named Fairchild—why?" as Cloud started, involuntarily, in the circle of her arm. "Do you know him?"

"I know *of* him, and that's enough." Then, in thought: "Did you get that, Nordquist?"

"I got it." Cloud was, as the Lensman had said that he would be, under surveillance every second. "Of course, this one may not be Fairchild, since there are three or four other suspects in other places, but from the horrible time we and the Vegians both are having, trying to locate this bird, I'm coming to think he is."

The dance went on until, some hours later, there was an unusual tumult and confusion at the door.

"Oh, the police are calling Vesta—something has happened!" his companion exclaimed. "Let's rush over—oh, hurry!"

Cloud hurried; but, as well as hurrying, he sent his sense of perception on ahead, and meshed his mind imperceptibly with Vesta's as well.

Her mind was a queerly turbid, violently turbulent mixture of emotions: hot with a furiously passionate lust for personal, tooth-and-claw-revenge; at the same time icily cold with the implacable, unswervable resolve of the dedicated, remorseless, and merciless killer.

"Are you sure, beyond all doubt, that this is the garment of my brother's slayer?" Vesta was demanding.

"I am sure," the Vegian policeman replied. "Not only did Zambkptkn hold it pierced by the first and fourth fingers of his left hand—the sign positive, as you know—but an eyewitness verified the scent and furnished descriptions. The slayer was dressed as an Aldebaranian, which accounts for the size of the garment your brother could seize before he died; his four bodyguards as Tellurians, with leather belts and holsters for their blasters."

"QX." Vesta accepted a pair of offered shears and began to cut off tiny pieces of the cloth. As each piece began to fall it was seized in mid-air by a Vegian man or girl who immediately ran away with it. And in the meantime other Vegians, forming into a long line, ran past Vesta, each taking a quick sniff and running on, out into the street. Cloud, reaching outside the building with his perceptors, saw that all vehicular traffic had paused. A Vegian stood on the walk-way, holding a bit of cloth pinched between thumb and finger-nail. All passersby, on foot or in any kind of vehicle, would pause, sniff at the cloth, and—apparently—go on about their business.

But Cloud, after reading Vesta's mind and the policeman's, turned as white as his space-tan would permit. In less than an hour almost every Vegian in that city of over eight million would know the murderer by scent and would be sniffing eagerly for him; and when any one of them *did* find him . . .

Except for the two Vegians and the six Tellurians, the vast hall was now empty. Vesta was holding a pose Cloud had never before seen—stiffly erect, with her tail wrapped tightly around her body.

"Can they get a scent—a *reliable* scent, I mean—that fast?" Cloud asked.

"Zertainly," Vesta's voice was cold, level, almost uninflected. "How long would it take you to learn that an egg you started to eat was rotten? The man who wore this shirt is a class A Triple Prime stinker—his odor is recognizable instantly and anywhere."

"But as to the rest of it—*don't* do this thing, Vesta! Let the law handle it."

"The law comes second. He killed my brother; it is my right and my privilege to kill him . . ."

Cloud became conscious of the fact that Joan was in his mind. "You been here all along?" he flashed.

"In or near. You and I are one, you know," and Vesta's voice went on:

". . . and besides, the law is merciful. Its death is instant. Under my claws and teeth he will live for hours—for a full day, I hope."

"But officer, can't *you* do something?"

"Nothing. The law comes second. As she has said, it is her right and her privilege."

"But it's suicide, man—sheer *suicide*. You know that, don't you?"

"Not necessarily. She will not be working alone. Whether she lives or dies, however, it is still her right and. her privilege."

Cloud switched to thought. "Nordquist, *you* can stop this if you want to. *Do* it."

"I can't, and you know I can't. The Patrol does not and cannot interfere in purely planetary affairs."

"You intend, then," Cloud demanded furiously, "to let this girl put her naked hands and teeth up against four trigger-happy gunnies with DeLameters?"

"Just that. There's nothing else I or any other Patrolman can do. To interfere in this one instance would alienate half the planets of Civilization and set the Patrol back five hundred years."

"Well, even though I'm a Patrolman—of sorts—*I* can do something about it!" Cloud blazed, "and by God, I will!"

"We will, you mean, and we *will*, too," Joan's thought came forcibly at first, then became dubious: "That is, if it doesn't mean getting *you* blasted, too."

"Just what?" Nordquist's thought was sharp. "Oh, I see . . . and, being a Vegian, as well as a Patrolman, and the acknowledged friend of both the dead man and his sister . . ."

"Who's a Vegian?" Cloud demanded.

"You are, and so are the other five of your group, as you would have been informed if the party had not been broken up so violently. Honorary Vegians, for life."

"Why, I never *heard* of such a thing!" Joan exclaimed, "and I studied them for years!"

"No, you never did," Nordquist agreed. "There haven't been many honorary Vegians, and to my certain knowledge, not one of them has ever talked. Vegians are very strongly psychic in picking their off-world friends."

"You mean to tell me that that bleached blonde over

there won't spill everything she knows fifteen minutes after we leave here?" Cloud demanded.

"Just that. You can't judge character by hair, even if it were bleached, which it isn't. You owe her an apology, Storm."

"If you say so, I do, and I hereby apologize, but . . ."

"But to get back to the subject," the Lensman went on, narrowing his thought down so sharply as to exclude Joan, "You can do something. You're the *only* one who can. Such being the case, and since you are no longer indispensable. I withdraw all objections. Go ahead."

Cloud started a thought, but Joan blanked him out. "Lensman, has Storm been sending—*can* he send information to you that *I* can't dig out of his mind?"

"Very easily. He is an exceptionally fine tuner."

"I'm sorry, Joanie," Cloud thought, hastily, "but it sounded too much like bragging to let you in on. However, you're in from now on."

Then, aloud, "Vesta, I'm staying with you," he said, quietly.

"I was sure you would," she said, as quietly. "You are my friend and Zamke's. Although your customs are not exactly like ours, a man of your odor does not desert his friends."

Cloud turned then to the four lieutenants, who stood close-grouped. "Will you four kids please go back to the ship, and take Joan with you?"

"Not on Thursdays, Storm," Joe said, pointing to an inconspicuous bronze button set into a shoulder-strap. "We both rate Blaster Expert First. Count us in," and Bob added:

"Joan has been telling us an earful, and what she didn't tell us a couple of Vegian boys did. The Three Honorary Vegian Musketeers; that's us. Lead on, d'Artagnan!"

"Bob and Joe are staying, too, Vesta," Cloud said then.

"Of course. I'm sorry I didn't get to tell you myself about being adopted, but I knew somebody would. But you, Joan and Barbara and Helen, you three had better go back to the ship. You can be of no use here."

Two of them were willing enough to go, but:

"Where Neal Cloud goes, I go," Joan said, and there was no doubt whatever that she meant exactly that.

"Why?" Vesta demanded. "Commander Cloud, the fastest gunman in all space, is necessary for the success of this our mission. He can, from a cold, bell-tone start, at thirty yards, burn the centers out of six irregularly-spaced targets . . ."

"Nordquist! Lay off! What in *hell* do you think you're doing?" Cloud thought, viciously.

"I don't think—I *know*," came instant reply. "Do you want her hanging on⁻your left arm when the blasting starts? This is the only *possible* way Joan Janowick can be handled. Lay off yourself!" and Vesta's voice went calmly on:

". . . in exactly two hundred and forty nine mils. Lieutenant Mackay and Lieutenant Ingalls, although perhaps not absolutely necessary, are highly desirable. They are fast enough, and are of deadly accuracy. When either of them shoots a man in a crowd, however large, that one man dies, and not a dozen bystanders. Now just what good would *you* be, Lieutenant-Commander Janowick? Can you fire a blaster with any one of these men? Or bite a man's throat out with me?"

For probably the first time in her life, Joan Janowick stood mute.

"And suppose you *do* come along," Vesta continued relentlessly. "With *you* at his side, in the line of fire, do you suppose . . ."

"Just a minute—shut up, Vesta!" Cloud ordered, roughly. "Listen, all of you. The Lensman is doing this, not Vesta, and I'll be damned if I'll let anybody, not even a Lensman, bedevil my Joan this way. So, Joan, wherever we go, you can come along. All I ask is, you'll keep a little ways back?"

"Of course I will, Storm," and Joan crept into the shelter of his arm.

"Ha—I thought you'd pop off at about this point," Nordquist's thought came chattily into Cloud's mind. "Good work, my boy; you've consolidated your position no end."

"Well, what do we do now?" Joe Mackay broke the somewhat sticky silence that followed.

"We wait," Vesta said, calmly. "We wait right here until we receive news."

They waited; and, as they waited the tension mounted and mounted. Before it became intolerable, however, the news came in, and Cloud, reading Vesta's mind as the ultra-sonic information was received, relayed it to other Tellurians. The murderer and his four bodyguards were at that moment entering a theater less than one city block away . . .

"Why, they *couldn't* be!" Helen protested. "*Nobody* could be *that* stupid . . . or . . . I wonder . . .?"

"I wonder, too." This from Joan. "Yes, it would be the supremely clever thing to do; the perfect place to hide for a few hours while the worst of the storm blows over and they can complete their planned getaway. Provided, of course, they're out-worlders and thus don't know what we Vegians can do with our wonderful sense of smell. Of course they aren't a Tellurian and four Aldebaranians any more, are they?"

"No, they are five Centralians now. Perfectly innocent. They think their blasters are completely hidden under those long over shirts, but now and again a bulge shows—they've still got blasters on their hips. The theater's crowded, but the five friends want to sit together. The manager thinks it could be arranged, by paying a small gratuity to a few seat-holders who would like to make a fast credit that way . . . he'll place them and it's almost time for us to go. 'Bye, Joanie—stay back, remember!" and she was in his arms.

"How about it, Helen?" Joe asked. "Surely you're going to kiss your Porthos goodbye, aren't you?"

"Of a surety, m'enfant!" she exclaimed, and did so with enthusiasm. "But it's more like Aramis, I think—he kissed everybody, you know—and since I'm not hooked like Joan is—yet—don't think that this is establishing a precedent."

"Well, Babs, that leaves you and me." Bob reached out—she was standing beside him—and pulled her close. "QX?"

"Why, I . . . I guess so." Barbara blushed furiously. "But Bob . . . is it really *dangerous?*" she whispered.

"I don't know. Not very, really, I don't think. At least I certainly *hope* not. But blasters are *not* cap-pistols, you know, and whenever one goes off it can raise pure hell. Why? Would you really miss me?"

"You *know* I would, Bob," and her kiss had more fervor than either she or he would have believed possible a few minutes before. And at its end she laughed, shakily, and blushed again as she said, "I've got sort of used to having you around, so be *sure* and come back."

They left the building and walked rapidly along a strangely quiet street to the theater. Without a word they were ushered up a short flight of stairs.

"Hold up, Vesta!" Cloud thought sharply. "We can't see a thing—wait a couple of minutes."

They waited five minutes, during which time they learned exactly where the enemy were and discussed every detail of the proposed attack.

"I *still* can't see well enough to shoot," Cloud said then. "Can they give us a little glow of light?"

They could. By almost imperceptible increments the thick, soft blackness was relieved.

"That's enough." The light, such as it was, steadied.

"Ready?" Vesta's voice was a savage growl, low, deep in her throat.

"Ready."

"No more noise, then."

They walked forward to the balcony's edge, leaned over it, looked down. Directly beneath Vesta's head was seated a man in Centralian garb; four others were behind, in front of, and at each side of, their chief.

"Now!" Vesta yelled, and flung herself over the low railing.

At her shout four Vegians ripped four Centralian shirts apart, seized four hip-holstered blasters, and shouted with glee—but they shouted too soon. For the real gun-slick, then as now, did not work from the hip, but out of his sleeve; and these were four of the coldest, fastest killers to be found throughout the far flung empire of Boskone. Thus, all four flashed into action even before they began rising to their feet.

But so did Storm Cloud; and his heavy weapon was already out and ready. He knew what those hands were doing, in the instant of their starting to do it, and his DeLameter flamed three times in what was practically one very short blast. He had to move a little before he could sight on the fourth guard—Vesta's furiously active body was in the way—so Joe and Bob each got a shot, too. Three bolts of lightning hit that luckless wight at once, literally cremating him in air as he half-crouched, bringing his blaster to bear on the catapulting thing attacking his boss.

When Vesta went over the rail she did not jump to the floor below. Instead, her hands locked on the edge; her feet dug into the latticework of the apron. She squatted. Her tail flashed down, wrapping itself twice around the zwilnik's neck. She heaved, then, and climbed with everything she had; and as she stood upright on the railing, eager hands reached down to help her tail lift its burden up into the balcony. The man struck the floor with a thud and Vesta jumped at him.

"Your fingers first—one at a time," she snarled; and, seizing a hand, she brought it toward her mouth.

She paused then as if thunderstruck; a dazed, incredulous expression spreading over her face. Bending over, she felt, curiously, tenderly, of his neck.

"Why, he . . . he's *dead!*" she gasped. "His neck . . . it's . . . it's *broken!* From such a little, tiny pull as *that?* Why, *anybody* ought to have a stronger neck than *that!*"

She straightened up; then, as a crowd of Vegians and the Tellurian women came up, she became instantly her old, gay self. "Well, shall we all go back and finish our dance?"

"What?" Cloud demanded. "After *this?*"

"Why certainly," Vesta said, brightly. "I'm sorry, of course, that I killed him so quickly, but it doesn't make any real difference. Zamke is avenged; he can now enjoy himself. We'll join him in a few years, more or less. Until then, what would you do? What you call 'mourn'?"

"I don't know . . . I simply don't know," Cloud said, slowly, his arm tightening around Joan's supple waist. "I thought I'd seen everything, but . . . I suppose you can have somebody take that body out to the ship, so they can check it for identity?"

"Oh, yes, I'll do that. Right away. You're sure you don't want to dance any more?"

"Very sure, my dear. *Very* sure. All *I* want to do is take Joan back to the ship."

"QX. I won't see you again this trip, then; your hours are so funny. I'll send for my things. And I won't say good-bye, Captain Nealcloud and you other wonderful people, because we'll see each other again, soon and often. Just so-long, and thanks tremendously for all you have done for me."

And Vesta the Vegian strode away, purring contentedly to herself—tail high.

Chapter 17

THE CALL

THE LENSMEN and their Patrolmen, having made sure that the body of Zamke's murderer was in fact that of the long-sought Fairchild, went unostentatiously about their various businesses.

The six Tellurians, although shaken no little by their climactic experience on Vegia, returned soon to normal and resumed their accustomed routines of life—with certain outstanding variations. Thus, Helen and Joe flirted joyously and sparred dextrously, but neither was ever to be found tete-a-tete with anyone else. And thus, Bob and Barbara, neither flirting nor sparring, became quietly but enthusiastically inseparable. And thus, between Joan and Cloud, so close even before Vegia, the bonding became so tight that their two minds were, to all intents and purposes, one mind.

The week on Vegia was over. The *Vortex Blaster II* was loafing through the void at idling speed. Cloud was pacing the floor in his office. Joan, lounging in a deeply-cushioned chair with legs stuck out an an angle of forty-five degrees to each other, was smoking a cigarette and watching him, with her eyes agleam.

"Confound it, I wish they'd hurry up with that fine-tooth," he said, flipping his half-smoked cigarette at a receptacle and paying no attention to the fact that he missed it by over a foot. "How can I tell Captain Ross where to go when I don't know myself?"

"That's one thing I just *love* about you, my pet," Joan drawled. "You're so wonderfully, so superhumanly *patient*. You know as well as I do that the absolutely irreducible minimum of time is twenty-six minutes from now, and that they'll probably find something they'll want to study for a minute or so after they get there. So light somewhere, why don't you, and unseethe yourself?"

"Touché, Joan." He sat down with a thump. "Has Doctor Janowick a prescription specific for the ailment?"

"Nothing else but, chum. That tight-linkage snooping that we've been going to try, but never had time for. Let's start on Helen and Barbara. I've snooped them repeatedly, of course, but our fusion of minds, theoretically, should be able to pick their minds apart cell by cell; to tap their subconscious ancestral memories, even—if there are such things—for a thousand generations back."

He looked at her curiously. "You know, I think you must have some ghoul blood in you somewhere? I tell you again, those girls are *friends* of ours!"

"So what?" she grinned at him, entirely unabashed. "You'll have to get rid of that squeamishness some day; it's the biggest roadblock there is on the Way of Knowledge. If not them, how would Nadine suit you?"

"Worse yet. She's just as good at this business as we are, maybe better, and she probably wouldn't like it."

"You may have something there. We'll save her for last, and call on her formally, with announcements and everything. Vesta, then?"

"*Now* you're squeaking, little mouse. But no deep digging for a while. We'll take it easy and light—we don't want to do any damage we may not be able to undo. As I told you before, my brain is firing on altogether too damn many barrels that I simply don't know what are doing. Let's go."

They fused their minds—an effortless process now—and were at their objective instantaneously.

Vesta was primping; enjoying sensuously the physical feel of her physical body even as dozens of parts of speech of dozens of different languages went through her racing mind. And, one layer down, she was wishing she were old enough to be a newlywed; wishing she had a baby of her own . . . babies were so cute and soft and cuddlesome . . .

Then Tommie. Cloud and Joan enjoyed with her the strong, rank, sense-satisfying flavor of a Venerian cigar and studied with her the intricate electronic equations of a proposed modification of the standard deep-space drive. And, one layer down, the Tomingan engineer, too, was thinking of love and of babies. What was all this space hopping getting her, anyway? It didn't stop the ache, fill the void, satisfy the longing. As soon as this cruise was over, she was going back to Tominga, tell Hanko she was ready, and settle down. A husband and a family did tie a woman down something fierce—but what price freedom to wander when you wake up in the middle of the night from dreaming of a baby in your arms, only to find the baby isn't there?

Then Thlaskan and Maluleme. They were seated, arms around each other, on a davenport in their own home on Chickladoria. They were not talking, merely feeling. They were deeply, truly, tremendously in love. In the man's mind there was a background of his work, of pilotry, of orbits and charts and computations. There was a flash of sincere liking for Cloud, the best boss and the finest figure-man he had ever known; but practically all of his mind was full of love for the wonderful woman at his side. In hers, at the moment, there were only two things; love of her husband and longing for the child which she might already have succeeded in conceiving . . .

Cloud wrenched their linked minds away.

"This is monstrous, Joan!"

"What's monstrous about it?" she asked, quietly. "Nothing. It isn't. Women *need* children, Storm. All women, everywhere. Now that I've found *you,* I can scarcely wait to have some myself. And listen, Storm, please. Before we visit Nadine, you *must* make up your mind to face facts— *any* kind of facts—without flinching and shying away and getting mental goose-bumps all over your psyche."

"I see what you mean. In a fully telepathic race there couldn't be any real privacy without a continuous block, and that probably wouldn't be very feasible."

"No, you *don't* see what I mean. You aren't even on the right road—your whole *concept* is wrong. There couldn't be any *thought,* even of privacy, no *conception* of such a thing. *Think* a minute! From birth—from the very birth of the whole race—full and open meetings of minds must have been the norm of thought. That kind of thing is—must be—what Nadine is accustomed to at home."

"Hm . . . I never thought . . . you go see her, Joan, and I'll stay home."

"What good would *that* do? Whatever you may be, my dear, I know darn well you're *not* stupid."

"Not exactly stupid, maybe, but I haven't thought this thing through the way you have . . . of course, if she's half as good as we know she is, she's read us both already, clear down to the footings of our foundations . . . but this thing of a *full* meeting of minds with anybody but you . . ."

"You haven't a thing to hide, you know. At least, *I* know, whether you do or not."

"No? How do you figure that? Maybe *you* think so, but . . . I've tried, of course, but I've failed a lot oftener than I succeeded."

"Who hasn't? You're not unique, my dear. Shall we go?"

"We might as well, I guess . . . I'm as ready as I ever will be . . . I'll try, but . . ."

"Please do, Master," came Nadine's quiet, composed thought, in a vein completely foreign to her usual attitude of self-sufficient aloofness. "I have been observing; studying with awe and with wonder. If you will so deign, revered Master, come fully into my mind."

"Deign?" Cloud demanded. "What kind of a thought is that, Nadine, from you to me?"

"Deign." Nadine repeated, firmly. Deeply moved, she was feeling and sending a solemnity of respect Cloud had never before experienced. "My powers are ordinary, since I am of Type One. The two greatest Masters of Manarka are Fives, and have been the greatest Masters of the past. This is the first time I have ever encountered a mind of a type higher than Five. Come in, sir, I plead."

Cloud went in, and his first flash of comparison was that it was like diving into the pellucid depths of a clean, cool, utterly transparent mountain lake. This mind was *so* different from Joan's! Joan's was rich, warmly sympathetic, tender and emphatic, yet it was full of dark corners, secret nooks, recesses, and automatic blocks . . . Huh? He had thought her mind as open as a book, but it wasn't . . . On the other hand, Nadine's was wide open by nature. It was cool, poised—although at the moment uncomfortably worshipful—and utterly, *shockingly* open!

His second thought was that Joan was no longer with him. She was there, in a sense, but *outside*, some way; she wasn't in Nadine's mind the way he was.

"I'll say I'm not!" Joan agreed, fervently. "Thank God!

I don't know what you did or how you did it, but whe
you went in you peeled me off like the skin of a banana
and I was clinging like a leech, too. I'm on the outside,
looking in. Did you see how he did it, Nadine?"

"No, but since I am only a One, such insight would not
be expected. I have called the Fives, and they come."

"We are here." Two close-linked minds linked themselves with the two already so closely linked. Each of the
two visitors was grave, kindly, and old with an appalling
weight of years; each mind bore an appalling freight of
knowledge both mundane and esoteric. "We are here,
fellow Master of Thought, to be of aid to you in the
clarification of your newly-awakened mind, to the end
that, in a future time, your superior powers will assist us
along Paths of Truth which we could not otherwise trav-
erse."

"Will you please tell me what this is all about?" Cloud
asked. "Starting at the beginning and using words of as
few syllables as possible?"

"Gladly. It has been known for some time that
Janowick is Type Three. Self-developed, partially-
developed, under-developed, struggling against she knew
not what, but still a Three. Now Threes as such, while
eminently noteworthy, are by no means phenomenal.
There are some hundreds of Threes now alive. Being
noteworthy, she has been watched. In time she would have
completed her development and would have taken her
rightful place in the School of Thought.

"You, however, have been a complete enigma to our
most penetrant minds. Since no mind of lower type than
Three can be an instantaneous calculator, it was clear that
you were, basically, at least a Three. However, unlike
other Threes, you did nothing whatever to develop the
latent, potential abilities of whatever type you might be.
Instead and excepting only the small and unimportant
item of computation, you used the tremendous powers of
your mind, not for any constructive purpose whatever, but
only for the application of such rigid controls and suppres-
sions that all the tremendous abilities you should have
shown remained completely dormant and inert.

"Nor could we do anything about it. We tried, but you
have blocks that not even the full power of two linked
Fives can crack; which fact showed that you are of a type

gher than Five. We were about to come to you in
person, to plead with you, when you met Three Janowick
and opened to her your hitherto impregnably-sealed inner
mind. She does not know, and you do not know, what you
jointly did; which was, in effect, to break and to dissolve
the bindings which had been shackling both your minds.
That brings us to the present. It has now become clear
that you have been Called."

"Called?" Cloud winced, physically and mentally. No
man likes to be reminded that he failed Lensman's Exam.
"You're wrong. I didn't make even the first round."

"We did not mean the Call of the Lens. There are many
Calls, of which that is only one. Nor is it the highest, as
we have just discovered, in certain little-known aspects of
that vast thing we call the mind. For, to the best of our
knowledge, no Lensman of the present or of the past is or
was of a type higher than Five. The exact nature of your
Call is as yet obscure."

"I'd like to buy that, but I'm afraid it's ..." Cloud
paused. Until he'd met Joan, he'd supposed his mind
ordinary enough. Since then, however ... all those extra
barrels ...

"Exactly. We are specialists of the mind, young man. We
perceive your mind, not as it is, but as it should be and
will be. It should have and will have a penetrance, a
range, a flexibility of directive force, and, above all, a
scope of heights and depths we have never encountered
before. It is eminently clear that you, and, very probably,
Three Janowick as well, have been developed each for
some specific Purpose in the Great Scheme of Things."

"A *Purpose?*" Cloud demanded. "*What* purpose? What
could *I* do? What could both of us together do?"

"We can not surely know."

"Does that mean that you can make a well-informed
guess? If so, let's have it."

"There is a very high probability that Three Janowick
was developed specifically to develop you; to pierce and to
dissolve those hampering barriers which were amenable to
no other force. Concerning you, there are several possibilities, none of which have any very high degree of probability, since you are unique. The one we prefer at the
moment is that you are to become the greatest living
Master of Thought; the Prime Expounder of the Truth.

But that is of no importance now, since in due time it will be revealed. Of present import is the fact that both your minds are confused, cloudy, and disorderly. We offer our services in reorienting and ordering them."

"We'd like that very much; but first, if I am going to develop into a mental giant of some kind—frankly, I have my doubts—why did it wait this long to show up?"

"The answer to that question is plain and simple. There is a time for everything, and everything that happens does so in its exact time. Let us to work."

They worked, and when it was done:

"We would like to dwell with you for long," the ancient Fives said, "but the time for such a boon will not come until you are much emptier of cares and much fuller of years."

The Fives split apart. "How do you type this new Master, brother? A full Six, I say."

"A full Six he is, brother, beyond doubt."

They fused. "In a time to come, Six Cloud, we will, with your help and under your guidance, explore many and many a Path of Truth which without you would remain closed. But we observe that there is about to arrive a message which is to you of some present concern. Until a day, then."

The Fives disappeared as suddenly as they had come, and Cloud began to test and to exercise the new capabilities of his mind; in much the same fashion as that in which a good belly-dancer exercises and trains each individual muscle of her torso.

"But what . . . I didn't . . . How did they . . .?" Joan shook her head violently and started all over again. "What did they *do* to us, Storm?"

"I don't know. It was over my head like a lunar dome. But it—whatever it was—was exactly what the doctor ordered. I can handle all those extra barrels now like van-Buskirk handles a space-axe. How about you?"

"Me, too—I think." She hugged his arm. "It shocked me speechless for a minute, but it's all settling into place fast . . . But that message? They could get it from your mind that you expected that fine-tooth pretty soon, but how could they know it's coming in right now? We don't— in fact, we know it *can't* get here for a good ten minutes yet."

"I wish I knew. I'd like to think they were bluffing, but I know they weren't."

"Hi Storm and Joan!" Philip Strong's face appeared upon a screen, his voice came from a speaker. "The Survey ship has just reported. Technical dope is still coming in. Communications is buzzing you a tape of the whole thing, but to save time I thought I'd call you and give you the gist. To make it short and unsweet, there's nothing there."

"Nothing there!"

"Nothing for you. They gave it the works, and all there is to that system, Cahuita, they call it, is one red dwarf with one red microdwarf circling it planetwise."

"Huh?" Cloud demanded. "Come again, chief."

"How could a micro-sun like that exist?" Strong laughed. "That had me bothered, too, but they've got a lot of cosmological double-talk to cover it. It's terrifically radioactive, they say. And even so, it's temporary. In the cosmological sense, that is; a hundred million years or so either way don't matter."

"No solid planets at all? Not even one?"

"Not one. Nothing really liquid, even. Incandescent, very highly radioactive gas. Nothing solid bigger than your thumb within twelve parsecs."

"And so it never has been solid, and won't be for millions of years . . . Oh, *Damn!* Well, thanks, chief, a lot."

Then, as the Lensman signed off: "Joan, that puts us deeper in the dark than ever. We had twice too many unknowns and only half enough knowns before, and this really tears it. Well, it was a very nice theory while it lasted."

"It's *still* a very nice theory, Storm."

"Huh? How do you figure that?"

"I don't have to figure it. Listen! First, that point is significant, with a probability greater than point nine nine nine. Second, no other point in space has a probability as great as point zero zero one. Whoever or whatever was— is—there, the Survey ship missed. We've got to go there ourselves, Storm. We simply *must.*"

" 'Was' is probably right. Whatever used to be there is gone . . . but that doesn't make sense, either . . . that planet has *never* been solid, Joan . . ." Cloud got up and began to pace the floor. "Dammit, Joan, *nothing* can live on a planet like that."

"Life as we know it, no."

"What do you mean by that?"

"Only that I am trying to keep an open mind. We simply haven't enough data."

"Do you think you and I have got jets enough to find data that the Patrol's best experts missed?"

"I don't know. All I am sure of, Doctor Neal Cloud, is this: If we *don't* go, we'll both wish we had, to the day we die."

"You're probably right . . . but I haven't got a glimmering of an idea as to what we're going to look for."

"I don't know whether I have or not, but we've simply *got* to go. Even if we don't find anything, we will at least have tried. Besides, your most pressing work is done, so you can take the time . . . and besides that . . . well, something those Fives said is bothering me terribly . . . the Purpose, you know . . . do you think . . .?"

"That my Purpose in Life is to go solve the mystery of the Red Dwarf and its Enigmatic Microcompanion?" he gibed. "Hardly. Furthermore, the coincidence of the Fives getting here just one jump ahead of the fine-tooth is much—*very* much—too coincidental."

Joan caught her breath and, if possible, paled whiter than before. "You may *think* you're joking, Storm, but you aren't. Believe me, you aren't. That's one of the things that are scaring me witless. You see, if I learned anything at all in my quite-a-few years of semantics, philosophy, and logic, it was that coincidence has no more reality than paradox has. Both are completely meaningless terms. Neither does or can exist."

Cloud paled, then. "You believe that *is* my purpose in life?" he demanded.

"Now it's you who are extrapolating." Joan laughed, albeit shakily. "To quote you, 'I merely stated a fact,' et cetera."

"Facts hurt, when they hit as hard as that one did." Cloud paced about, immersed in thought, for minutes.

"I can't find any point of attack," he said, finally. "No foothold. No finger-hold, even. But what you just said rocked me to the foundations . . . you said, a while back, that you believe in God."

"I do. So do you, Storm."

"Yes ... after a fashion ... yes, I do ... Well, anyway, now I know what to tell Ross."

He called the captain and issued instructions. The *Vortex Blaster II* darted away at full touring blast.

"Now what?" Cloud asked.

"We practise."

"Practise what?"

"How should I know? Everything, I guess. Oh, no, the Fives emphasized 'scope,' whatever that means. 'Scope in heights and depths.' Does that ring any bells?"

"Not loud ones, if any. All it suggests to me is spectra of some kind or other."

"It could, at that." Joan caught her lower lip between her teeth. "But before we start playing scales, let's see if we can deduce anything helpful—examine our points of contact and so on. What have we got to go on?"

"We have one significant point in space. That's all."

"Oh no, it isn't. You're forgetting one other highly significant fact. The data fitted the growth-of-population curve *exactly,* remember."

"You mean to say you *still* think the things *breed?*"

"I can't get away from it, and it isn't because I'm a woman and obsessed with offspring, either. How else *could* your data fit that curve, and what else fits it so exactly?"

Cloud frowned in concentration, but made no reply. Joan went on to: "Assume, as a working hypothesis, that the vortices are concerned, in that exact relationship, with the increase in some kind of life. Since the fewer assumptions we make, the better, we don't care at the moment what kind of life it is or whether it's intelligent or not. To fit the curve, just what would the vortices have to be? Not houses, certainly . . . nor bedrooms . . . nor eggs, since they don't hatch and the very oldest ones are still there, or would have been, except for you . . . I'm about out of ideas. How about you?"

"Maybe. My best guess would be incubators ... and one-shot incubators at that. But with this new angle of approach I've got to re-evaluate the data and see what it means now."

He went over to the work-table, studied charts and diagrams briefly, then thumbed rapidly through a book of tables. He whistled raucously through his teeth. "This gets

screwier by the minute, but it still checks. Every vo
represents *twins*. Never singles or triplets, *always* twi
And the cycle is so long that the full span of our data isn
enough to even validate a wild guess at it. Now, Joan, you
baby expert, just what kind of an infant would be just
comfortably warm and cosy in the middle of a loose
atomic vortex? Feed *that* one to Margie, chum, and let's
see what she does with it."

"I don't have to; I can work it in my own little head.
An exceedingly complex, exceedingly long-lived, exceedingly slow-growing baby of pure force. What else?"

"Ugh! And Ugh! again. That's twice you've slugged me
right in the solar plexus." Cloud began again to pace the
floor. "Up to now, I was just having fun . . . I'm mighty
glad we don't have to let anybody else in on this, the psychs
would be on our tails in nothing flat . . . and the conclusion would be completely justifiable and we've both blown
our stacks . . . I've been trying to find holes in your theory
. . . still am . . . but I can't even *kick* a hole in it . . .

"When one theory, and only one, fits much observation-
al data and does not conflict with any, nor with any
known or proven law or fact," he said finally, aloud, "that
theory, however bizarre, *must* be explored. The only thing
is, just how are we going to explore it?"

"That's what we have to work out."

"Just like that, eh? But before we start, tell me the rest
of it—that stuff you've been keeping behind a solid block
down there in the south-east corner of your mind."

"QX. I was afraid to, before, but now that you're
getting sold on the basic idea, I'll tell all. First, the planet.
There are two possibilities about that. It could have been
cold a long time ago and this race of—of beings, entities,
call them whatever you please—with their peculiar processes of metabolism, or habits of life, or something, could
have liquefied it and then volatilized it. Or perhaps it
started out hot and the activities of this postulated race
have kept it from cooling; perhaps made it get hotter and
hotter. Either hypothesis is sufficient.

"Second, the Patrol couldn't find anything because it
wasn't looking for the right category of objects; and
besides, it didn't have the right equipment to find these
particular objects even if it had known what to look for.

"Third, assuming that these beings once lived on that

net, or on or in its sun, perhaps, they simply *must* live ere yet. Creatures of that type, with such a tremendously long life-span as you have just deduced and as methodical in thought as they must be, would not move away except for some very solid reason, and nothing in our data indicates any significant change in status. Tracking me so far?"

"On track to a micro, every millimeter."

"And you don't think I've got rooms for rent upstairs?"

"If you have, I have too. Now that I'm in, I'm going to follow this thing to its logical conclusion, wherever that may be. You've buttoned up the vortices themselves very nicely, but they were never the main point at issue, Joan. That spherical surface was, and still is. *Why* is it? And why such a terrifically long radius? Those have always been the stickers and they still are. If your theory can't explain them, and it hasn't, so far, it fails."

"I think you're wrong, Storm. I don't think they'll turn out to be important at all. They don't *conflict* with the theory in any way, you know, and as we get more data I'm pretty sure everything will fit. It fits too beautifully so far to fail the last test. Besides . . ." her thought died away.

"Besides what? Unblock, chum. Give."

"I think those things fit in, already. You see, entities of pure energy can't be expected to think the way we do. When we meet them—if we can understand them at all—that surface, radius and all, will undoubtedly prove to be completely in accord with their mode of thought; system of logic; their semantics; or whatever they have along those lines."

"Could be." Cloud's attitude changed sharply. "You've settled one moot point. They're intelligent."

"Why, yes . . . of course they are! It's funny I didn't think of that myself. And you're really sold, Storm."

"I really am. Up to now I've just been receptive; but now I really believe the whole cockeyed theory. I suppose you've figured out an angle of approach?"

"You flatter me. I'm not that good. But perhaps . . . in a very broad and general way . . . Heights and depths, remember? And superhuman scope therein or thereat? But *we* don't do it, Storm. *You* do."

"Uh-uh. Nix. You and I are one. Let's go!"

"I'll come along as far as I can, of course, but son.
thing tells me it won't be very far. Lead on, Six Cloud!"

"Where'll we start?"

"Now we're right back where we were before. Do you
still favor spectra? Of vibration, say, for a start?"

"Nothing else but. So let's slide ourselves up and down
the frequencies, seeing what we can see, hear, feel, or
sense, and what we can do about 'em."

Chapter 18

CAHUITA

ON THE PLANET CAHUITA, unreckonable years before this story opens, an entity brooded.

This entity, Medury by symbol, was not even vaguely
man-like; in fact, he—the third person singular pronoun,
masculine, is used very loosely indeed; but since it is
somewhat better than either "it" or "she" it will have to
do—was not even vaguely corporeal or substantial.

Man's earliest ancestor, it is believed, came into being
through the interaction of energy and matter in the waters
of the infant seas of Earth. The first Cahuitans, however,
originated in the unimaginably violent, raw, crude energy-
flare of an atomic explosion.

This explosion did not take place on Tellus, nor in any
time known to Tellurian history. The place of occurrence
was a planet in the spiral arm of the galaxy across the
tremendous gulf of empty space which we now call Rift
Two Hundred Forty; the time, as has been said, was in the
unthinkably remote past.

Cahuitans are not, strictly speaking, immortal; but as
far as mankind is concerned, and except for exceedingly
peculiar violences, they might as well be.

Medury brooded. His problem was old; it had probably
been considered, academically, by every Cahuitan then
alive. But only academically, and no Cahuitan had ever
solved it, for the philosophy of the race had always been
(and still is) the simple one of least action—no Cahuitan
ever did any job until it became necessary; but, converse-

, once any job was done it was done as nearly as possible or all time to come.

Medury was the first Cahuitan to be compelled, by one of the basic urges of life, to deal with the problem as a concrete, not an abstract, thing. The problem was, therefore, his. His alone.

His world, the only planet of its sun, was old, old. The last atoms of its fissionables had been fissioned; the last atoms of its fusibles had been fused; no more fires could be kindled.

The Cahuitans in general did not care. For the adolescents, the time of need for a source of high-level quanta had not yet come. For those already fulfilled* it had passed. While entirely gaseous, the planet would stay comfortably warm for a long time. Its energies, with the outpourings of its parent sun, would feed billions of people instead of the mere hundreds of thousands comprising its present population. Jobs*, businesses*, commerce*, and industry* went on as usual, unaffected.

But Medury was affected: basically, fundamentally affected. The time had come when he should progress into completion, and without a new fire the Change was impossible.

For a time which to a human race would have been fantastically long Medury brooded, considering every aspect of the problem; then stirred himself to action. Converting a tiny portion of his non-material being into three filaments of energy, he constructed a working platform by attaching the ends of these three filaments to the cores of three widely-separated suns. Thus assured of orientation, he launched into space a probing needle of pure force; a needle which, propagated in and through the sub-ether, covered parsecs of distances in microseconds of time. And thus for days, years, what might have been centuries and millennia as we of Tellus know time he searched; and finally, he found.

Pulling in all his extensions, he shot a tight beam to a fellow-being, Litosa by symbol, and tuned his mind precisely to hers. ("Hers" being perhaps a trifle better than either "his" or "its".)

---

* The reader will please understand that I am doing the best I can with words we all know. E.E.S.

"For some little time you too have felt the need fulfillment," he informed his proposed complement level, passionless thought. "You and I match well; there being no duplications, no incompatibles, no antagonistics in our twelve basics. Our fulfillment, Medosalitury, and our products, Midora and Letusy, would all three be super-primes."

"Yes." What a freight of rebellion against fate was carried by that monosyllable! "But why discuss it? Why reach for the unattainable? From now on we die—we *all* die—unfulfilled and without product. All life in this universe—in this galaxy, at least—ends with us now here."

"I hope not. I think not. There are many solar systems . . ."

"To what end?" Litosa broke in, her thought a sneer. "Can you kindle utterly frigid fuel? Can you work in a sun's core? Or can you, perhaps, take a piece of star-core stuff through empty space to a cold planet and . . ." The thought changed in tone, became what would have been on Earth a schoolgirl's squeal of rapture:

"You CAN! Or you wouldn't have brought up such a harrowing subject. You REALLY CAN!"

"Not that, exactly, but something just as good. I found sparks and kindling on a cold, solid planet."

"NO!" The thought was ecstasy. "You DIDN'T!"

"I did. Whenever you're ready, we'll go."

"I've been ready for CYCLES!"

The two beings linked themselves together in some fashion unknowable to man and shot away through the airless, heatless void. Heatless, but by no means devoid of energy; the travelers could draw sustenance enough for their ordinary needs from the cosmic radiation pervading all space.

Across Rift Two Hundred Forty they flew and on through interstellar space. They reached our solar system. On the third planet, our Earth, they found several atomic power plants. There were no loose atomic vortices—then.

"Hold on! Wait!" Litosa exclaimed, and the strangely-linked pair stopped just short of the glowing bit of warmth —the ragingly incandescent, furiously radiating reactor in the heart of one of Earth's largest generating stations—which was its goal. "There's something funny about this. How could there possibly be even one little

rk like this, to say nothing of so many, on such an
.erly frigid planet, unless some intelligent being started it
nd is maintaining it for some purpose? There MUST be
intelligence on this planet and we must be intruding
shamefully. Have you scanned? Scanned. CAREFULLY?"

"I have scanned. Carefully, completely. Not only on this
planet's surface, but throughout its depths. I have
scanned, area by area and volume by volume, this sun and
its every planet, satellite, and asteroid. There is no intelligence here. More, there is no sign whatever of any kind of
life, however rudimentary, latent, or nascent. I have been
able to find nothing whatever to modify our conclusion of
long and long ago that we are the only life, intelligent or
otherwise, in existence. Scan for yourself "

Litosa scanned. She scanned the sun, the planets, the
moons and moonlets, the asteroids down to grains of sand
and particles of dust. Still unsatisfied, she scanned all
neighboring solar systems, from Centralia to Salvador.
Then, and only then, did she accept Medury's almost
unacceptable conclusion that these providential sparks
were in fact accidental and were in fact, by some process
as yet unknown to Cahuitan science, self-balancing and
self-sustaining.

Medury and Litosa, woven into a fantastically intricate
and complex sphere of ultra-microscopic filaments, flashed
into the heart of the reactor, which thereupon went instantaneously and enthusiastically out of control.

And from the pleasant warmth of the incubator-womb—
to us of Earth the ravening fury of the first loose atomic
vortex—there emerged the fulfillment Medosalitury. This
entity, grave and complete and serene as an adult Cahuitan should be, wafted itself (there is no question as to
which pronoun is to be used here) sedately back to its
home planet.

And in the pleasant warmth of that same incubator-
womb the two products, Midora and Letusy, began
very slowly to gestate.

* * * * *

Joan and Storm, minds in fusion, set out to regions
never before explored by man. Downward first. One cycle

per second. One per minute. One per hour; per day
year; per century . . .

"Hold everything, Storm! You're getting out beyond
depth. Anyway, what *use* are they in what we're after?"

"None at all, that I can see; but it's *new knowledge*.
Nobody ever dreamed—correction, please: nobody ever
published—anything about it, or I'd've heard of it. Maybe
the Fives know all about it, though; I'll check with them,
first chance I get. QX, we'll jump up to the radio band."

"There wouldn't be any radio waves out here, and you
couldn't understand the language if there were."

"How do you know? We'll go where there are some and
find out. Maybe we can understand *any* kind of language
now—maybe that's one of the natural abilities of a Type
Three-Six fusion. Who knows?"

In an instant they were receiving a short-wave broadcast at the Heaviside Layer of a distant planet. They could
receive it, could de-louse it, could separate signal from
carrier wave, could read the information; but they could
not understand it.

"Well, *that's* a relief," Joan sighed. "I was getting more
than half afraid that a Type Six mind would be omnis-
cient."

"If I'm a Six you needn't worry; there's altogether too
much to know. Where do you want to go from here?"

"Let's look at the infra-red and the ultra-violet. I've
often wondered what colors they would be."

The fusion looked, and saw things that made both
participants gasp. That is, they did not really *see*, either.
None of the six ordinary senses—of perception, sight,
hearing, taste, smell, or touch—were involved. Or rather,
perhaps, all of them were involved, or merged with or into
some other, brand-new sense possessed only by high-type
minds in full action.

"As a semanticist, Joan, can you write a paper on that?
That would make any kind of sense, I mean?"

"I'll say I can't," Joan breathed. *"Especially* as a semanticist, I can't. No words, no symbology, in any language.
But weren't they *beautiful,* Storm? And wonderful, and
. . . and awful?"

"All of that. I'd like to write it up, or make a tri-di of it
. . . or something . . . but of course we can't. What next?

we flirt a bit with the cosmics and ultras, or had we
.er jump right into the channels of thought?"

"Thought, by all means; the more practise we get, the
.etter, and they'd be on a terrifically high band, don't you
think?"

"Bound to be. The logical conclusion of this whole
fantastically cockeyed set-up is that they've simply never
even suspected that we exist; any more than we have that
they do."

"Would the . . . the bodies, if I can call them that,
radiate of themselves, or just thoughts?"

"Not of themselves, I don't think . . . no. An entity of
pure energy would have to be held together by forces of
magnitudes we can't even guess at; much too intense to
permit bodily radiation. Something like the binding energies of particles, I imagine; but different and very probably even more so."

The fusion leaped then to the bands of thought. It
sought out and seized the thoughts of various of the ship's
personnel; gripping, molding, working, analyzing. Joan and
Cloud were not reading minds now, at all; they were
studying the fundamental mechanisms of the thoughts
themselves. How they were generated; upon what, if anything, they were heterodyned; how they were transmitted;
and, above all, exactly how they were received and exactly
how they were converted from pure thought, couched at
least in part in the symbols of language, into usefully
assimilable information.

And, such was the power of that fusion, it succeeded.

Then up and up and up the scale of thought the fused
minds went; seeking, finding, mastering. And up and up
and up, into regions where no thoughts at all were to be
found. And up and up, and up . . .

"Stop it! Let me go! I'm burning out!" Joan shrieked
aloud. "My God, Storm, is there no limit at all to your
ceiling?"

Cloud stopped; loosed her mind. "I'm sorry, chick, but I
was just getting nicely organized. We've got a long ways
to go yet, I'm afraid."

"I'm sorry, too, Storm, sorrier than you'll ever know,
but I simply can't take it. Three seconds more of that and
I'd've gone stark, raving mad. And when we get to Cahuita I don't know what I'll do. I may blow up completely."

"You may think so, but you won't. You're not the t
And we aren't going to Cahuita—at least, not in the fle
When we hit that band we'll be there automatically."

"Not quite automatically, of course, but we'll be there
yes. I want to stay with you, more than I ever wanted
anything before in my whole life, and I want to help you
... couldn't we loosen the fusion just a little, so that I can
pull away when the going gets too rough for me? Just
enough to keep away from a burnout, but close enough to
see and perhaps to help a little?"

"I don't know why not ... sure, like this." He showed
her.

Again the fusion went up and up and up, and this time
it did not stop at Joan's ceiling. She pulled away a little,
but not enough so that she could not sense and understand, in a way, what was going on.

Cloud, every muscle set and eyes closed tight, sat in a
chair, his hands gripping fiercely its arms. Joan lay face
down upon a davenport, her face buried in a pillow, her
fists tight-clenched.

And the linked minds—linked now, not fused—went up
... and up ... and up ...

And, finally, they reached the band upon which a Cahuitan fulfillment was thinking.

It would probably be too much to say that the fulfillment was surprised. An adult, fulfilled Cahuitan is so
serene, so sedate, so inherently stable at any possible level
of stress, that it is probably impossible for it to feel any
such sensation or emotion as surprise, even at the instantaneous unveiling of a whole new universe of thought. It
was, however, in a calm, passionless, and scholarly way,
interested. Not what could be called intensely interested,
perhaps, but really interested, nevertheless.

As had been foreseen, the modes of thought of the
Cahuitan and the linked Tellurians were different indeed.
As has been shown, however, there were some points—the
fulfillment could remember the emotions of its component
products, even though it could no longer feel them—upon
which even such divergent minds as those could find
common ground. Also, it must be borne in mind that the
Cahuitan was an able and seasoned thinker, trained for
many millennia in the art, and that Neal Cloud was a Type
Six mind; the only such mind then to be found in all

…lization. Hence, while it would serve no useful purpose …re to go into detail as to how it was accomplished, a …orking understanding was at last attained.

Cloud came to understand, as well as any being of material substance ever could, the beings of pure energy. The Cahuitan learned, and broadcast, that intelligent life could and did exist in intimate association with ultimately frigid matter. While the probability was small that there would ever be any considerable amount of fruitful intercourse between the two kinds of life, some live-and-let-live arrangement should be and would be worked out. There were thousands, yes, millions, of planets absolutely useless to anybody or anything known to man; planets harboring no life of any kind. The Patrol would be glad to set up, on any desired number of these barren planets, as many atomic power plants as the Cahuitans wanted; with controls set either to let go in an hour or to maintain stability for twenty five thousand Galactic Standard years.

The Cahuitans would immediately extinguish all vortices not containing products, and would move all living products to the new planets as soon as the promised incubators were ready.

"Products indeed—they're *babies!"* Joan insisted, when Cloud stepped the information down to her level. "And how can they possibly move them?"

"Easily enough," the fulfillment told Cloud. "Blankets of force will retain the warmth necessary for such short trips, provided each new incubator is waiting, warm, and ready."

"I see. But there's one question I want to ask for myself," and Cloud went on to explain about the unbelievably huge sphere that crossed Civilization's vast expanse of space. "What's the *reason* for it?"

"To save time and effort. The product Medury devoted much of both to the evaluation of a sufficiently productive, esthetically satisfying, and mathematically correct construction. It would not be logical to waste time and labor in seeking a variant or an alternate, especially since Medury's work showed, almost conclusively, that his was in fact the most symmetrical construction possible. Now symmetry, to us, is what you might, perhaps, call a ruling passion in one of your own races."

"Symmetry? The first twelve vortices were symmetrical, of course, but from there on—nothing."

"Ah—that is due to the differences between our thinkings; particularly in our mathematical and philosophical thinkings. The circle, the sphere, the square, the cube—all such elementary forms—are common to both but the likenesses are few. The differences are many; so many that it will require several thousands of your Galactic Standard years for certain of my fellows and me to tabulate them and to make whatever may be possible of reconciliation."

"Well . . . thanks. One more question . . . maybe I shouldn't ask it, but . . . this that we have laid out is a wide-reaching and extremely important program. Are you sure that you are able to speak for all the Cahuitans who will be affected?"

"I am sure. Since we are a logical race we all think alike—logically. On the other hand, your race does not seem to me at the moment to be at all a logical one. Can you speak for it?"

"In this matter I can; and you, in my mind, will know that I can," and in this case Cloud could indeed speak for the Patrol. Philip Strong, after one glance in Cloud's mind, would issue the necessary orders himself and would explain later—to anyone capable of accepting the true explanation.

"Very well. We will destroy the empty incubators at once, and will go ahead with the rest of the project whenever you are ready."

The Cahuitan broke contact and vanished.

In the ship, Cloud got up. So did Joan. Without exchanging a word or a thought they went hungrily into each other's arms.

After a time, and still keeping one arm around his Joan, Cloud reached out and punched a button on his intercom.

"Captain Ross?"

"Ross speaking."

"Cloud. Mission accomplished. Return to Tellus, please, at full touring blast."

"Very well, sir."

And "Storm" Cloud, Vortex Blaster, was out of a job.